What's Remembered

a novel by

ARTHUR MOTYER

Cormorant Books

THE CANADA COUNCIL | LE CONSEIL DES ARTS
FOR THE ARTS | DU CANADA
SINCE 1957 | DEPUIS 1957

ONTARIO ARTS COUNCIL
CONSEIL DES ARTS DE L'ONTARIO

The publisher gratefully acknowledges the support of the
Canada Council for the Arts and the Ontario Arts Council
for its publishing program. We acknowledge the financial support
of the Government of Canada through the Book Publishing
Industry Development Program (BPIDP) for our publishing activities.

Printed and bound in Canada

NATIONAL LIBRARY OF CANADA CATALOGUING IN PUBLICATION

Motyer, Arthur
What's remembered / Arthur Motyer.

ISBN 1-896951-68-6

I. Title.

PS8576.O858W43 2004   C813'.6   C2003-907269-X

Cover and Text Design: Tannice Goddard
Cover image: Detail from *The Blue Check Tablecloth*
by Joseph Plaskett (1982)
Printer: Webcom Ltd.

CORMORANT BOOKS INC.
215 SPADINA AVENUE, STUDIO 230, TORONTO, ON CANADA M5T 2C7
www.cormorantbooks.com

For Alasdair

Our birth is but a sleep and a forgetting:
The soul that rises with us, our life's star,
Hath had elsewhere its setting,
And cometh from afar.
— WILLIAM WORDSWORTH

I

"Think I don't know what your world was like?"

Legitimate question or statement with answer implied? Peter wasn't sure. If question, he should respond. If statement, he need not. His world? It was like everyone else's, full of the usual traps and rewards. But he was not like everyone else. He looked for his own way through, trying to remember whatever it was Shelley's baby forgot.

"My world? How could you know? Some things, maybe, but not all. You might be surprised. But you go first. Tell me about yourself. I know nothing except what you said just now in the gallery. Three hours ago we hadn't even met."

They had walked around the corner from the vernissage of paintings by Christopher Lewis at a nearby gallery to a trendy little restaurant called Hats Off, tucked into a side street just off Avenue Road in Yorkville. They were seated at one of the booths towards the back.

The atmosphere was relaxed and friendly, with the waiters charmingly aware of their talents. Glossy black and white photographs of male movie stars adorned the magenta walls behind discreet and darkened booths. Clark Gable, Walter Pidgeon, Humphrey Bogart, Gene Kelly, Fred Astaire, and Cary Grant smiled upon their admirers. Lights with Tiffany-style glass shades in every booth produced a warm glow, and patrons were encouraged to linger.

"You're younger than I am," Peter continued.

"I was, if you want to know, a post-atom-bomb baby, born August 27, 1945."

"That makes you thirty-six," said Peter.

"And you?"

"Forty-nine. That's the difference, and it's enough. A lot went on before you were around. The world makes progress, tiny bit by tiny bit, as a friend of mine once put it, but it's sometimes hard to tell."

It was almost midnight. The waiter had brought their food — salmon steaks baked in foil, with toasted French bread on the side — and a modestly priced bottle of white wine from Bulgaria.

In the first hour that followed, and even as he ate, Peter listened without interruption to everything he heard, saying only at the end, without explanation, that he wanted to remember what Shelley's baby forgot. It was then that he began his own story.

He spoke about his father, saying that he had been in the church and had told him none of the things he had needed to know as a boy about sex. The first time he had a wet dream, he didn't even know what it was. He thought something was wrong and maybe he should see a doctor, but he was too embarrassed to mention it to anyone. His father maintained that he had been called to his ministry by a demanding God who was making him pay for a single childhood sin. He had been given the name of Charles by God-fearing Ontario parents who had a limited view of English history and believed the name itself would pour on him the light and blessings of a king. But even a name that suggested power and dominion had never been enough to banish the darkness he carried within for the sin he thought he had committed, one not immediately disclosed. Like Peter himself, he had been the only boy in the family.

"Were you an only child?" Peter asked, interrupting the story he was telling.

"No, I've one sister. She's older. Married to a lawyer and they've got twin girls. Beautiful, too. Still live in Vancouver. I see them whenever I can, though not as often as I'd like."

It was this simple, direct, and unaffected way of responding, which Peter had earlier observed in the art gallery, that disarmed him, and he hesitated slightly, keenly aware that he was talking to someone who had nothing to hide, whereas he had spent too much of his life not disclosing his full self to anyone.

"Go on. Don't stop. I want to hear. Tell me anything you like."

"You might regret saying that."

"Me? No. I'm a good listener, and we've got all night."

"True enough. We've got all night."

"You haven't said anything yet. I only know your father was a reverend, and you didn't know what a wet dream was."

"I'll go on. That was only the beginning."

"I'm listening. You first said you wanted to remember what Shelley's baby forgot, whatever that means."

"I'll get to that, but first, there's more you should know about my father."

My father was born in 1900, so he was only fourteen when the heir to the Austrian throne was assassinated in Sarajevo, the world then muddling into war, nation after nation, an inglorious chain reaction leading to death. All over Canada and everywhere else, young men were called from their homes — maybe your father was, too, or was he too young? — called from farms on the prairies, called from valleys and mountains, summoned from coastal fishing ports, so they could get killed in places they couldn't even pronounce and buried in rows with little white crosses as the only statement that they had ever lived.

So anxious to do the right thing, so unwilling to wait his turn to die, my father falsified his records in 1916, lying about his age by two years to get into the army. After early training at a camp just outside Niagara-on-the-Lake, he eventually saw action in France, and survived. Though he never had to pour out "the red sweet wine of youth" so that someone else could write a poem about it, the small diaries he kept record, nonetheless, a few of the horrors he witnessed. He had no patience with anyone who romanticized war. Beautiful young poets with fair hair, like Rupert Brooke, sickened him.

Though he could hardly bear to speak of it, he told of the dummies they used for bayonet practice, dummies that spilled out sawdust, never real guts and blood. Even so, he had vomited often enough at such sights to be accused of moral cowardice, a condition of nerves not far removed from that disorder which led others to desert and then to face a firing squad. Well disciplined soldiers were kept busy that winter, killing their own.

When the war was over and Versailles was done and Germany was punished, my father went back to the world he had left and decided to enter the church, for his own very private reasons, which related to the childhood sin he thought he had committed. After taking his theology at Trinity College, here in Toronto, he was ordained in 1926, and in the year following married my mother, Hazel, an English nurse he had met when on leave in Surrey and who had emigrated to Canada to be with him. They settled down together in their first rectory in Parkhurst, Ontario, not far from Stratford, where my sister, Rosemarie, was born in 1930, and I was born two years later.

In that Ontario town, everything seemed small to me, and flat. No great ocean was in sight. Could it possibly have been more different from what surrounded you in Kelowna? No oceans for you, either, I know, but mountains and lakes and glories beyond anything that can be reduced to a picture on a postcard. No wonder your spirits were early to take off. For me, Parkhurst was a circumscribed place with its one drug store, three churches (Anglican, United, and Roman Catholic), one school, one grocery store (which sold all the things I never wanted to buy in later life, like tinned peas, baked beans, and sliced peaches), one traffic light (turned off every Saturday at midnight to save the town money), one small bookstore (with the books only adults were supposed to read high on a top shelf), a number of Victorian-Gothic houses (made of yellow brick, not red) and smaller bungalows of more recent vintage for families of modest means. It seemed to me an oppressive place, but I was too young to understand why. I only knew that there were oceans in the world and I had yet to cross them.

The rectory itself was not yellow brick, but clapboard painted grey with a front door painted black. The rooms inside were sparsely furnished, my father always complaining that there was never enough money for anything better. There were two sets of candlesticks in the dining room and framed religious pictures everywhere. Does Holman Hunt mean anything to you? The name would mean nothing to me if I hadn't been brought up in a rectory. He painted storybook art, moral pictures, pure Victoriana, where the titles say it all. The three I remember best were *The Light of the World* near the door going into the parlour, *Strayed Sheep* in my bedroom, and *The Shadow of Death* in my parents' room.

You told me you have one sister. I had one, too, named Rosemarie. Yours is older. So was mine. I don't know if you and your sister did what we did, but we would often play "house", and take turns at being mother and father. When it was my turn to be mother, I would ask my mother if I could borrow a dress, because she had so many pretty ones. She always said yes when my father was out and no when he was home in his study. One day, when he had a funeral to conduct, she agreed to let me borrow a dress, before she went off to do some shopping.

I was not a budding transvestite. It was just that I loved dressing up in my mother's clothes, which hung in a dark cupboard until I put on the light. They were so far above my head when I was five years old that I had to stand on a chair to get the dress I wanted. It was never an easy choice, because my mother loved colours, all kinds of colours, and it was hard to make up my mind.

There were golds and reds and purples, deep cobalt blues and the palest of lemon yellows. I must tell you, though, that the dress I loved best was the one that felt like the smooth skin of a peach when I touched its sleeves. It had a full long skirt. Carefully, I would take it from its hanger, and pretend that I was a real lady, with a lot of friends, just like my mother. There were also shoes and hats, lots of them — shoes with high heels, hats with brims and hats with flowers — and belts I could wrap twice around my waist at that young age. A little Eden, I suppose, where everything was as enchanting to me as the apple must have looked to Eve before she took a bite. But the dresses were too long and the shoes were too large, and when I tried to walk, I couldn't do it without falling.

My mother had always been there to pick me up, of course, but on this particular day she wasn't. It was my father who appeared instead and saw me in her dress. Until that moment, I had always thought him gentle and quiet. It had not been difficult to sense that he moved in some sort of darkness, but it was his own grief, something I knew little of at the time.

"What in God's name?" he shouted, seizing me. "This isn't natural."

I began to cry.

"Be quiet. I don't want to hear from you."

He noticed Rosemarie, dressed in a pair of his old trousers, which she'd gathered around her in folds and inadequately secured with a too-tight belt, and a jacket that hung to the floor, and a clerical collar that might better have fitted her waist. He pushed her with a force that sent her flying from the room.

Then he was back at me, for I was crying louder than ever: "Take those things off now ... right now ... Want to grow up a girl?"

I did as I was told, but without understanding what I had done wrong. It seems always to have been that way. But while I have remembered what my father said to me, I later wondered if he remembered his own words to Rosemarie and how he had pushed her forcefully away from him, without allowing her to explain? If he did, what must he have thought the following year when Rosemarie, riding her bicycle on a quiet dirt road just outside the town, was killed outright by a car. The driver said she had suddenly swerved to the left, directly in front of him.

There was an official explanation, of course. Rosemarie had an old carrier on the back of her bike, because my father couldn't afford to buy her a new one. She had tried to make it more secure by tying a piece of heavy string around it, but it had come undone and got caught in the spokes. This had caused her to swerve. It came out at the enquiry. Things like that aren't supposed to happen. But they do.

An RCMP officer came to my parents' front door with news of Rosemarie's death. I was reading *Winnie the Pooh*. What did I know of death until then? I only knew that Pooh and Piglet, Kanga and Roo, Owl, Eeyore, and Rabbit were not supposed to die. Christopher Robin had made them promise they would never forget about him, not even when he was a hundred. "Whatever happens, you will understand, won't you?"

But I could only watch and not understand. Watch my mother's grief. Watch my father's stoicism as he insisted on taking the service himself. Watch Rosemarie not open her eyes when they closed the lid of her coffin. Not understand what was meant when my father pronounced the words, unfamiliar to me at the time: "Ashes to ashes. Dust to dust" — whatever could that mean? Not understand why I had to throw a handful of dirt on top of Rosemarie down below, not understand the assurance of words my father spoke but did not himself believe — as I later found out — that Jesus Christ would change my sister's corruptible body to be more like His own, which was glorious.

Though assured at the funeral service that I shouldn't be upset or ignorant about those who only slept, how could I be anything other than ignorant of my sister, asleep in her casket, her corruptible body something I would never see again?

Silent, not explaining, my father went out the following week and bought a chicken, a live one, from one of his parishioners, and brought it into the house. He held it upsidedown and came at me with it, squawking in his hand. He grabbed me with his other hand, and hauled me into the backyard, saying he wanted to show me something, something my grandfather showed him: how to make a sacrifice. It was something I should know about, though again no explanation was given.

He took the axe that was propped against the stump of an old tree, deftly flipped the chicken so that its neck was on the stump, and chopped off its head, letting go of its legs at the same time. We watched the chicken run about until it collapsed on the ground, with a necklace of bloody feathers where its head used to be.

He declared that I had better get used to it, I would see worse things in my life. He certainly had. Sometimes we had to make sacrifices. God always expected a sacrifice. I had to remember that. For days afterward I tried to understand, but did not.

When war came again in 1939, my father once more joined up, but this time as a chaplain. He went overseas, leaving my mother and me to carry on. I sent letters to him, tucking them in with those my mother wrote. My own desire to please him, to say something he might want to hear, seems evident now, and yet he never answered me directly, only by way of a postscript, usually on the outside of an envelope addressed to my mother. He'd write: *P.S. Tell Peter his letter reached me.* There was never a thank-you.

I've got boxes full of papers, letters with memories, both happy and sad, old invitations, and newspaper clippings, everything stashed away in folders and envelopes. The force of the original emotion may remain, but it's the joy that often dissipates.

I remember, at the age of eight, beginning one of my letters with *Dear Daddy*, which prompted him, via my mother, to tell me that was too childish. Addressing him, therefore, as *father* in my next letter and trying to be more grown up, I asked if he would like me to play Beethoven's "Für Elise" for him when he came home. His reply, on the back of another envelope, was that I should learn some Bach.

My mother said not to mind all this. It didn't really matter, even when it did — to me and, I think, to her as well. But that's the way she was. She was never openly critical of my father. Aware of her position in the community, a clergyman's wife, she was an exemplar for everybody, a healer of ruffled feathers, someone who could make sandwiches, pour tea and attend church bazaars with an easy grace. Sometimes she was asked to give out prizes at school; she'd always wear my favourite dress. Yet to me she was more than all these things.

One day, just before my father returned from the war, when I was thirteen, she gave me a hug, when I came home upset after school. She said there was nothing I could tell her that she didn't already know. Mothers were like that. She loved me because I had been part of her, and I still was part of her, even though I was also myself. I was the boy God gave her, and that would always be true. She couldn't quite imagine what God was like — "I can't quite picture what God is like." I heard her say that many, many times in the years that followed: but she knew He had done this for her, and she loved me.

Such love notwithstanding, and despite the fact that I was the student to whom most of the prizes were presented at school, my life in that small town was one I longed to escape. That didn't happen until I finished high school and went on to study English at Trinity College in the University of Toronto, where I was lucky enough to win a big scholarship.

My father had, in the meantime, moved up the ecclesiastical ladder from Parkhurst to take over the rather more prestigious, and certainly bigger, Anglican church of St. Martin's in Stratford. The stained glass windows in that holy place may have been witness to eternity, but the righteous were also sure that Sodom and Gomorrah got what they deserved, and they were even more sure once artists and actors started that year to take over the town.

II

At Trinity, I continued to be an A student, once I got past the challenges and adjustments required in that first term. Most of my professors seemed to like me. One of them was Willie Wilcox, spelled with a "c-o-x" at the end, but it got altered pretty often to "c-o-c-k-s" on envelopes addressed to him by male undergraduates who thought their own deliberate misspelling better reflected Willie's interests and what a joke it all was.

I got on with him well enough. In my sophomore year, he would invite me to his apartment on Saturday afternoons to listen to the Texaco broadcasts of the Metropolitan Opera, and always he sat very close to me. I knew what he wanted, of course, but (foolishly, I think now) considered him too old for me. He was thirty-two, very tall and very thin, and had a moustache I didn't like. He chain-smoked cigarettes, at forty-five cents a pack, no warning label to tell him it was deadly, which, five years later, it proved to be.

I regularly swam naked in the Hart House pool, soaped myself in the showers, and longed for adventure, but the fleshpots of Toronto continued to elude me. My fellow students were forbiddingly academic, though what they may have done in their double rooms late at night was cause for endless speculation on my part. Night after night, in my single room, I would fantasize about every good-looking guy I had seen that day, ending always with sheets that the maids must have noticed the next morning were stained.

When my peers weren't reading Spenser's *Faerie Queene*, with its endlessly boring allegorical lessons artfully concealed in stanzas of unbelievable monotony, or keeping their deadly research alive with minor contributions to undergraduate magazines that no one else would ever read, they would pray in that splendid Trinity chapel to be enlightened scholars, just like those who taught them.

The sensible, blue-stockinged girls, of course, were all safely across the road in St. Hilda's.

There was, however, a different sort of establishment I later discovered, advertising itself in the yellow pages, under "B" for Baths, where another sort of education was accessible for anyone who could pay the modest entrance fee. It was there, on several occasions after Christmas in my second year, I learned first-hand about lust, persuading myself at the same time (wrongly, as it turned out) that any place with the name Continental must somehow be sophisticated in a good European way. I would enter late at night through a dimly lit front door, hoping no one would see me, and leave a couple of hours later with a mixture of relief and shame, vowing never to return.

Such exciting but guilt-producing experiences made me wonder if I shouldn't make a conscious effort not to be homosexual. No one much used the word "gay" at the time: this was 1953, remember, when you would have been only eight years old. I should change my orientation through willpower, especially since reputable psychiatrists said that a cure was not just desirable, but possible. Homosexuals, they claimed, led desperately unhappy and sordid lives, but if they sought a psychiatrist's help, they had every chance of turning themselves into decent, happy, well-adjusted and compassionate human beings, just like all the heterosexuals of the world. My own life was obviously going to be a mess if I continued my decadent ways. Furthermore, because Canada's Criminal Code remained unchanged, I might even end up in prison, like Oscar Wilde, though he got there for other complicated legal reasons. But then I was not about to go out and look for a doctor somewhere, and aversion therapy had absolutely no appeal. No one was going to attach electrodes to my testicles while I was made to look at pictures of naked men.

How to cure myself was the question. Where were the fleshpots that contained women who could teach me how to be a man? On Jarvis Street, I learned, listening to macho-talk in the dining-hall one evening. That's where I could pick up a girl. What I needed was a girl to show me the way. I could learn to be a man, a real man, as my father had told me I should be when he came upon me in my mother's dress.

I found my way to Jarvis Street and stood on a corner at midnight, but nothing happened. The whole area looked deserted. There were no Amsterdam-style hookers of either sex looking from windows, standing in doorways, luring me with smiles into bedrooms with fake silk sheets and artificial flowers, the sort of thing I had read about. Yet I had twenty dollars in my pocket, and a bit of loose change.

I hailed a passing taxi and asked the driver, in a voice which I hoped would project worldly confidence and immense experience, if he knew where I could find a woman, believing it preferable to say "woman" rather than "girl." He said he sure did, and went on to tell me that she lived quite close and he used her himself. She had the biggest tits he'd ever seen and a cunt that could take whatever a real man had to give her, revving his engine to imitate sexual thrust. Only nine dollars an hour, too, he added.

Immediately I felt trapped. He drove very fast to a semi-detached house not far away. The house appeared to be in darkness, but a beer-bellied, cigar smoking man in jeans and a T-shirt opened the door when I rang the bell. The girl wasn't there, we were told, but would come right back when summoned by Mr. Beerbelly, whose name was actually Fred. Hers, I learned, was Sulena.

I was assured by the driver that Fred would look after me until the girl got back, and I shouldn't bother "with no tip either," when I paid him out of the loose change I had in my pocket. Left alone with Fred, I asked if nine dollars was right for the girl, and he told me not to worry, I'd get my money's worth. She did everything, and he meant every-thing. She would even suck me off if I asked her "real good," and I wouldn't have to lick her pussy either, if I didn't want to. I liked a good blow job, didn't I?

I tried to form a sentence in response, but nothing came out. I could feel myself breaking into a sweat and thought I might vomit. He said okay, I didn't have to tell him, it was none of his business, and I could just do whatever I felt like doing. He then led the way up a narrow, uncarpeted stairwell to a small bed-sitting-room, sparsely furnished with a couch that was folded open, two chrome and bakelite chairs set against one wall, and a table covered with pink oilcloth against another. A geranium without blooms was in the window and Jesus with a crown of thorns hung over a door going into the kitchen. Fred leered at me with his brown tobacco-stained teeth and made his exit. By now I felt really stupid being there.

Minutes later the downstairs door opened and Sulena appeared in the room, a sex professional immediately ready for work. She kicked off her shoes, undid the side button on her skirt and sat on the couch beside me, saying I didn't have to be shy. She pulled her short skirt, loosened already at the waist, high above her knees, and turned her body towards me so that her right leg, folded under, pressed against my left side. She then took my left hand and placed it on her upper thigh, her legs now spread so far apart as to reveal she wore nothing underneath.

She was dark-complexioned and short. Her close-cropped hair framed a face that might have been pretty with less make-up, but as it was, the rouge, lipstick, and heavy mascara declared her profession. Any straight man would, undeniably, have found her attractive. Her large firm breasts needed little support, which she proudly and immediately demonstrated by unbuttoning her blouse to expose herself fully.

Taking my face in her hands, she kissed me with her lipsticked mouth, trying to force her tongue between my lips, then starting to tug at my belt and undo the buttons of my shirt.

Realizing how unnatural all this was for me, and how far removed I was from my true self, I said I shouldn't have come; she only laughed at this, thinking I meant something else. She had met men before who couldn't wait. I'd have to pay her just the same.

Again, I thought I was going to be sick. I said I'd pay her, all right, I had the nine dollars. I reached into my pocket for one of my two ten dollar bills, not waiting to see if she offered me change. Embarrassed, ashamed, mortified, humiliated — pick any word that conveys all that, and that is how I felt as I escaped the scene.

My shirt was hardly tucked in or my fly zipped before I found myself running down the stairs, dropping the other ten dollar bill en route, and out into the night. I didn't know where I was, but instinct must have pushed me in the right direction, because within five minutes I found the College streetcar heading west, and used my last ticket. Once off, I walked north across the great open space in front of University College, under the Hart House tower, and across the road to my room at Trinity. There I fell into a deeply troubled sleep, waking every half hour for what remained of the night, a night of dreams, in which nipples were pushed into my mouth and lipstick was smeared all over my cock, and a beautiful boy from Stratford, unable to help, was obliged to watch. He was tied to an old chrome chair from that kitchen and positioned in the doorway below Jesus with a crown of thorns.

You're the first person, believe me, to hear this story. I told not a soul about that night, for there was no one to tell, not even at graduation time, when William Wilcox, more attractive now, I realized, because I was older myself, confided in me, after many drinks, that he was a homosexual and hoped I would understand and not be shocked. He wasn't sure why he was telling me, but he hoped I had not mistaken his intimacy for crude desire. He had only wanted to be with me.

I said yes, I understood, I really did, but nothing more. Considering his end not so many years later, it was an embarrassingly ungenerous response. But I began at last to

understand how my failure with a woman who was supposed to turn boy into man had been a triumph of sorts, a
test, another step — a vital one that confirmed my true self.
My mother had implied that I should follow my own heart,
and I would try to do just that.

Another thing happened that same year that further confirmed my natural feelings, even when I was quite thrown
off balance by the circumstances. Quite unexpectedly —
and believe me, I wasn't cruising — I met someone, a man
this time, and not in the baths either. He was a graduate
student, slightly older, introduced to me at a residence party
simply as Tom — full name Thomas Alexander Spence, I
learned later — younger brother of one of my high-school
teachers in Stratford. I knew right away what would happen
as soon as we looked at each other, and it did. The chemistry
was not to be suppressed. We went to bed together a scant
hour later in the second-floor room of his boarding house
nearby in the Annex. Until that night I hadn't thought
myself promiscuous, just highly sexed, despite some of the
things I'd done in the baths, but now another door had
opened, and I have to admit I rushed through it.

I wanted to be honourable, but was always aware that I
had to be secretive. After all, I was living in a country that
made my private sexual life a criminal offence. Here, however,
was someone who gave every appearance of loving me, not
just having sex with me, because he was able to talk and
seemed sensitive to my needs, using terms of endearment to
ask if I had ever done this or that, as we shared the joys of
a Kama Sutra for homosexuals. When I left him in bed at
half past three in the morning, he said he would call the
next day, and I believed him. When it didn't happen, I found

myself gripped by an emotion I had not experienced before — sexual obsession.

I've an aunt Gertie who likes to say about almost anything, "You have no idea," and while you may have some idea what I'm talking about, I confess that for almost a month, when I was twenty-two and you were only nine, I became obsessed with Thomas Alexander Spence just because he didn't call me when he said he would. I'm amazed I got through it at all.

I had gone back to my room at Trinity that night, deliriously happy because love had taken hold of my heart. I knew he would call me again. He loved me. The universe would open its doors to further discovery, and I would go through them. I would take lessons in voice at the Conservatory. I would go to Massey Hall as often as I could afford a ticket and listen to all the great singers of the world and be inspired by them. I would sing in the shower and eventually prove myself a star at La Scala and Bayreuth. No operatic role would be beyond me, not even Tristan. When hordes of admirers clamoured for my autograph, I would graciously accede to every request. All this because I was instantly in love with someone who loved me.

The next day I waited in the residence for the phone to ring. I skipped all my classes, but the phone did not ring. Neither was there a call the day after that, despite my being there, being faithful, just waiting, but no longer singing in the shower. The day after that, I walked in the direction of the Annex, but couldn't find the house. I had been there only late at night and had taken no note of the number. I phoned Tom's brother in Stratford and tried to be casual. "Can you give me Tom's phone number?" I asked. He didn't have a phone was the answer and why did I want it? I was not prepared for that question, and Tom had told me that no one in his family knew about him. I didn't know how to answer, so I made up something about a mutual friend I had met who wanted to get in touch with him, and ended the call that way.

Another two days passed — sleepless nights and skipped lectures — and I walked back to the Annex, thinking that if I tried really hard I might recognize the house, and I did. I rang the bell, and the landlady answered. No, she said, Tom wasn't there. He had moved out the day before, and she didn't know where he had gone.

I felt quite frantic. Why had he done that? Was it because of me? Where was he? Why hadn't he phoned? What had I done wrong? Didn't he love me? Had he met someone else the very next day?

I walked back to my own place, besieged by phantom autograph hunters along the route, but turning them all aside, no longer gracious. I cancelled my contract at La Scala. I drew a curtain over the heavens and vowed never again to enter a concert hall. I felt so sorry for myself that I sat down and wept. Only at the end of a self-indulgent month, when I was back in Stratford for a visit, did I learn from Tom's brother that Tom had moved in with his girl-friend, who lived in Etobicoke.

So much for obsession that grips with such force we lose sight of the whole wondrous world around us. I determined that I would never again be a victim.

It was the September following that I left for Oxford, lucky again to have won a big scholarship. With it, I vowed to continue the search for myself and the search for love in another land. But I learned that we take ourselves with us wherever we go and we leave nothing behind.

It was in Oxford, you see, that I first heard the story of Shelley and the baby, and it was in Oxford that some perverse destiny led me to Clifford Hughes.

III

The enchantments of the Middle Ages were alive in that city of dreaming spires, jostled now by the modern world. It was a society of scholars, brilliant conversations over dinner, games of cricket, punting on the river, afternoon tea at the Mitre Hotel, tutorials and lectures, bowling on the lawns, coffee in the Junior Common Room, and glasses of port late at night. Oxford, crowned by the glorious sweep of the High, that most beautiful of all curved streets in Europe, lined with splendid churches and colleges. On one side of the High stand Queen's, All Soul's, and Magdalen, and on the other, Oriel College and University College, this last known simply as "Univ."

It's at "Univ" that Shelley wrote his pamphlet, *The Necessity of Atheism*, and got himself expelled for it. He insisted on sending copies to assorted Oxford authorities who couldn't tolerate the challenge to their thinking. But now, in a mausoleum-like space within that same college, his sculpted figure is revered. He who dreamed of an answer that was always beyond reach. A white marble effigy of his slight and naked body lies on an equally white marble slab, dimly lit behind protective railings which keep out those who might be tempted to deface that innocent young poet with graffiti. Undergraduates had been known to add colourful bits to his nipples and shrivelled genitalia. But now he lies just as he was found washed up on an Italian beach, not far from the Bay of Lerici where he drowned in 1822. It's worth gaining access to his old college just to see the effigy, though it's certainly not high art.

I enjoyed all the celebrations of May Morning, with traffic stopped on the High before dawn and the cherubic choir boys of Magdalen College singing a Latin anthem from their Gothic tower: "Te Deum Patrem colimus/ Te laudibus prosequimur." They've been doing that since the eighteenth century, and everyone below listens to their peerless treble voices floating over the early morning mists on the river.

Did you know that all this went on? Would you ever guess that Magdalen is not pronounced the way it's spelled and the way it sounds when you say, for example, Mary Magdalene? No, in Oxford it has to be "Maudlin," just as Cirencester is sometimes "Sisista" and Gloucester becomes "Glosta." None of us lives in a wholly rational world, though Oxford professed to be a rational place.

On May Morning, after the choristers have sung, there's Morris Dancing and general celebrations all up and down the High. Happily inebriated undergraduates, still in evening dress from parties the night before, are all crushed together, laughing and drinking, men with their bow ties undone drinking Mumm's directly from the bottle, and girls in trailing gowns consuming their share. Others in punts on the Cherwell, under the bridge, try to keep warm while eating a cold breakfast, washed down with white wine.

I would like to tell you all this, and to tell you that my first meeting with Clifford Hughes occurred in such a place, where time was marked by the chimes from Merton's tower and the sweet bells from Magdalen and the deep tolling notes of Great Tom at Christ Church. That's the immense bell that was brought from Osney Abbey to its new life in the splendidly elaborate, phallic-shaped, tower of grey stone, designed by Sir Christopher Wren. The tower had been left unfinished for over a hundred and fifty years, but had long been the principal entrance to Christ Church from St. Aldate's, the street outside, perversely pronounced "St. Old's." All of these bells and chimes seem somehow synchronized to strike a few seconds apart so that each will be heard.

Our first meeting should have been magical in such a place: the unmistakeable look, the first, "Hello, my name is Clifford," "Hello, my name is Peter, how do you do?" Proprieties observed sure enough. Instant bliss right there and recognized. But it was not that way, not in the world I knew, not in the Oxford world of intellectuals, where I longed for something to be real, longed for love, longed for an adult version of love.

On my arrival at Christ Church, I gave my name to the porter at Tom Tower entrance who saw, from checking his list of new students, that I was from Canada and welcomed me accordingly. I might like to know, he said, that there were two other gentlemen from Canada in the college, but they had their rooms in Peckwater Quadrangle, whereas mine were in Meadows, there being between the two residences, as I later found out, a social distinction as well as an architectural one. Peckwater, an eighteenth century classic for aristocrats and the elite; Meadows a neo-Gothic Victorian pile, easy to denigrate.

He told me I should go straight through Tom Quad and

over to the right, under the dining-hall arch, and then keep going. My scout would be there and he would show me the ropes.

My scout? The very word set off alarm bells. My father had forbade me any contact with Scouts — boys who could tie deadly knots — an imperative which used to baffle me. The porter explained that my scout was my manservant, though one never called him that, of course. He was there to look after me and seven other gentlemen on a staircase of eight. His name was Ewing, and I would find him in Meadows 3, where I had been assigned my rooms. Meadows, he added, was a lovely old building. Very quiet, with wonderful views down to the river, though one couldn't actually see the river with all the trees in the way.

I had arrived three days before term began and knew I would have plenty of time to look around. Indeed, my rooms, when I found them, had views in one direction — from my sitting-room to the south — of Constable-like meadows, complete with grazing cows, and the river Thames — or Isis, as I learned to call it in Oxford — with its tributary, the Cherwell, just behind the long line of trees. In the other direction, northwards from my bedroom windows, were rooftop views of this most magnificent of all Oxford colleges. It began its life under Cardinal Wolsey as Cardinal College in 1525, but was taken over by Henry VIII when Wolsey fell from favour over the king's divorce. In 1546 it became known as Christ Church. It was Wolsey who had lopped off one end of the small Norman cathedral already on that site, shortening its nave to make way for the great quadrangle he had envisioned as cloistered, but which remained unfinished and open and is even more splendid that way.

Because the dining-hall of unsurpassing beauty — thought now the finest in England outside Westminster — was built first, local wags, aware of Wolsey's gourmandizing capacities, spread the word: "Your Cardinal a college plans, but builds a guzzling hall." Though he and Henry were no more, their great creation yet stood, arrogant testament to genius.

Unpacking my things and listening to my scout tell what was expected of me, a gentleman, I wondered how I might cope, surrounded with such grandeur. Who would be there if human comfort were needed? I had thought there must be other homosexuals in Oxford, but where were they? Would they even show themselves? Laws were still in effect which made buggery — that repellent word so loved by legal experts who had no more intimate knowledge of it than I did of childbirth — a criminal offence. Two years were yet to pass in England before the enlightened few who worked with Sir John Wolfenden would publish their report, recommending changes in the old repressive laws. Though I knew that sodomy was still a criminal offence in Canada, I was surprised that it remained a criminal offence in England in 1955, and yet I didn't care. Never would the law be a deterrent to love. Though Oscar Wilde was no more, he had left his mark not just on Oxford and Magdalen, which was his college; he had left it on a world in which I hoped I might live as an authentic person.

I arranged to meet my tutors, but first set about the business of making new friends. To that end, I addressed and deposited in their mailbox slots, at the foot of the stairs, "At Home" invitations for the seven who lived on my staircase, inviting them all for sherry some ten days later at five p.m. These were, as I came to know them: Edward,

Sir Edward Troy-Jeffers, the only titled aristocrat who had chosen to live in Meadows and never moved to Peckwater, who wore thick glasses and did the *Times* crossword puzzle every morning at breakfast in half an hour flat, assured that he would one day inherit a baronetcy and would never have to work for a living; Harvey, a Rhodes Scholar from Michigan, who was always hungry because he played rugby every weekday afternoon, a new game for him, quite unlike the American football he was used to, and one which increased his appetite, he claimed; Roger, a fair-haired, fresh-complexioned youth of nineteen, an Etonian and, thus, a public schoolboy with undoubted sexual experience, but someone too young, even too pretty, for my tastes; Alan, a well-built, somewhat stocky Englishman, defined by an accent which even I could tell would keep him forever in a lower social bracket, unless Professor Higgins could be resurrected to teach him those vowels which, correctly pro-nounced, would forever gain him access to more tea parties than Eliza Doolittle ever attended; Cecil, a Rhodesian Jew, who, especially by contrast with Alan, had an accent more British than the British and wrote long, boring poems in ottava rima, after the style of Byron, as all of us later distressingly discovered, and hoped that the name of his native land would never be changed to anything less redolent of the old British Empire, already in the process of breaking up; Pieter — that's spelled P-I-E-T-E-R — an art historian from Germany, with a name too much like my own, despite the spelling, who spoke in jewelled sentences about the Renaissance without any discernible accent, and I wondered how he could. Finally, there was the history student who lived on the opposite side of the staircase, two floors down from my own rooms. He was Clifford Hughes.

As for my two tutors, one for language, the other for literature, whom I saw once a week over the next several terms, they were invariably cordial but distant. Always I sat in a chair opposite them while reading whatever I had written about "The Vanity of Human Wishes" or the conventions of medieval courtly love or the sixth century Beowulf who had come from Sweden to destroy the ogre Grendel in Denmark and returned home to rule for fifty years, only to die at last in mortal combat with a fire-breathing dragon. All this in a language I was required to learn and translate for myself, which might just as well have been Old High Norse.

I was beginning to wonder if I could stand it. What had this to do with my inner life? I doubted that I was even supposed to have one. Never once in those years did either tutor sit close to me or confess later that he was homosexual. They listened and talked and analyzed, told me what books to read on whatever topic had been assigned for the next week, and advised me mostly to stay away from formally delivered university lectures, held in various locales, unless given by someone truly distinguished, for they were otherwise a waste of time. Better to stay home and read, they said, or go to the library to study; but if I wished, I could find out who was lecturing on what by looking at university notices. They thought that C.S. Lewis's series of lectures, *Prolegomena to Renaissance Poetry*, might prove worthwhile, even if he dictated everything word by word, including punctuation, as though it were a privileged preview of his next book; or I might wish to hear J.R.R. Tolkien speak about vowel changes in Middle English because he was clearer on that vital topic than the less well-known Otto Jespersen.

For all such good advice, whether I took it or not, I expressed deep gratitude, at the same time vowing to continue the journey I had started in search of myself. That began with the sherry party.

When beer was not being drunk in a pub, sherry was the favoured aperitif; Ewing let it be known that I was expected to buy for my gentlemen friends only the real thing from Spain, no substitutes from South Africa allowed. He was sure I would want it very dry, and he'd be happy to pick up some bottles for me from the buttery, if I would like him to do that. This is how he put it when he arrived one morning with a kettle of hot water to pour into the china basin in my bedroom, in order that I might shave, there being no running water in any of our rooms. An old-fashioned toilet, flushed by pulling a long chain, had its own space on the landing outside. The bathtubs, big enough for two, required going down the stairs in one's dressing gown to the cold outside, carrying towels and soap, past four other sets of staircases to another entrance which led to basement tubs discreetly positioned behind wooden partitions. One wondered by the end of the journey why one had wanted a bath in the first place, especially when the hike to cleanliness involved doing the whole marathon all over again, this time in reverse, still with soap but now with damp towels in hand, in order to get back to one's far-distant rooms. Neither were there any showers, once one got to that washing heaven, eliminating even the possibility that some Greek god might there be found soaping himself.

My first party went pretty well, I thought, once the day arrived, with all present consuming, within fifteen minutes, at least two glasses of the very good sherry Ewing had secured for me from the college buttery. I knew he would be pleased when I told him later that my gentlemen friends confirmed his choice.

All about me there was a conversational buzz, enabling me to hear mostly trivial snatches of this and that as I moved among my guests, decanter in hand. Even now I can hear that babble of voices, which I have never been able to shut out, even inconsequential bits like: "She's having a baby, who's the father?" "Take your pick," at which everyone laughed a great deal, and I went on pouring sherry.

There was talk of going in a punt on the river and everyone screwing the same girl, mixed in with other talk about the Italian Renaissance and the poet Shelley. Someone said that that most romantic of all poets, when up at Oxford himself — and presumably before he told everyone they should be atheists — had seized a baby one day from its mother, who was walking along the High, and demanded that the poor little thing tell everything it knew about the eternal beyond. The mother must have been terrified, and I doubt the child was very forthcoming. All this, you understand, was counterpointed at the party with talk about the best place to hire punts to go on the river.

"Sounds foolish to me. What happened to the child?" I heard someone ask before Sir Edward explained that Shelley actually believed, like Wordsworth and many other poets of the time, that babies came into this world trailing clouds of glory but wouldn't talk about it or couldn't because they hadn't learned their words yet. So why not give a little shake to see if anything would come out before the poor child forgot everything? Very romantic, isn't it? As babies we know everything about love because we come directly from heaven, but get it all messed up later on because we can't remember how it's supposed to work, and life's experiences get in the way.

The story has haunted me ever since. It may be apocryphal, who knows? It doesn't matter: it's still truthful. You can't live without being aware that there's got to be something more, something behind the little we know, something more than the shadows cast by prisoners in Plato's cave. And here's this baby who knows everything but says nothing.

Back to my Oxford party — I heard the well-built Alan say that he swam quite a lot, which was the perfect non-sequitur to the story about Shelley's baby. He tried, even as he said it, to disguise his obviously lower middle-class accent.

When Roger, the pretty Etonian, asked Alan where he swam and got the answer that it was the borough pool in East London, he simply said "Oh dear!" He took the occasion to add, however, that when he was at Eton, the boys used to see the Queen quite often; it was one of the benefits of being at school right next to Windsor Castle. Bad of me, I know, but I wondered if the excitement led him to jerk off every night when he got into bed, at the mere thought of royalty. I was almost sorry he was not my type.

By this time, Harvey and Cecil were comparing the heights of Niagara Falls and Victoria Falls, Harvey boasting that more tourists saw Niagara than Victoria, and there were statistics to prove it.

I heard Cecil ask rather airily why anyone would even want to keep statistics about such a thing — it was so terribly American — so I chimed in to ask Michigan and Rhodesia if they were having an argument, but they seemed to be enjoying themselves. Purely academic, they said. Just a discussion. No offence.

Roger was insisting by now that Alan hear about the time he had to sit right next to the Queen, when she came to have dinner at the school. Alan quite understandably said he wouldn't have known what to say to her, but Roger finished his story, undeterred, saying that all he managed to get out at the end of the meal was, "Would Your Majesty like to eat a peach?" She said yes, she would be charmed to eat a peach, so he peeled one for her and ate it himself, he was so nervous. He was, however, very young at the time and didn't expect the Queen would remember. At least, he hoped not.

The noise grew louder as I continued to pour the sherry. There was talk of the Proms in London's Royal Albert Hall and how bad the seats were and how tiresome it was that Elgar got played all the time because it was hardly a land of hope and glory any more. There was talk of where one should go skiing in the Christmas vac. No one called it vacation which would have sounded too much like time off, which it wasn't supposed to be; the word vac disguised it more. Gstaad being the favoured resort in Switzerland, because that is where Prince Aly Khan showed up with his retinue of hangers-on, though he and Rita Hayworth had been divorced for two years and he could no longer slalom with that particular sex goddess. What snobbery! I was beginning to fear there might be nothing more to Oxford talk. Nothing for me.

There was laughter again, this time when Sir Edward declared, not recognizing it as funny himself, that the first girl born in every British family should be called Elizabeth and the first boy Philip.

Roger said something about a picnic and punting up the Cher as far as Parson's Pleasure, which was always quite divine. Because I was a parson's son, I asked what Parson's Pleasure was, and learned it was that spot on the Cherwell where the river bends and men bathe in the nude.

Good news at last! I wondered if this could lead to something.

Roger explained there were partitions in place to screen the area off from women; if you had a girl in your punt, she had to get out and walk around to meet you at the other end, while you punted your way through a world of naked men and boys. It was a very sensible arrangement, he concluded, and I should see it sometime.

Yes, I thought, I should, but refrained from saying as much, and instead offered to see what was on the radio, which Edward reminded me was called wireless in England.

Mixed babble was all around me, a confusing mélange of subjects as varied as the Palace of the Doges and Parson's Pleasure and abortions and Titian's Giorgionesqe nudes which constituted the very apotheosis of art and pseudo-philosophic questions about ambition. Was it essential for good living? Could a man be truly good if he lacked ambition? The answer being, of course, both yes and no, but mostly yes. And whether a good man could also be dishonest? The answer coming from Edward being yes. What, after all, would it be like if everyone ran about saying exactly what he thought? It would be truly appalling, he claimed. A certain level of hypocrisy was absolutely essential for the smooth running of society.

It was Pieter and Edward who were talking at this point; the rest of us were listening or only partly listening to Schubert's *Die schöne Müllerin* on the radio. Roving had been also my delight, of course, but I had never thought of asking a flower or star to tell me what I so much wanted to know. I would find out for myself. The miller loved a girl, as I certainly did not, and the angels cut their wings off, coming every morning down to earth. Did the brook even know what it was to be in love? That was the plaintive question which found an echo in my heart.

Suddenly I was aware of someone right behind me who must have just come in. There had been only seven of us, and I had not noticed. There should have been eight.

"Hello," the newcomer said.

I turned around.

"Looks like a good party."

I thanked him.

"My name is Clifford."

I said I knew that. I had invited him. I wasn't so drunk that I didn't know his name.

"Me either."

I told him that my name was Peter, but of course I didn't have to remind him. He knew that. He had received my signed invitation.

And that was that: just an empty, somewhat foolish exchange, but I've not forgotten a word. Neither of us knew what to say next. We just stood there, looking at each other, amused somehow, smiling.

The earth had not tipped. No planets fell out of orbit. Neither did the level of light increase in the room. It was the briefest of low-key exchanges. Nothing more. But the genie of obsession must have escaped at that precise moment from his bottle, and there would be no putting him back.

Was the decanter still in my hand? It was, so I held it out.

He said he couldn't stay but appreciated having been asked. He had a tutorial in the morning and hadn't finished his essay.

I asked him what it was on, and he said, "The rule of the Raj."

I told him I was in English.

"Can't all be in history, can we?"

We stood there. He didn't leave. Was there anything more to say?

What about a game of tennis the next day, he enquired. He'd book one of the college courts, if I liked.

Somehow I managed to say yes.

He said not to get the wrong idea. He was not a great player. Just a keen one, adding — I remember his exact words: "I really miss Caroline. When she comes to visit, we'll have to find a fourth and have a game of doubles. See you tomorrow."

He left, and that was it.

There were no goodbyes to anyone else, if there was even anyone else in the room, which I was not aware of.

But who was Caroline?

Sister? Cousin?

Suddenly I was aware that I no longer felt like eating dinner. I tried to remember who else was actually in the room, but confusion took hold. Was the borough pool really all that bad? How high were Niagara Falls? Was I a dishonest person? Did I lack ambition? Who was Titian, anyway? Why didn't the Queen grab her own peach? And what could any brook possibly know about love?

It was not long after the others had left, with Noël-Coward-like assurances that they had been to a marvellous party, that I went to bed early, without going to dinner, assured that Ewing would come the next morning to clean up.

I also tried *not* to think about Caroline, whoever she was.

IV

For someone unused to grass courts, I played reasonably well that next afternoon, though Clifford beat me in two sets, 6–4, 6–3. He had, after all, a stronger serve, was a bit taller than I, and was five years older. His hair was very thick and dark, his eyebrows equally so; his eyes were an unusual hazel colour, his nose aquiline, looking as if it had been broken and mended, which had happened, I learned later, when he was in India, at the age of nineteen, serving briefly in the British army. His two lower front teeth were slightly out of alignment, the rest appeared perfect when he smiled; his full mouth was ripe for kissing, and his Adam's apple was pronounced in a long neck. His thin, hollow-chested body of unimpressive physique was, nonetheless, supported by strong, hirsute legs, and I could tell he was not wearing a jockstrap, because I looked closely. He congratulated me on my game, even as he claimed it had not been very sporting of him to win, and maybe we should play again, which we did the following week and the week after that. We won and lost on a fairly equal basis and considered ourselves a good match for each other.

In that second week we also visited the nearby Botanic Gardens, which can be reached by walking from the Meadows or from the High, opposite Magdalen. They're the oldest in

Britain, started as a place to grow medicinal herbs in the
seventeenth century, but now contain the most compact and
diverse collection of plants in the world. I would love to
show you these, if we were ever in Oxford together. It was
an easy step from there to walk back into Christ Church
meadows, past the building where we had our rooms — an
edifice "mercifully clothed in creepers," said those who
didn't like the "prickly pile of brick" — then down the long
avenue of chestnut trees to the river Isis where all the
college boathouses are located. Some of them are actual
river barges, colourfully painted and decorated with flags,
others more contemporary structures on the bank. We would
find ourselves soon on a path beside the Cherwell, which
wound its way from the upstream paradise where men
bathed in the nude. Large willows overhanging the path
created the canopy we walked under and the filigreed shadows we stepped on. It was truly an extended bower of bliss.

One unusually warm Sunday afternoon we went, on the
spur of the moment, across the Parks to Parson's Pleasure,
where we swam in the nude and lay together afterwards in
the sun, although I had to roll over onto my stomach so
Clifford wouldn't see what was happening. After a little
while, I noticed that he rolled over, too.

If we wanted to buy books, we would ride our bicycles
along the Cornmarket to Broad Street, known in Oxford as
"The Broad", where Blackwell's was located, surely the most
famous bookshop in the world. Always a bit of a muddle,
actually, but everything is there, and no one ever asks if
you actually want to buy what you can stand there for so
long reading. Just browsing can be an education in itself.
We would often cycle further through North Oxford to the

Trout Inn, that most picturesque of pubs, where we would drink and talk about such historical figures as Clive of India and Lawrence of Arabia and why Gallipoli had been such a failure and what the United Nations might do to redistribute the world's wealth and anything else that came into our heads.

As the year progressed, we went for most of our meals together, sitting below portraits of the great and famous in Wolsey's spectacular guzzling hall. We ate the meringues that Christ Church is famous for, brought up on wooden trays by ancient servants from the kitchens far below. We sat in the Master's Garden to read books, propping our backs against the small flowering crab tree that stood in the centre of the velvet lawn, and we concentrated not at all on scholarship. Certainly, my mind was elsewhere, and I hoped Clifford's might be there, too. We watched the boat races in Eights Week, when the Trinity summer term arrived, and ran along the river's edge with every other cheering person in Oxford. Some were on bicycles, urging on their college crew with whistles, bells, and hooters; we disappeared under Donnington Bridge and came out the other side, yelling with excitement if the Christ Church eight succeeded in touching or "bumping" the boat just ahead. In that case, that college eight would move up one place in the day that followed, there being only four such days in Eights Week for a boat to improve its river standing in any given year.

To appease our cultural appetites, we went to films and plays and concerts throughout the year; to Christmas music in the chapel at Brasenose, that college anxious to change its image as a place mostly for athletes or "hearties"; to carols in the hall at Balliol, that most intellectual of all colleges, where Benjamin Jowett, the greatest moral teacher of his age, had reigned supreme in mid-nineteenth century Oxford; to a performance of the St. Matthew Passion in Oxford's Town Hall, sung by local choirs; and to evensong and Sunday morning services in the Cathedral Church of Christ, the only cathedral in England to be also a college chapel, thanks to Wolsey. There the ancient and scholarly Cathedral Canons would dress for winter, against the cold, in layers of pyjamas and dressing gowns, all of which could be glimpsed clearly under their cassocks and surplices. With slow and measured pace, we would watch them walk unsteadily towards their elaborately carved wooden stalls in this intimate Norman cathedral where cherubic-looking choirboys projected an innocence I had long since lost and could hardly remember.

It was in this way that the terms of Michaelmas and Hilary and Trinity all passed in that first year, and still the name of Caroline had never again been uttered. But neither had I been able to get Clifford into my bed. Did he even think about the possibility? I don't know. Did I? Yes, definitely. But what was this slow mating game, or was it a mating game at all? Had I met an Englishman with raging passions never to be acknowledged and always covered up? What did he do for sex? He never said, and though you may think it odd, I never asked. What I did, when I got into bed, was to think of him and take myself in hand. I had to be patient. My time would come. I convinced myself that waiting would be worth it.

As I said just now, the name of Caroline had not been mentioned since that first day we met. I had, therefore, put her from my mind, or I had tried to. Surely she didn't even exist, and her name had been mentioned initially only to make me think there was someone else important in Clifford's life, a character he had quickly and instinctively created to protect himself, to make me aware that I shouldn't aspire to take any such person's place. But my own place was secure, I thought. Walking together, being together, anywhere, everywhere, we always managed to touch somehow, easily, lightly, instinctively, a hand brushing past, a felt knee at a concert, a leg in a church pew, a shoulder in contact with another shoulder, the feel of one finger in simple contact with another when passing a hymn book.

By all such little things, obsession grows, disguising itself as love.

One day in Trinity term, when we were out for one of our walks by the river, he stopped and said, "I've asked Caroline to the Commem. Ball."

My only response was, "Oh!"

The Commemoration Ball was the big social event of the term, when no expense was spared and everyone appeared in their best finery.

He said he thought we should go. Didn't I want to?

I said I hadn't thought of it, whereupon he replied that I should.

It was then I forced myself to ask who Caroline was.

She was his girlfriend, I learned, someone he hadn't talked much about, not to me anyway. Thought it might upset me somehow. Didn't know why.

"It doesn't upset ..." I started to say, my voice trailing off, for great waves were now rolling over sandcastles on my beach. Like a child who had created something, I was unaware of the tides.

In that case, why didn't I find someone to ask? There was Claire at Lady Margaret Hall. I liked her well enough, didn't I? She had been to many of our sherry parties, and she would probably love to go. I should ask Claire.

"I'll think about it" was my answer.

He said that was good and it was bound to be fun. Stylish, too. Trust the House to do things in style. Marquees would be set up in the quad. There would be lashings of champagne and food in hall after midnight. Dancing until dawn. Breakfast on the river after that. Not much chance for sex, though, Clifford went on, blundering now into the secret world of my heart, unless Caroline were to get there a bit early on the day. It was not my problem, though. It was his, and he would work something out. We would have to rent tails, or did I have some? Had I brought them from Canada, maybe? If not, Moss Brothers was the place, referred to always and only as Moss Bross, that great establishment in London where formal wear could be rented. Half the men who went to garden parties at Buckingham Palace went there first.

There were bigger and bigger waves now, and not much left on my beach.

I thought about it, and at last realized there was no way I could imagine not going, not being with Clifford, even if he was with Caroline, no way I could endure not seeing him, even with someone else in his arms, no possible way of detaching myself from myself. I would have to go. The heart allowed no choice. I never thought it was obsession. I knew it was love.

Can you believe all this, you who sit there so quietly listening? Even I find it difficult to understand why I did the things I did, putting myself into situations where I invariably ended up only wounding myself. Perhaps I was a masochist back then, though at the time I thought I was a lover. Unfulfilled — rejected, maybe — but a lover nonetheless.

Claire was free. She would like very much to go. She thanked me.

I rented tails.

The day came. I picked her up.

Caroline arrived. She was late. She gave Clifford a knowing look.

We all said hello.

We all got dressed up. We all said what fun it was going to be.

The four of us laughed and drank champagne and ate slices of smoked duck breast at midnight and danced until the sun began its day. We breakfasted on peaches with cheese and baguettes and hot tea and more champagne in a punt on a river unknown to Ophelia.

When it was over, I escorted Claire back to Lady Margaret Hall, not even kissing her goodnight, while Clifford, very openly, made a point of saying that he and Caroline were going back to his rooms. I had watched the build-up to it all that night, playing to perfection my role of recalcitrant voyeur until dawn.

The tides had now demolished everything.

It was then, in the early morning light, sitting at my window, looking down to the river, that I picked up my pen and wrote a quick note to the only homosexual I had met in Oxford, an older student at Exeter College, a gentle Scot, whose name was Angus. He was perfectly open about his orientation even among those who weren't, and overhearing his conversation at a party in his college, his words had carried the force of an evangelist moving mankind to his new vision of love. We had been only quickly introduced on that occasion, but our eyes, when they met, held the gaze longer than reason might have allowed. I had encountered him only a few times more, when walking down the High, wearing his cape and sporting a gold-tipped cane, which made heads turn, because he was also beautiful to look at. Not quite "Piccadilly with a poppy or a lily in his medieval hand," but Wildean enough for the time. Where might I turn, in all of Oxford, if human comfort were ever needed? I had asked myself so many months earlier.

To Angus, I now hoped.

I addressed the envelope to "Angus McKay, Exeter College," with my letter inside, asking if he might possibly come to my rooms later that day, after it grew dark, for I urgently needed to see him.

I walked out Canterbury Gate through narrow Blue Boar Street before I crossed the High to that other old and narrow street, the Turl, bearing the note myself, not trusting the inter-college mail service to get it there on time. I delivered it personally to the porter at the gate, who was surprised to see me there at such an early hour.

Would Angus agree to visit someone he hardly knew late at night? I was not at all sure. Should I, on the other hand, have been surprised when, some hours later, he answered my reckless call for help, having sensed my genuine desperation?

Promptly at eleven o'clock I heard my outer door open and then get locked from the inside. I was already in bed. He walked over, sat on the edge, and felt for my hand. Then gently, ever so gently, I heard him say:

"You're in trouble. I can tell."

I tried to make some sort of response but couldn't.

Sshhing me, he said I didn't have to talk.

Again I began, but he cut in with:

"Not now. Maybe later. Not now. Let's be very quiet."

He stood up, took off all his clothes, and then got into bed, holding me naked and shivering against him. He must have sensed that I was crying.

What he said next has stayed with me exactly as he said it and has become for me a sort of creed, something I believe or want to believe:

"It'll be all right. Eventually it will be all right. I promise it will. It takes time, that's all. Time. We have to learn to love. All of us have to learn. Don't let the sex bit fool you. Love a man. Love a woman. It hardly matters which, as long as it's love, and only you know that. No one knows, as you do, what's in your own heart, and what's there is all that ever matters. I know. Believe me."

It was not the night of passion I had anticipated. It was, instead, my simple epiphany.

We slept together, curled up against each other, spoon-positioned and warm, without having sex. In the morning, he simply kissed my lips and kissed my cock, just long enough to awaken it, and left. Nothing more.

You might ask what had changed? Had I changed? No. Had Clifford changed? No. At least, not on the surface. I sought out Clifford's company more than ever, but that, after all, was not difficult to do, for he also sought out mine; and again we were inseparable.

What had happened with Caroline? Did they go to bed? He never mentioned it. Maybe it had been a failure. Maybe he now wanted me but didn't know how to make his feelings known. As for me, should I then have made my move, made my own feelings clear and invited him to my bed, where he might really have wanted to be but didn't know how to let me know? What was I afraid of? I did want to seduce him, didn't I? And he wanted to be seduced, didn't he? The only thing that was clear was that Caroline had returned to Norwich, and Clifford and I remained in Oxford. That was clear, and it was to my advantage. I convinced myself I might win if I could just hold out, last long enough, endure my private Stalingrad, though no interior battle lines had ever been drawn.

In the natural course of events, over the next many months in our second Oxford year, we still had meals together, walked together, studied together, cycled together, took trips to France and Ireland together, almost dissolving into each other the way two lovers become one; we did everything together except going to bed together, though once, on a cycling trip through the south of France, Clifford and I were pushed by circumstances into sharing the same bed in a hostelry near Avignon, and we came close.

When the owner offered us a room with only one bed, I said immediately it would do, before Clifford could demur.

Later that night, under the shelter of great folds of mosquito netting which hung from the ceiling, I was aware that Clifford, in his sleep, had turned towards me like a lover and had placed his left leg over mine and thrown an arm across my chest. His breathing was regular, but mine almost stopped. I had to lie very still, but with my left hand, I reached down to touch and even hold him while, with my right hand, I brought myself off, which he never noticed.

Everything but sex, I have said. But life, as we all know, is forever in flux.

There were to be a number of performances of *Love's Labour's Lost* in Merton College that summer term, and I asked Clifford if he would like to go some evening. I would get the tickets, if he did.

That was now my way, always doing things for him, inviting him here or there, suggesting a special lecture or concert or play, leaving small gifts I thought he might like — a bunch of fresh daffodils bought in the market, a small box of chocolates or truffles, a travel book from Blackwell's so that we might plan a trip to Ireland. And there were little notes from me to him, sometimes even his replies. "Gone for my tutorial," I would write. "See you later ... Come for sherry ... Did you sleep well? ... Tea at four, but my rooms this time ... Would you like this? ... Would you like that? ... Peter Pears is singing tonight. I'll try to get tickets ... Here's this ... Here's that ..." There was always something to communicate.

All of this seemed to be working, and Clifford and I were happier than ever to be together. Whenever we walked, our shoulders still touched, and I could always feel the charge of energy which came from one of his arms when I arranged for my body not so casually to brush against his. I had only to be patient and wait. I would keep the coverlet on my bed turned down, ready for him.

We went to the play, which was performed in Merton gardens just next door. In due course, after the opening scene, the Princess of France arrived with her ladies, only to be rejected at first by the smart young men of abounding wit who had vowed to give up love, as if that were even possible.

Characters, fantastical or otherwise, with names like Holofernes and Jaquenetta and Don Adriano de Armado and Berowne, which is made to rhyme with moon, walked on and off, stating their positions, retreating, playing games, revealing themselves or hiding behind masks, all under trees that were centuries old and had seen it all before.

When the natural light of a fading summer sun gave way to well-concealed theatre floodlights and spots, the transition was so smooth that none of us noticed we were anywhere other than in an enchanted garden. In the growing darkness, I was also able to place my left leg against Clifford's right, our chairs being so close together as to make it seem natural, and I was very aware that he didn't move his leg away. In fact, I felt him press against me.

"Sing, boy," said Don Adriano to his little pageboy, Moth, "my spirit grows heavy in love." But none of the lovers got what they wanted when the play was over. A dark cloud passed over them all when the Princess of France received news of her father's death. The ladies would have to return home, and the men would have to do penance. Love's labours were lost, at least for the moment. They would all be obliged to wait for one whole year.

"Are we not all in love?" asked the King, and to myself, I quietly answered yes. Would I, too, have to wait for another whole year, like those in the play?

As we walked from the darkened gardens of that oldest of Oxford colleges back to Christ Church and Meadows, by way of Canterbury Gate, Clifford remarked that the evening had turned quite cool, and suggested I go back to his rooms for a nightcap. He had a good bottle of single malt scotch, which his father had sent as a special present. Who better to share it with than me?

Was this a significant invitation, I wondered, the one I had been waiting for, and was he trying to tell me something? Was he leading up to something? I accepted. A coal fire in his study, with the curtains drawn, warmth, security, and the radio on, this time Beethoven's Violin Concerto, the Larghetto movement just begun and the violin singing its pure song of joy.

Scotch in hand, we sat and watched the fire, talking little. I knew what was happening to me and felt sure the same thing was happening to him. Once again I felt the pressure of his leg against mine as we sat together on that small sofa, where we had sat so many times.

When the concerto was finished, he announced that he would turn in, but I didn't have to go. I could stay on for a bit, if I liked. Have another drink. Just put the lights out when I left and sport his oak, which, I had learned in my first Oxford week, meant close the outer door for privacy.

I wasn't sure whether he was suggesting I leave or simply making certain that no one else would come in.

"Sleep well," I said, as nonchalantly as I could.

For the next few minutes I could hear Clifford getting ready for bed, because he had not closed the door between the two rooms. I could hear each shoe he dropped on the floor, the soft rustle of his shirt as he removed it, the sound of his zipper pulled down, the soft thud of clothes thrown somewhere — maybe onto a chair? — and finally the smooth, sweet noise a naked body makes as it settles between sheets.

Silence. Total silence. Just the thumping of my own heart.

"Peter?" he called out. "You still there?"

Yes, of course I was still there.

"I was just thinking," came the voice out of darkness. "Thinking about the play, thinking about love, if it means anything."

I murmured something like, "I hope so," then said it a second time, in case he hadn't heard me.

"Come in here for a minute," was his response. Was it his invitation?

"As I was saying ..." he continued, when I entered the bedroom, but he interrupted his own thought when he saw me looking around and told me to sit down. There was plenty of room on the bed. He was wondering if there really was such a thing as love? He meant pure love, or did it always have to get mixed up with everything else — sex, lust, desire? Look at the play. Nothing worked out. What did I think?

Astonished by a question I thought uncharacteristic, but which also gave me hope, I waited a long time before answering, aware of his naked body under the thin sheet and so close to my own.

It was difficult, I admitted, always difficult.

"Bloody difficult. You're right. It gets in the way of everything."

Intensity was where it hadn't been before.

"Every goddamned thing."

As he was not given to profanity, I could only guess at the depth of a distress he couldn't articulate, because he didn't know what it was himself or where it had come from. On the other hand, I did.

I reached out to hold his hand.

"It's all right. Everything works out somehow," I said, echoing unconsciously what Angus had said to me. "It's all going to be all right."

I said this to comfort him and to persuade myself at the same time. I went on holding his hand while he lay on his back, eyes shut, a sheet covering his body. I thought he was fighting back tears.

Minutes passed. Nothing was said. Then I noticed, noticed him, noticed his erection.

Still holding his hand, I shifted my position so that I could kneel beside the bed, and I put my other hand under the sheet. He still said nothing and still did not move.

Quietly I pulled at the sheet, moving it down to below his knees. Then, hesitating only slightly at the wonder I saw, I lowered my head to take him in my mouth, as inevitably as river finds ocean.

I felt two hands placed softly on my head playing with my hair, pulling strands gently, turning them into curls, slowly at first, then twisting faster and faster as pressure mounted, digging deep into scalp and gripping at the last with passion equal to my own.

There was silence when I finished, total silence, just the sound of breathing, mine and his — but only for a moment.

There was also relief and joy, on my part as well as his, I thought, when I had finished — but only for a moment.

Then came his words: "What the hell do you think you're doing?"

I froze in horror, more abashed than I can tell you. What had I done that was so terrible? This was something he had welcomed, I thought. What was I doing? I thought I was loving him. I thought he knew that.

I had to get out of there, so I pulled the sheet back over him and I left the room, saying nothing, and turning off any lights. The last thing I did was to sport his oak, as he had asked me to do, and I returned to my own rooms, more anguished than at any other time in my life, shocked and tearful, my whole body shaking like an epileptic.

The few months that followed were my last in Oxford and brought only swings from anguish to joy and back again. There was no escaping either. Night after night, I thought only of one man, and night after night I brought myself off — when I was not again kneeling beside his bed.

Everything had changed radically, but on the surface nothing had changed. Clifford and I remained inseparable. Still we shared everything and went everywhere together; for even undeclared wars can end in declared truce. The tension between us, however, was palpable.

If we weren't together, I would run to my windows when I thought he might be passing, just to see the top of his head, the swing of his arms, or to my door if I thought I heard his footsteps, by then as familiar as my own. I would walk outside my building when it was dark, in the hope of seeing a light from his window, or make up excuses to call on him during the day. The truce we had worked out was broken over and over again, because I could not keep it and neither could he.

When it came time, months later, for writing my final exams in that lavishly designed, forbidding structure on the High, now compulsorily and ridiculously dressed for the occasion in what was called "sub-fusc" (dark suit, white shirt, white collar, white bow tie, black shoes, dark socks, academic cap and gown), scratching out nine three-hour papers in five days, covering all I knew or didn't want to know about Lady Macbeth's illegitimate children, the questions were a blur and seemed, in my state of mind, entirely unimportant and irrelevant to life.

Would you say that a mastery of the verb or of the adjective is the more common characteristic of the great prose stylist?

Screw you, I wanted to answer.

It ought to be the first endeavour of the writer to distinguish nature from custom; or that which is established because it is right, from that which is right only because it is established.

You, too, Dr. Samuel Johnson.

Blake's position was an insecure form of compromise from which he despised both science and religion proper; it was also one which helped to reduce his art to confusion and failure.

Whatever Shelley's baby might have said when shaken for answers was not revealed.

V

Returning to Canada by ship — the cheapest mode of transport I could find, Liverpool to Montreal — I had plenty of time to contemplate my future, though I was so seasick I wondered if I would have one. The small Greek Line vessel appeared not to have enough lifeboats to save even Lilliputians, and had been named the S. S. Mykonos. That's the Aegean island, as you may know, which is fast becoming a haven for sophisticated homosexuals who want to get away from it all and lie about naked on secluded beaches, drinking retsina and ouzo whenever they feel like it. On stormy North Atlantic seas, however, where the smell of too much bad food fried in rancid olive oil hung heavy, invading every cabin, even Mykonos had little appeal for me. It might have been a helluva lot better, though, than Parson's Pleasure, which is mostly full of corpulent dons who read books while they display themselves to others who might not be interested in reading books. What if I had gone there again with Clifford, I wondered: would that have made any difference?

As it was, I felt only sick, day after day for a week, and when I was able to stand at the stern of the ship, looking down on the constantly churning wake, I was more aware of what I was leaving behind than what I was going to. But if I had any future at all, I wasn't going to allow myself to fail again. There would be no traps now. I was aware of them all. I would not be obsessive. I would learn to love. Everything would be different once I got back, because Canada, after all, was home. For three years I had been a displaced person in a foreign land, trying to fit into a society where I didn't belong, but now that Vincent Massey, our first Canadian-born Governor General, had been in office for six years, the signs were good that Canada was at last growing up, except for one thing: the sex life I was leading, or wanting to lead, was still a criminal offence.

I had written to my parents, of course, and they had written to me, or, at least, my mother had. She told me that my aunts Fannie and Gertie, her sisters-in-law, who never got married and lived together on the old farm which had been my grandfather's, came for lunch every Sunday after church, and my father, who said little enough at the best of times, said even less on these occasions, and would just go on drinking sherry. He maintained that he had said all he had to say in his sermons and preferred silence. Fannie, who had gone quite deaf, despite, as a child, eating lots of carrot soup, which was supposed to be good for eyes and ears, didn't mind that; but overweight Gertie, fat from all the peanut-butter sandwiches she had consumed in her youth and who still had two helpings of everything, as though she didn't know where her next meal was coming from, did.

In all such letters, my mother usually specialized in presenting facts, without editorial comment, but in one exceptional letter she wrote that Stratford had changed. World stars came now to its door, and a new theatre had replaced the old tent which had been used for four years. The legendary Tyrone Guthrie had gone, but Michael

Langham was there with new directing skills and experience. The future looked bright.

My mother's letter told how two actors, both men, had been found down by the river the week before, late at night, and were apparently taken to the police station for questioning. At least, that's what her friend Isabel, who was the social columnist for the Stratford paper, had said, and they could both only guess at the reasons. The names hadn't been released publicly, but Isabel had heard they were both very attractive men. Her gossipy column, which appeared only on Wednesdays, was immensely popular. "One wonders what goes on sometimes," concluded my mother, though she expressed the hope that the two men wouldn't come to any harm. That would be bad for the Festival. She was just glad I was quite safe where I was and was having such a nice time with my friends.

This letter reached me the week after I had gone to see *Love's Labours Lost* with Clifford, and though it did nothing to relieve the distress of that terrible night, I took it as a gentle warning given by a mother who loved her son. "You don't have to say anything," she had told me that day when I was thirteen, just before my father came home from the war. "I know, and it's all right."

After all my mother had written and said over the years, I was persuaded that the whole world would be a better place if it were run by women, and I still think that. I'm not sexually attracted to women, but that has nothing to do with it. I'm convinced women are wiser judges and teachers and doctors and clergy and leaders of nations than most men, because they're not driven by testosterone to aggression and wars and locker-room jokes about pussies and cunts.

They're usually much better than men when it comes to embracing the diversity in life.

Still, I needed a university job, and it was exclusively men — never a woman among them — I had to face in interviews to get one. I scoured the ads and looked for a teaching position somewhere in Ontario, but not Toronto, Hamilton, London, or Kingston. I wanted a small place near a river or a lake. In Mason College, I found such a place.

Seen at first from across the river, when approached from the town of Preston, the red brick buildings are dwarfed by evergreens, planted when the site was given its basic shape in 1892. It took ten minutes to walk there from the Preston Inn where I had spent the night, prior to all the scheduled meetings and interviews which followed upon my successful application. I had to cross two sets of railway tracks, where lights were flashed and gates were dropped when any train approached, and cross an iron bridge badly in need of paint, to reach the campus. Once there, I had some time to wander about on my own, entering an open quad-like space where various structures stood without much architectural relationship to each other, the whole obviously not designed by Sir Christopher Wren, no mini-Tom Tower in sight. Neither were there colonnades, triumphal arches or outdoor sculptures to remind one of Napoleon.

There was a post-war, functional, flat-roofed gymnasium, which was locked; a chapel, neo-Gothic in appearance, built at the time the college was founded, which was not locked; two academic buildings, one for arts, the other for science, the latter with unsophisticated, poorly equipped labs. I walked about and looked in the various buildings, with no one to stop me or ask questions. There was a residence for men, again made of brick, again neo-Gothic, with window frames that rattled in the winter, as I later found out, and a decrepit iron fire escape at the back. The more comfortable women's residence was more recent.

The whole interview process at Mason was more reasonable than I might have expected, though I had to jump through a number of pretentiously contrived academic hoops with committees and deans before the tricky finale with the president.

The president, Dr. Alan Hibbert, was vertically challenged, preferring to sit behind his desk where his lack of stature would not be noticed and from which position he leaned forward to shake my hand on arrival. He sat on a ringed cushion to relieve pressure on his haemorrhoids, had a bit of a cough, and a thin layer of hair plastered over the top of his head. I estimated his age at fifty going on seventy-five. His aim was to be polite and to please, when not in his I-need-your-money mode. He had a wife but no children; they liked to grow gladiolus and label them in mango chutney jars which they proudly displayed on their mantelpiece for faculty members to admire at receptions.

It was the president who said, towards the end of the interview: "I understand you're not married?"

I said no, I was not.

While I was obliged to be honest, I had also to be careful. It was 1958, remember, and not just the state but everyone else was allowed in my bedroom. I certainly didn't want Dr. Alan Hibbert there. The penalties were still severe. Homosexuals were banned from teaching. The safest place to be was the closet.

He segued into a lecture about how important it was at

Mason to develop the whole person, to have well-rounded people on the faculty as role models for students. I would surely agree there was nothing wrong with that.

"Being well-rounded?" I asked from the old armchair with broken springs where I had been assigned to sit. No, there was nothing wrong with being well rounded.

He went on to say that they liked to have married faculty members at Mason College. He also hoped I had enjoyed my little tour of the campus. They were very proud of their buildings, most of them built using donations from their dedicated alumni, and "Where would we be without them?" leaving me to wonder if he meant buildings or alumni. He wanted me to know that they had an annual campaign, which in the previous year had raised over $180,000, though he wasn't sure of the exact figure. Most of it was earmarked for the library, where there was a real shortage of books about the seventeenth century, which he thought was my period. I didn't stop to inform him that I really didn't have a century: I was not a specialist and proud of it. But he went stumbling on, telling me that they always tried to encourage their faculty members to do research, not just any old research, of course — there was all too much of that around — but research of the best kind that made a real contribution to human progress, which was why they normally tried to hire well-rounded married persons. In my case, though, they were happy to make an exception. After all, I would get married some day, wouldn't I? I was quite young, he believed, but just how old was I?

I learned later that he received an additional four hundred dollars a year beyond his administrative salary for being the Mason Professor of Religious Studies, an obviously insufficient amount to guarantee clear thinking, for he started to look in my c.v. for the answer, as though I weren't present to tell him.

"Twenty-six," I interrupted.

He announced that I was quite right, I was, indeed, twenty-six, he saw it written down. He went on to note that my academic credentials were first-class. No doubt about that, which was a good thing, for that was really what they were after. Scholarship, good sound scholarship, of which only the most disciplined minds were capable. He had written a number of articles himself over the years, but had time to write only one book. Maybe I knew it — and he managed a false, self-deprecating little smile when he gave me its title — *Fragments of Essence*. Can you believe it? *Fragments of Essence*. He had no idea it was funny.

He continued that they would also be pleased to offer me accommodation in the men's residence, which he thought might be convenient for me.

This interested me at once.

There would be other duties, I was told, in return for free rent; not onerous, but duties, nonetheless. Just checking up on the men. Making sure they were all right. Inspecting their rooms from time to time. Being a good listener. They were young, so they always had problems — though, didn't we all? — and I might have to comfort them from time to time. Be a sort of father figure when necessary. But then he didn't suppose he would have to tell me anything about all that, because he was sure I must have had a loving father.

Still, my chief purpose would be to act as an academic leader. I had to inspire the students to perfection. Not allow shoddy work. Wherever one looked these days, it seemed that standards were slipping and we had to hold the line. I did agree, didn't I?

Yes, yes, of course. I would do all I could to hold the line and even do more, I assured him.

"Good fellow!" was his commendation. I should be back there by the last day of August. Always lots to do before term started. He would look forward to seeing me then. He was sure I would get on very well at Mason, so I thanked him and actually meant it. After all, I had to have a job.

He remained in his chair. I left. It was only sometime after this that I learned the president's cure for insomnia was to run through the names of all the Books in the Bible backwards, from The Revelation of St. John the Divine to Genesis, seeing how far he could get before falling asleep. He boasted that he rarely got past Habukkuk and never reached Obadiah before starting to snore, or so his wife would tell him the next morning, her insomnia increasing in direct proportion to the remedy he was using for his own. Esther and Ruth were never called upon in the night, and Eve remained safely in Genesis.

I called my parents to tell them I got the job and would be coming home for the weekend, thinking that the news would make them happy. But when my father answered, he simply said he'd tell my mother. No pleasure was expressed. He would meet my bus at 5:05. I called back to say I had decided not to go. I didn't supply a reason and wasn't asked for one.

My new colleagues were an even more eccentric bunch than I might have expected, many of them riddled with prejudices and insecurities that made university teaching their only safe haven. The one exception was Gerald Walton, who was at that time a young lecturer in English, like me, and an aspiring poet. He had just arrived to teach at Mason, and would ultimately have, I felt sure, the sort of career he's now having. He soon became my friend and was someone my own age I could talk to, someone who understood. His hair was just as brown and curly as it is now and his eyes just as sharp and clear. He was always a little sloppy in dress, but physical appearance never seemed to matter to him, any more than it did to me, because I was so strongly aware of his inner qualities.

The others were the usual mix: Joe Gaudry, a lecturer in French who told me in a quiet moment that he had written his doctoral thesis on André Gide, but I intuited that he remained in the closet himself; Sheila Kemp, a librarian who had recently caught a seventeen-year-old male student adding sexual marginalia with a red ballpoint pen to a medical dictionary; Dennis Grant, an unmarried professor of psychology who confessed to me, in a quiet corner, that his recurring dream was to run naked over an acre of bare-breasted Congolese women; Bob Fletcher, a sociologist who had an especial liking for bathtubs with claw feet and coffee urns with spigots, the latter causing him to worry that he might have a repressed desire to interfere with small boys; Tom Burton, a fundamentalist historian who believed in spanking the many children he had thoughtlessly added to the world's population; Carl Hollen, a biologist who spent more time bird-watching than teaching because even the flight of a bumblebee gave him pleasure, set to music or not; Samuel Bean, an art historian who compared notes with the president on how best to deal with insomnia, his own highly recommended method being to list alphabetically as many eighteenth century painters as he could, starting with the gently cloying Boucher but always excluding Hogarth, whose realism he dismissed as a vulgarity too distressing to promote sleep.

Surrounded by such learning, was it any wonder that I took immediately to Gerald, whose highly developed intuition caused him to recognize at once that I was homosexual and whose honesty led him to declare that he was not. This understood, we became firm friends and are to this day. We could always confide in each other, in the same sort of instinctive way I seem to be confiding in you now. When he wasn't telling me about any one of the girls who had fallen for his insouciant good looks, as indeed I might have done had his orientation been otherwise, I liked hearing him talk, especially about poetry.

To be a poet was to see, he told me. That's all it was, really. Well, that and a bit of technique thrown in. You had to be able to say what you wanted in a tight space, with each word carrying a lot of baggage — unless, of course, you were writing *Paradise Lost*, and even there every word had to count for something. Words were never things to be thrown away. But the seeing was the important thing, seeing what others didn't see. An ordinary person might look at a flower, a daffodil, say, and see only a daffodil, but a poet saw that daffodil as part of something bigger, and when a poet wrote of love, a whole world was opened up. Whether you believed in God or not hardly mattered when you were made aware of the eternity you carried within.

Our favourite place for talking was a small café we happened upon by accident in Preston, not knowing at first its hours for business. We had been looking for lunch and were inspecting a menu outside the Paper Doll Café when the glass door suddenly opened and we heard a female voice ask if we were looking for lunch. We said yes and entered.

She said her name was Rachel, and told us what was on special that day, chewing gum all the while and rolling a curl up over her forehead. Her shape reminded me of an hourglass set in blonde wood, with bleached hair gathered on top to stand in a mass of loosely formed curls. Her teeth came slightly forward, with lipstick covering more of her mouth than her actual lips, and her manicured hands, with fingernails bitten below the quick, displayed only half-nails painted red. Yet there was an air of elegant vulgarity in every step she took and every gesture she made. Indeed, "elegant," as we quickly discovered, was her favourite adjective.

When we said we'd have the hot chicken special and a beer to go with it, she asked if we wanted an elegant glass. Assuring her that we did, she smiled and so positioned herself that each elegant foot followed the other through the swing door into the kitchen, toes pointed like a ballet dancer's.

Happily for us, no interior designer had altered the pre-war décor of that unpretentious place, which became our second home. In front of an arborite-covered counter to the right, eight stools were fixed to the floor, while a vaguely suggestive art deco plywood panel was to be seen on the wall behind. Four booths stood against one side wall, four on another. Donuts, pies, and date squares were on everlasting, unembarrassed display, while at the counter to the left you could buy cigarettes and chocolate bars, as well as postcards with local views of barns in the country and geese on lakes. Any magazines found on the adjacent wall held nothing erotic for me and little enough in those days for Gerald, despite his always looking in a casual way for something to satisfy his pictorial lusts. While we did not share Rachel's view of what was truly elegant in this world, it was the unguarded simplicity of a place that did not pretend to be anything other than what it was that so much appealed to Gerald and me. Away from prying university eyes at two or three o'clock in the morning, we could always be assured that at least two people we knew wouldn't be there, the president and Samuel Bean, for they would be safely home in bed, muddling up Fragonard with Jeremiah — or was it Goya? whoever came first — as they tried to fall into sleep.

It was Gerald, in that place, who said he was in love again, only this time with someone truly beautiful; and it was to Gerald, in that place, that I confided something else. I couldn't say I was in love again, but I could say I had met someone called Martin. There was, you see, a dangerous aspect to that. He was a student of mine.

VI

I suppose I could say it began on a chilly day early in that November of my second year at Mason. That would make it 1959. Low clouds had threatened rain but it hadn't arrived. The leaves were off the trees by then, and the campus looked pretty desolate. Even the single swan, which had been swimming in circles since August, looking for its mate, which had died that summer, had been taken from the pond and put into further seclusion for the winter.

I had just returned from a weekend in Toronto, driven by sexual frustration — as I had been for that whole first year at Mason — to visit the city's baths. I had discovered by then one in particular, superior to anything continental, just off Yonge Street, which had become my favourite, perhaps because it was the most accessible. It was discreet, low-key, and secure in its clientele. I always gave a false name, of course, as I assumed everyone did, when I checked in at the door. I would pay my ten dollars, collect my towel and key, and proceed to my assigned cubicle, impelled by lust, sheer lust. I'm certainly not proud of going, but I never thought of them as male brothels, which I suppose they were. For me, they were just places I could visit and simply be myself, with no one there to ask any questions or condemn me to hell's flames. There was no real fulfillment there, no atonement, and I knew there never would be; just momentary sexual relief, after which the loneliness would return.

All manner of men — doctors, lawyers, judges, teachers, physiotherapists, star athletes — were there, stripped of identifiable clothing when they walked those dark and narrow corridors in silence, clad in towels only, folded carefully so as never quite to cover the genitals. Figures in slow motion, spirits in limbo from Dante's world, gliding past each other, always looking, sometimes touching, glancing into any cubicle with a door ajar, hoping to see an obliging occupant lying, standing, or sitting in the position appropriate for the kind of sex desired.

"Do you want company?" was the standard question.

"Come in, yes," or, "Not just now," were the standard answers.

The possibilities for yes or no were equal. Life went on teaching its lessons.

"So thick, abject and lost lay these," I thought to myself, as I kicked the leaves on my way to class, remembering all the rebel angels who had fallen, preparing myself for another lecture on Milton — *Comus* this time, not *Paradise Lost*.

"Today I want to talk about *Comus*," I announced, as soon as I got to the lectern, "presented at Ludlow Castle in 1634." Twenty-five hands wrote name and date in notebooks just because I spoke. Terrifying! What if I had been wrong? Who did they think I was? C. S. Lewis? If I had said, "This is a very pretty little poem," would twenty-five hands have recorded the same for posterity? I read from the text, though I hardly needed to, because I already knew it by heart:

Here dwell no frowns, nor anger, from these gates
Sorrow flies far: See, here be all the pleasures
That fancy can beget on youthful thoughts,
When the fresh blood grows lively, and returns
Brisk as the *April* buds in Primrose-season.

Those were the attractive words of Comus, I told them,
son of Circe and Bacchus, wildest of parents, as he tried
to seduce someone simply called the Lady, who was very
much a virgin. He had captured her in the woods when she
became separated from her two brothers, and had deceived
her into thinking that his "low but loyal cottage" was a place
of safety. Once he got her there, of course, he was very
much on the make: "Why should you be so cruel to yourself
/ And to those dainty limbs which nature lent / For gentle
usage and soft delicacy?" It was the seductive approach
echoed later, I reminded the class, in Marvell and in others:
"Had we but world enough, and time / This coyness, lady,
were no crime." But, returning to Milton, it was clear that
Comus had found his match in this particular Lady. It might
be unkind to describe her as a professional virgin, but it
wasn't far from the truth. Listening to her sermon on the
"serious doctrine of Virginity," which Comus described later
as "mere moral babble," was for him the equivalent of being
dipped in a "cold shudd'ring dew," enough to cool any man's
passions. Nothing like a cold shower. But Milton would
have us believe that the Lady was right. Her arguments were
the ones he meant to be persuasive. We were not to be
seduced by Comus any more than she was.

Having said that, a hand went up, and a voice questioned:
"Why not?"

Did the speaker want to be seduced by someone like Comus? I asked, whereupon everyone in the class laughed. They thought I'd made a joke, but as soon as I said it, I realized I'd asked the wrong question. The hand belonged to a boy in the back row, sitting between two girls.

"Sounds like fun," he said. "What is chastity, anyway?"

That was just the point, I replied, and I gave my little sermon about chastity suggesting temperance, the proper use of the body, the purification of nature through virtue, not just doing whatever one liked, any time of the day or night, though I felt hypocritical and even a bit pompous as I said it, aware that twenty-four hours earlier I had spent a whole night in the baths.

One of the girls agreed that chastity implied restraint, but another went further, saying that the Lady was negative, totally negative. She was wooden, rigid, and static, and probably thought there was never a right time.

I partly conceded it was an unsatisfactory debate. The Lady went as far in one direction as Comus went in the other, and Milton would have liked to suggest a balance, but didn't quite get there.

"Then you agree?" the boy asked. "There is a time and a place. It *can* be okay?"

Feeling myself by now a little trapped and even uneasy that he might have been personally focussing on something more than this abstract argument, I moved on to a discussion of the court masque and the stylish sets of Inigo Jones.

After the lecture my student approached me directly, saying that it had been an interesting debate, even before he introduced himself as Martin, Martin Alexander Pearson, but no relation to Lester B., in case I was worried, a remark which made me smile.

I said I was glad he liked the poem, which he replied wasn't true: he didn't much care for the poem, it was too stuffed with classical references for his taste, and he guessed that only academics liked Milton. There was no disrespect intended, but did I really like Milton, or was I just saying that because it was my business to say that?

Who are you? I thought to myself. I know your name. You're in my class. But who are you? Why are you asking me these questions?

I did like Milton, yes, I answered, whereupon he said that that figured: there must be something to Milton if I liked him, and did I think he ever would?

I told him he might, when he grew up, teasing him a little. It wasn't easy stuff, and he should know that. His answer was that he did know that, and could I help him to like Milton? Could he, in fact, come and talk to me about it, and when? The sooner the better, he hoped.

I had a meeting to attend that afternoon, I replied, but I would be in my apartment that evening, if he wanted to come up after dinner. I lived in Osborne Hall.

"I'll be there," he shot back, giving a look that stripped me bare as he left, or was I indulging a fantasy? Has such a thing ever happened to you?

I checked my records immediately. Pearson, Martin Alexander. Age eighteen. I sat down, aware by now of the obscure chemistry which sent blood up to my cheeks and down to somewhere else. It was a signal I recognized, and when it came, it always came unprompted. With Clifford it had been a constant torment, and I knew I could be entering dangerous territory again.

In memory, I went instinctively back to Christ Church, catching my breath, as I always did when I entered that grandest of all Oxford quads with the simplest name — Tom. Then past the hall itself, with its portraits of the great — Wolsey, Henry VIII and daughter Elizabeth, John Locke, Gladstone, and Peel — all watching and listening, silent and equal in death. And the gentle lecturer in mathematics who told his stories for the Dean's daughter and made for her a wonderland. "'Tut, tut, child!' said the Duchess. 'Everything's got a moral, if only you can find it ... and the moral of that is — Oh, 'tis love, 'tis love, that makes the world go round!'"

Still in memory then, past the residence of Meadows to the serenely walled garden beyond, and the deep booming bell from Tom Tower, a sound never silenced, not even in war, and just over the wall, the gardens of Merton, where love's labours were lost on that terrible night.

Kneeling now by Clifford's bed, my own spirit grown heavy in love. My hand under the bedclothes. I love you. I love you. The thought formed, the words unsaid. Hand moving to its destination. Head and mouth following hand. The sweet taste of love. Subsiding flesh. The quiet moment. Then the shock. Achievement and loss in one. Clifford's voice, annihilating me with bullet-like words: "What the hell do you think you're doing?" But he added what I didn't tell you earlier: "Don't you know that's disgusting, really disgusting?" Blow job was not in my vocabulary then, and I would still consider it a coarse term thus to describe what I so naturally gave him. But disgusting? Had I done something disgusting?

Putting memory aside, what could I expect to happen this time? I finished my meal and waited for Martin to arrive. Had I eaten too much garlic with the sausage I cooked? I gargled with a good mouthwash. I put on a clean, loose-fitting shirt, a pair of casual slacks and, finally, my red socks.

Cushions were fluffed, candles were lit, and from my not very large record collection I chose Kathleen Ferrier's English Songs and Folksongs, singing to myself one of them in advance: "I know where I'm going / And I know who's going with me." But did I really know? My mind was a tumble of questions. Should I even be doing all this? What if I were found out? I was breaking the law. I could lose my job. What would Martin think when he came in? Too obvious? Or was I merely setting the stage for a play he had already written? Who, after all, was playing Comus, Martin or me? What if I had misjudged? What if he reported me? I could be taken to court, given a jail sentence.

Promptly at nine o'clock, there was a knock on my apartment door. The residence itself was friendly and open, allowing me quiet and privacy in my own space if I simply shut an outer door, much like sporting one's oak at Oxford, which I did after admitting Martin. No one was around to witness his entrance.

He walked into the small, modestly furnished living room with its two soft chairs, coffee table, bookcases and two prints over the couch, a Rouault and Van Gogh. He liked the Old King especially. He didn't get off on cypress trees, though they were a bit phallic, didn't I think?

He asked what two other contemporary-looking prints on the opposite wall were all about. Just a jungle of leaves and vines, tying themselves in knots, I told him. Nature unleashed sort of thing.

"They shouldn't be tied in knots," he said.

What did he mean?

"Anything natural ought to be free, that's all."

Again I wondered. Who was this boy, that he would talk like this as soon as he came into the room? I was his professor. He had only ever seen me in class, but he seemed to know about me.

He was only of average height, about five-nine or -ten, but obviously strong and muscular. Below heavy eyebrows, his brown eyes flashed intelligence, and his lips, unusually red and full for a boy, were clearly designed for sex. This much was evident from the beginning. That he might also be petulant and demanding and selfish never occurred to me. Already I was gripped by passion, fearful of no consequences.

Martin sat on the couch. He said it was warm in the room, and did I mind if he took off his sweater? I said he should make himself comfortable. Throw it over one of the chairs, which he did. He wore very tight blue jeans and a red, somewhat thin T-shirt, so form-fitting I could tell his chest was hairless. He kicked off his shoes and then readjusted his position so that he sat cross-legged at one end of the couch but turned slightly towards me. The move had caused his jeans to get pulled partway up his legs, which I then could see were unusually hirsute, as were Clifford's. The bulge in his crotch was now conspicuous, and I tried not to look, even as I turned to hide my own growing erection.

Because there was wine left over from dinner, I asked if he wanted some, and when he said yes, I poured two glasses and brought them to the coffee table, kicking off my own shoes as I sat beside him.

"Who were you thinking about?" he asked, though he must have known the answer.

"You," I told him. "I see you're wearing red socks." But then I was, too, and he had noticed that.

"What do you want to know?" he asked, and my answer was quite simple: "Who you are."

I thought it best, you see, to be direct.

In just this way, I started a voyage that would take years to complete. In those first years, you would have been growing up in the Okanagan Valley, discovering yourself, learning who you were meant to be, and then going on to Europe. You were lucky.

VII

Once Martin got started, I realized I had no idea what I was getting into. He told me, for example, that his mother was a social worker as well as a witch, and when I asked him what he meant by "a witch," his answer was simply that she liked cats and cast a spell on his father who was an alcoholic. But the spell didn't work, and because his father continued to drink, she took to religion, thinking that might be another way to cure him, which it wasn't. Martin had a twin sister, Jane, who was still at home with his mother and the cats, and an older sister, Hope, who had married and got out of the house as soon as she could, in an effort to fulfill the promise of her name. His father had left when he and Jane were only ten years old, after saying how much he hated all the goddamned cats because they just slept all the time, and he was jealous. Martin could not decide whether he missed his father or not.

All this came out very quickly, even a little incoherently, just the way I've related it, and I must have appeared startled by its strangeness. When he asked what was wrong, I told him that I wasn't expecting to hear so much. Not all at once, anyway. It was unusual. In that case, he said, to balance things, I should tell him about myself. As he leaned forward for his glass of wine, he managed to brush against my leg.

That was enough to bring back my erection and, I could see, to confirm his own.

Trying to get this potentially explosive situation under control, I reminded him that he had come to learn about Milton, not me, and I changed the subject by asking where the home he had been talking about actually was. It turned out to be a small place just outside Montreal, St. Abel — English despite its French name — and that's where he went to school until he was twelve. The school wasn't any good, he claimed, so his mother sent him to Montreal for a real education. She also wanted to get him away from the town because of stories about his alcoholic father, and he thought he had made a good start in escaping all that.

On the surface, there was something easy and natural when he told me these things, but there was also a growing intensity which turned the exchange that followed almost into cross-examination. He was eighteen, going on nineteen; how old was I? Truthfully I said I was twenty-seven. Could he call me by my first name? Was that okay? Peter, wasn't it? Was he being too forward?

I said I didn't mind, providing others didn't hear him addressing me as Peter in public: it would be bad for discipline. He replied that he didn't believe in all that, he didn't believe in keeping everyone in their place. The Jesuit fathers had tried that with him at Loyola, and it hadn't worked. We ought to be free to express ourselves, which, of course, is exactly what he was doing.

When I said he sounded a bit like Comus, he countered that Comus wasn't all that bad. I should allow him a few points. He knew what he wanted, and he knew where he was going, which, I replied, was exactly nowhere.

"I wouldn't say that," he answered. "It seems to me he had a lot of fun trying. Which one would you rather be, Comus or the Lady?"

Without thinking, I answered that I could hardly be the Lady.

In that case, he cried, I had to be Comus, and looked as triumphant as a courtroom lawyer who had just tripped up a witness.

Surprised by the nature of this exchange, I got up for another bottle of wine, which I proceeded to open, for we had finished my dinner's leftovers. We both heard Ferrier's voice in the silence: "Where have you been all the day, my boy Willie? / Where have you been all the day / Willie, won't you tell me now?"

Not surprisingly, I found myself asking a similar series of questions. Certainly Martin was very much at ease in my company. He was obviously enjoying himself, but I wondered if I was ready for anyone so uninhibited, anyone so young? I hardly thought it possible for a mere boy to lead me happily to the place I had aspired to reach with Clifford. Martin was trying to escape, he admitted, and there was now the implicit invitation to escape with him, to sound the trumpets, make the walls fall down, and enter Jericho. "We have to learn to love," Angus had said in my Oxford bedroom, holding me in his arms when I had felt myself abased, and that was surely true.

Martin had taken these intervening moments to stretch out on the sofa and close his eyes, as he listened to that incomparable voice: "Feather beds are soft / And painted rooms are bonny; / But I would leave them all / To go with my love Johnny."

I opened the other bottle of wine, which was better than the first, and he teased me by saying I was corrupting the young, and he would drink to that. I must have frowned at a remark so near the edge. That was no joke, I told him a bit sternly. He touched his glass to mine.

"Then, to Socrates!"

"To youth!"

How sweet that sounds! To youth! But this boy was my student. I was in charge of his moral and intellectual upbringing. There were values to be passed on, principles to be inculcated, opinions to be formed that would have to be clear and just and far-reaching in their consequences. I had to be sure of what I was doing. However powerful the sexual attraction — and it was certainly that — he was still just a boy, still a student, and I was the adult who could be taken to court for sexual assault, for sodomy, for corrupting the young, even locked up, which was theoretically possible, though I hadn't heard of anyone who actually was. I should have been terrified, but something in me overrode my fears, and I went ahead anyway. He scrambled from his position and sat on the floor, turning himself to look up at me, one arm and elbow on the sofa where I sat. His strong presence was palpable. He asked if I thought he had come just to talk about Milton, when, quite frankly, his true purpose was to talk to me.

He asked if he had done anything to upset me, because he had seen my negative reaction when he talked about his mother and religion. I assured him that he had not. In fact, I had been thinking about my father, though I didn't want to get into all that. Too much in my past remained unresolved. Like the ghost of Hamlet's father, my own father was there on the ramparts of my life, forever stalking me. It was another potentially explosive situation I had to control.

"And girls? What about girls?" Martin asked.

I said I'd tried but it hadn't worked.

I could hardly have been prepared for his direct line of questioning and his assured intuition. It was all quite unlike anything I had ever experienced, even at Oxford, because it was entirely free of social restraint and intellectual affectation. I was beginning to realize that here was a truly free spirit, someone determined to be only himself, not a copy of anyone else. This was 1959, remember. It would be another ten years before drag queens and queers would riot in New York at Stonewall and proclaim the right to be themselves. It hadn't happened yet, which put Martin well ahead of his time. Yet now something was happening to me; a mere boy was about to change my life.

Martin claimed always to have known who he was. What was the use of pretending? From the time he was a very little boy, he knew what he wanted and how to get it. Neither did he see any reason to be ashamed. It was very beautiful. It was like seeing yourself in someone else, something you recognized as true.

I told him I had known that once, but I had forgotten, because the world had intervened. What did he want by coming to see me? I was startled when he replied that what he wanted was me. Unequivocally he wanted me.

I asked what he would do if he wanted someone but found out that person didn't want him? What if that person claimed he was disgusted by you?

"I'd feel sorry for that person if it was true," he replied, "and if it wasn't true, I wouldn't care. I don't disgust you, do I?"

"No."

"And you don't disgust me."

We had crossed our Rubicon.

I looked down at my left hand, which I had placed on the sofa, not far from Martin's right hand. Our fingers were almost touching. In the three-inch gap that separated his hand from mine, I could feel the charges of electricity that connected us, a horizontal Jacob's ladder that might take us to heaven if we journeyed along it carefully.

I remembered an incident with Clifford. We had gone on a cycling expedition to Ireland, straight across to Connemara, where he used to spend his summers as a child and where the inhabitants admitted never to rain but only to "a fine soft day." There had been for a time an emotional truce between us, during which we had passed through the town of Galway, pushing further to the coast, past Clifden, near the little village of Cleggan. Clifford had extracted from me there a promise not to touch him, and I had agreed, even when I knew how much he longed for what he denied.

We had stopped for a break beside a field overlooking the ocean, and there Clifford lay down on his back, with me on my stomach, four feet away, although it might as well have been four miles. Despite our agreement, I knew only the old agony and longing. I looked across the immense distance between us and studied the profile I had long committed to memory — the mass of unruly hair encroaching on his forehead, his nose silhouetted against a rare blue Irish sky and positioned between thick eyebrows above flashing dark eyes, closed for the moment, his unkissed mouth with lips now slightly parted, a strong chin that expressed all his determination never to surrender to me, his thin neck with prominent Adam's apple, and so down and down and further down his long lean body, past nipples I had gently touched, down and further down, past hollowed chest to navel and that thin line of hair leading to his cock, savouring its sweet-salty taste, holding it all in my mouth, my private joy in that most private place.

He turned at that point on his side towards me and opened his eyes, his right hand only inches away from my left. I plucked a blade of grass, held it for a moment, and then began to move it very slowly towards him, towards his right hand, inch by inch, both of us now focussed on this single act. It made a journey slow enough to be a microcosm of oriental theatre, my whole world held now and concentrated in a blade of grass.

It stopped when it reached its destination, but there I continued to hold it, my body alert and tense, my penis firm against the ground, his own in evidence.

For Clifford, the blade of grass might just as well have been the Trojan horse, a massive deception which would undo him forever. Did he really fear the Greeks, even when bearing gifts? It was a long suspended moment of choice, and in this dreadful pause I thought the universe exhaled and feared to take another breath. For me, a whole lifetime passed before he changed his focus abruptly, looked across the miles between us, removed his hand, rolled again onto his back and closed his eyes in pretend sleep. For the longest time I didn't move, but when I did, I threw the blade of grass against the winds that blew in from the Atlantic and lost it forever.

Now it was Martin who was beside me with a different blade of grass, more real than the real one. I reached for his hand and felt the rush of life. The walls shuddered and fell in a cloud of wasted years, and the city at last lay open. "I once loved a boy," sang Kathleen Ferrier, "and whether he loves me or loves me not / I will walk with my love now and then." I leaned forward to kiss him on the mouth, and assured him there was more ahead for both of us. The future would certainly come. The world would shudder from crisis to crisis, but still go on. The future was ours.

When I asked him to tell me his dreams, he repositioned himself in one easy move from floor to sofa, so that he lay with his head on the upper part of my leg, and only then spoke of a single and recurring dream. It was about a house where there was a party going on. It was a big house with lots of rooms. The guests were always very beautiful, some with children and some without. There was a cat there, too. There was always one cat, curled up, alert, and watching everything. Inside the house, there was music and laughter, and no one was ever ill or talked of illness, and the whole place was lit by candlelight. Outside, there was a garden with terraces. And when the party was over and all the candles had guttered to an end, the walls became doors, and everyone moved into the open garden space and said goodbye, leaving him alone.

With his eyes shut, I could believe that he was again back in his dream, and I waited some time before I replied, asking as gently as I could if I was at the party in his house. Yes, I was. Were there others there? Not at that moment. Had they gone? Yes, they had all left. Was he ready to leave? He was. Could I go with him? Yes. He would not be alone any more, but then neither would I.

Both of us were standing. He said nothing and I said nothing, as he carefully undid my shirt, button by button, allowing it to fall around my hips, so that it was held by the belt at my waist. He knelt to undo the buckle, then the top button of my trousers and the zipper, so that both shirt and trousers fell to the floor. He supported me while I stepped clear of all my clothes.

His was the ritual of an instinctive lover, and what he did seemed almost ceremonial. Each move he made was choreographed with delicacy and grace, and nothing was said until I stood naked before him. He looked up at me and smiled before he took me in his mouth for what was only a moment but could have been forever.

He got to his feet and stood in front of me so that I might do what he did. His shirt, when I removed it, revealed a torso as hairless and smooth as I had imagined. When I pulled his tight blue jeans down to his ankles, so that he stood as unashamed in front of me as I in front of him, I was reminded of a small statue of the Youth of Marathon, a boy rescued from the Aegean sea, with a bronzed body that seemed to have been smoothed by the hands of hundreds of lovers. My own hands followed now the line of Martin's smooth back and the curve of each buttock, before I knelt to take him in my mouth, this time without any fear of a reproving voice.

I took him to my bed, telling him that we must never lose what we were discovering, for a judgmental world would make every effort to take it away.

There were no more walls, I whispered, facing him on the bed, just doors and windows open to the light. It was no longer a dream. We had come through. There was no world more real than the one we were entering. Did he know what was best of all? Nothing was ever lost. Nothing could ever be truly lost if it was there in the first place. It remained forever. He should remember that. So should we, you and I, who are here in this place tonight.

He shifted his position and gently turned me over so that I lay on my back. Very slowly, sitting astride me, he let down the whole weight of his body so that I entered deep within him. I had no thought at all that I was committing a criminal act, quite simply believing that I had made another long journey to get home.

Some moments later, with Martin still in my arms and partly sleeping, I made for him a special name, something that might speak of youthful love — agile, erotic, uninhibited, and free.

"I've got a name for you," I said. "I'm going to call you my Arab Boy. It suits you."

After thinking for only the briefest moment and telling me he liked the name, he asked, very seriously, if he would always be my Arab Boy.

"Yes," I promised him, "you'll always be my Arab Boy."

VIII

You might guess I was sensitive the following morning to what were surely innocuous questions asked over coffee in the faculty common room. They came out in the usual way but somehow seemed pointed at me, as though everyone knew what I had been doing the night before. Instead of the usual hello, good morning, how are you? I was hearing, How did you sleep? Have a good night? Never can wait to get to bed myself, no place like it. I wondered if I was going to be able to cope, and feared I might now become paranoid. I would have to be careful skating on this particular pond.

The first person I was aware of talking was Carl, the biologist. He was saying he had heard of the Canada Warbler, but not until the day before had he learned there was also a bird called the Red-faced Warbler, and of course I wondered if he might be thinking of me, even though I knew he could have no idea of what I had been up to the night before, and I had no cause to feel embarrassed. He warbled right on, of course, about how these birds jerked their tails sideways, making only a thin sound when they sang. But that was not at all a description of Martin and me: our sounds were pretty robust and our actions more varied than that.

I noticed Joe Gaudry just then, sitting in a corner by himself reading *Corydon*, André Gide's painful but brilliant dialogues on sexual differentiation. I had read the book myself, and I had some genuine sympathy for someone else in the closet, though I had never found it possible to speak directly to him and felt guilty about that. Gide hoped his book would tear down the lies and hypocrisy found everywhere about homosexuals. He quite bravely and truthfully said we were an important part of humanity and were certainly not contemptible.

That was in 1911, mind you, and by 1959 I guess attitudes hadn't much changed in that little town, though they have since, I hope, in some ways. Back then, Joe would have to continue his own quiet reading, and Martin and I would have to continue to conceal ourselves, trusting no one to see us as we truly were.

The further sight of Bob Fletcher approaching the coffee urn with enthusiasm and turning slightly pink when he touched the spigot, and Dennis Grant talking about sex in the Congo, made me think I couldn't stay there another minute.

I disappeared in search of Martin, meeting him, quite fortuitously, in the corridor a few minutes later, as he came from a lecture. With other students around, I tried to sound offhand when I told him I had that book for him. It was in my apartment, and, if he liked, he could come up and get it right away.

"Be there in a minute," he replied, and he was. Within another minute we were back in bed, all our clothes hastily thrown onto the floor. His question was insistent: Would I fuck him if he was Lester Pearson's son? Yes, yes, I would want to fuck him, no matter whose son he was, and we both laughed and laughed, almost uncontrollably, so happy to be escaping the world.

So much laughter. Yes, we were happy then, and, as a result, I tried to put Clifford out of my mind. We had, however, to scheme to keep the world around us out. There was always the desperate need for secrecy, and at first we found it easy to deceive.

My bedroom in Osborne Hall was on the second floor, with a fire escape made of iron just outside my window, which we put to good use.

He would come to "learn more about *Comus* and the serious doctrine of Virginity" as many times a week as our different schedules allowed. It was easy for him to arrive at my door at nine or ten o'clock at night with a casual hello to anyone he might meet. No one would ever think to keep track of whether he had made a later exit or not. Once inside, my locked outer door guaranteed security. When he finally left, he would simply put on his clothes, go to the window, climb out onto the fire escape, move down to the point six feet above the ground where the iron ladder stopped, and jump. Always I stood at the window until I heard the thud at the bottom. Martin would look up, whether visible to me or not, and blow a kiss, and I would do the same. It was one of our many rituals, and whenever we talked about it, in more rational daylight hours, we called it our Romeo and Juliet act, and always laughed at how ironic it all was.

"Methinks I see thee, now thou art below, / As one dead in the bottom of a tomb."

I never said those lines, of course. I only thought them.

Because Martin had entered the college with credits, he began his last year at Mason in the fall of '61, and in that October, two matters of consequence happened within days of each other.

Gerald remained the friend I told everything to, and Gerald was the person I arranged to meet late one Sunday in the Paper Doll Café when Martin had to stay in residence to work on an essay for his sociology course due the next day. He said it was on birth rates in Quebec, and he knew nothing about the subject, which was true. He would have to pull an all-nighter.

The café would be quiet for Gerald and me at midnight, or so we thought, but it wasn't. Three tough-looking kids, scruffily blue jeaned and T-shirted, all about sixteen or seventeen, two of them with thin beards in progress, the third with a wispy moustache, were giving Rachel a hard time when we arrived, and she looked relieved to see us.

Forever pushing one large curl back into place, she quickly came to our booth with menus, whispering at the same time that she wished to hell those guys would get out. She apologized for inelegant language used in front of elegant patrons like us, but going past their booth on her way back to the kitchen with our order of beer and rings, she told them, nonetheless, to go fuck themselves.

That was enough to make them stop for a moment, thank God, so I started to tell Gerald about a confrontation I had had that morning in the common room with Tom Burton who claimed that not all of Hitler's methods were necessarily bad. Some people deserved their fate, even if they happened to be Jews or homosexuals. He did, however, disapprove of gas ovens, and thought hanging would have been better, spewing his venom as he went out through the door.

"No wonder the world gets in a mess, with men like you in it, you stupid ass-hole," said a small female voice from the corner where none of us had noticed Sheila sitting with a list of library fines she was preparing to send out. For emphasis, she added, "Screw you." But the sadistic Tom Burton was well out of earshot by then, beyond her not so beneficent imperative. Sheila simply looked up at the rest of us who just stood there, more stunned by her riposte than Tom's original outburst, and said rather sweetly that she wondered why so many students had overdue books. The rest of us cheered and congratulated her on doing what we had failed to do.

Gerald, who always avoided the faculty common room, regretted that he had not been there to witness so rare an event and started to tell me about his day, when into the Paper Doll Café walked someone who might have been a high-school student and quickly went for a vacant booth, looking around and behind him as he did. My reaction to this young man's obvious beauty caused Gerald to tease me immediately, reminding me I had Martin already, and wasn't one enough?

I said yes, yes, of course, but he was beautiful, wasn't he? One had just to look at his eyes and his hands. Though I knew Gerald wasn't gay, he could surely recognize beauty when he saw it, couldn't he? Beauty of either sex. Plato said you could always recognize it, if it was the real thing.

The young man looked distracted and nervous where he sat, nearer the rowdies than us, and they, in turn, started to snicker and whisper and point disparagingly. The young man looked pale as well as fidgety, and when he picked up the menu, having felt for it first, it was obvious that he couldn't easily read it, despite the thick glasses he put on.

I whispered my suspicion to Gerald that the boy might be blind, but Gerald said no, he couldn't be blind, because he had got in there, though he probably didn't see much either. Poor kid, I thought. Still, other people could see him, and that was a dividend for the rest of us in this poor old world.

The trio of teenagers who had not gone off to fuck themselves, as Rachel had so elegantly suggested, went on looking and started putting their heads even closer together.

When Rachel came for his order, the young man said he'd have a coffee and that would be all, thank you. She went back to the kitchen, and he reached into his windbreaker pocket and pulled out a piece of heavy twine, its two ends already tied together in a knot.

Continuing in his distracted mode, not even looking at his own hands while doing it, he started to play cat's cradle, fingers looping up strands, tightening them, releasing them, creating a network of triangles and diamonds, too small to endanger any grown cat but something that could ensnare a kitten if it got its claws entangled. He did this three times while waiting for his coffee, but suddenly stuffed the whole thing back in his pocket, got up and left, followed almost immediately by the three kids who had been looking at him.

When Rachel returned with the young man's coffee, she lowered her voice and told us confidentially that some people said the boy was a queer, a homo, a fruit, but it made no difference to her. She wanted people to be just whatever they were.

"Bless you," I said, meaning it, as we said goodnight.

I was late getting to the common room the next morning, where everyone had already heard about it.

"A boy in the town, son of the station master," began Carl, whose perspective on most things was reasonably balanced and who could always be relied on to give a fair account. The police found the boy dead early that morning. Murdered in a dead-end alley just a couple of blocks from the Paper Doll Café. He must have been cornered. Hit over the head with something heavy. Probably died instantly. His hands had been tied behind his back with a piece of heavy twine. His zipper had been pulled down and his penis taken out. Just left there, hanging out. It was awful to see, the police said. No clues, no suspects, no motives either. In that town, who would have thought anything like that could happen?

I went to the police immediately, and within hours, three boys had been picked up for questioning. The mother of one of them was very surprised. "He wouldn't hurt a fly," she protested when the police came to her door.

Some months later I learned they were given only minimal sentences because they were all juveniles. There were no actual witnesses to the crime, and no murder weapon had been found. It had all been a terrible mistake, the judge said. He didn't think anyone had anything against homosexuals, certainly not in a small Ontario college town, not in 1961.

It was on the Wednesday following the murder that the second thing happened, with potentially darker consequences for Martin and me.

Despite pulling an all-nighter, or maybe because of it, and despite the buzz of gossip and conjecture surrounding the murder, Martin was ready for my bed by mid-week, but his nerves were a bit frayed from work and from hearing so much talk. But in the twenty-first year of life, confidence runs high, and he was certain no one knew anything about his relationship with me; he exercised not even his usual caution when he came after eleven to my door that night. His knock was bolder than I was used to hearing it, and when I opened the door I heard loud voices from a nearby room occupied by a student called Ronnie Price. I had been obliged to warn Ronnie about excessive noise on several other occasions. Clearly, he was entertaining in his room yet again, during what were supposed to be quiet hours. The smell of beer was also obvious.

"Here I am," Martin said brightly and loudly, adding for emphasis, "Sir." And then, "May I come in?"

I spoke rather loudly myself, for the benefit of anyone who might be listening, assuring him I had the book he wanted to borrow, which was always my line. If Martin had been seen at all by the party crowd, it would be as well for them to think he had come on academic business, and they would quickly forget about him.

I closed the outer door and the inner door, grabbed Martin, gave him a deep kiss, and was quite prepared to fuck him right there in the hallway, standing up, a position we had perfected over many months. I was in such a state of excited tension from all that had been going on, that I convinced myself that only hard driving sex would bring relief after four days of abstinence. But just as suddenly, I came to my senses and said it was really important that we talk. I led Martin into my living room. He'd heard about the murder, hadn't he? He admitted that he had, but what could he do about it?

I could see his mood change as I told him, in detail, what went on in the Paper Doll Café and what I felt sure had happened right afterwards. I had gone to the police, I told him, and they were investigating. There were serious implications for both of us as individuals, though in different ways, and for both of us together. We lived in a dangerous world, I explained. Martin could be attacked like the young man who was murdered, and I was engaged in sex with a student, which could cause me to lose my job. It was more important than ever that we maintain a strict guard over all we said and did. Did he understand? "Whatever happens, you will understand, won't you?"

I reached the end of all I had to say, and led a sober Martin once more to my bed, but what we did there seemed now more fragile, even tarnished by the world we had tried to keep out. Even so, I gave an honest answer to his question as I watched him dress, before making his usual exit. Yes, he would always be my Arab Boy. He dropped the last six feet into darkness before I returned to my bed, still deeply troubled.

When I got up late that Thursday morning, there was an envelope tucked under my door, which at first I thought must have come from Martin, but the crude handwriting was not his, and my surname, Lindley, was missing the "d." On a piece of pink paper inside were the words: *We know what's going on.*

If life has its defining moments, that was one of them. Everything around me immediately looked different, innocence turned to threat and scrutiny caught me in a searchlight. I wondered how I might extricate myself from the several skeins that were tightening around me. Had someone done the equivalent of taking a black and white picture of me? If so, I knew that such things could never be reversed, for what has been revealed can simply not dissolve again, fade away in solutions until it is no more, wind itself back onto a reel, unphotograph itself, and unclick the camera. Escape was not possible.

I needed to talk to Martin and tell him of my fears, everything compounded by what had happened earlier in the week in that dead-end alley near the Paper Doll Café. When he came to my bed again that night, after passion had been satiated, I told him that we had to be sensible.

It could only have been Ronnie Price who wrote that note, I argued, though others might be implicated. But Ronnie couldn't possibly know anything. How could he? Martin had spoken to him when he went by his room, but so what? He was probably asleep when Martin left. I couldn't believe he was waiting for Martin at the bottom of the fire escape. Was he? Hiding behind that large tree at the corner, perhaps?

"Sure, that's just where he was," Martin hit back. Hadn't I seen the guy? He had jumped right out, pulled Martin onto the grass, sucked him off, and gone running back to his room to write that note. How could I possibly think ...

Irritated, I said this was no time for a joke.

"You're the one who's joking," he answered. "I want you to be serious."

I was being serious, I protested.

I wasn't, Martin argued. Ronnie Price might be a little shit, but why would he do a thing like that, even if he thought I didn't like him? It didn't make sense. How did I know, furthermore, that Martin himself hadn't written the note? Maybe he wanted a little excitement, something to keep me guessing. We didn't want our life together to become routine, did we? Which seemed, when he said it, like hitting below the belt.

Routine? Was that what he thought? By then I was starting to feel angry. Was it just routine for him?

"Stop, stop," he commanded. I was upset. He knew that, and he was sorry. He could get upset, too, but it wouldn't do any good. He loved me and I loved him. That was all that mattered. We couldn't fuss and worry ourselves into early graves because of a little anonymous note under my door. We had to move beyond fear.

I was the one who had to stay, I reminded him, whereas he was the one graduating. There were lots of rooms in his house, and he had to explore them all, find out what was in them, live in a wider world than the one he knew at Mason with me. He had to go. He had to move beyond all this. He asked where he would want to go, and I told him he'd find out. Wherever it was, he had to remember he'd always be my Arab Boy. Was I sure? Yes, I was sure.

With tension defused, I looked again at Martin, the mouth I loved to kiss, the hair I loved to run my fingers through, his nipples, his ears, his neck, his armpits, his abdomen, his cock, even his toes and fingers, all so precious to me, all so intimately known, as my own body is known to me. That night, unlike some that had been characterized by lust, we did more than have sex, we made love.

For Martin's remaining months at Mason, I was in agony, torn by the desire I had to keep him in my arms and the fear of being discovered. There was no sure way of interpreting events, either in that small place or in the greater world outside. It had also been in the beginning of that final year, just as Martin had been getting ready to return in September, that a massive wall, mostly concrete, nine feet high, had been constructed in Berlin, almost overnight. No one knew what it really meant or for how long it could possibly remain. The world looked forbidding and dangerous, and for all that final year at Mason, whenever Martin left my bed and dropped six feet into darkness, I thought my own thoughts and feared finding another note under the door. High walls, steep drops, and ropes filled my dreams. But he, somehow, coped better than I. All I could do was to make a private vow never to fail him, to stay with him always, even as I set him free.

On the night before his graduation, he came once more to my rooms, and again we made love, tenderly now and with an awareness that it might be the last time. He was leaving the next day to travel — destination undisclosed, he said, but it would be somewhere south of the border after he hitchhiked across Canada. He would look for a job, any job that would allow him to travel the next mile. He was going in search of the other rooms in his house, and he hoped I would feel free to search in mine.

I told him I liked the room I was in.

He liked it, too, he said, but there were other rooms. We'd stay in touch. We'd always be close. He'd write and I'd write, and in that way we'd never lose each other. I would always be the man he loved above all others, because I was the first man he loved. He kissed me goodbye, climbed down the fire escape and jumped into the dark.

At his graduation, I watched him cross the stage with mortar board and gown to pick up the parchment that would release him into a bigger world and take him away from me, even though I knew it could only be into a world of danger. I tried to understand, I really did, and I tried to accept that another chapter was over. There didn't seem much left. But I know now one should never say that. Lots more was to happen, and tonight's another night.

IX

As you might expect, it was Gerald I turned to more and more in those first two years after Martin's graduation, and it was Gerald who was my comfort. We spent hours and hours talking; not just in the Paper Doll Café — sometimes he came to my place or I went to his, but wherever it was, I must tell you that any happiness I had at that time came because he was my friend.

Martin, you see, had taken my advice to heart and had gone off on his own to explore as many rooms as he could in the large house of his dreams, while I remained in mine — small, dark, and increasingly closet-like. Unluckily for me, Gerald also moved from Mason the following year to take up a position in Toronto as manager of a Bloor Street bookstore owned by his uncle. Despite having to keep business hours, he knew he would have more time to write, and he began to get published in small journals. His presence in the big city, though, gave me an excuse to get away from the college any weekend I could.

The lure of cheap sex was strong, but those who moved in silence, like me, through the dimly lit spaces of a bathhouse world, might just as well have been looking for gold in the Yukon. Glimpsed in full-length mirrors, positioned at corners to heighten expectation when turning them, none of us looked happy, only desperate. Reading pornography at other times or seeing pictures of smooth, naked men and taking such pages to the privacy of my bedroom brought only shallow relief and further frustration. Hunks with perfect teeth and abdominal muscles, all of them endowed like horses, lay stained beneath my covers and further trans-mogrified into animals I had lusted to ride. It was Martin I missed.

Between lectures on Comus and Chaucer and the imagery in Blake, this was my world: dark, anonymous, sterile, without joy, dreaming of an ideal, pursuing the opposite. I thought of Martin, hundreds of miles away, and I remembered Clifford, aware that I would never be free of him. I thought, too, when I left the darkened corridors of sex, of the harsher light I had always to face: my father on my infrequent visits home. It was, however, the magnet of sex that held Martin and me together for all those years we were apart. Whatever the distance between us, we could always feel that pull. I would be back in his bed one day. I felt quite sure of that.

He wrote to me from wherever he was about the men he had met, and I wrote to him about my own sordid adventures, tame by comparison. His voracious and indiscriminating sexual capacities, even greater than my own, had led him to indulge almost professionally, and not just with men, as I later found out. Although he invariably had his favourites for a week or two, he changed his partners with all the élan of a dazzling virtuoso, so that no one was at the top of his hit parade, as he called it, for very long. No one, that is, but me. For me he professed an undying and genuine love, and I believed him. I loved him too.

In the early summer of '64, two years after his graduation and after working as a waiter in Buffalo, where he was at the time of Kennedy's assassination — like everyone else, he remembered exactly what he was doing when he heard the news — Martin had headed for the Big Apple, undeterred by a major article on homosexuality that had just appeared in the June 26th issue of *Life* magazine.

He phoned from New York, which he rarely did because rates were so high. Our usual method of communication was by mail. At that time letters within Canada cost only five cents and letters into Canada from the United States cost eight. He urged me to pick up that copy of *Life*, which I did, but he told me nothing of its content or tone.

I could hardly get past the first double-page black and white picture, with minimal sidebar text, of jacketed, capped, and blue jeaned young men in a smoke-filled San Francisco leather bar, without fearing immediately for Martin's well-being. On one page, I read about brawny young men in leather caps and shirts and pants who were practising homosexuals, men who turned to other men for sexual satisfaction, men who were a part of what was called the "gay world," though it was, according to the article, actually "a sad and often sordid world."

Can you believe it? Maybe you even saw that issue, because you would have been nineteen by then and interested. It alarmed the hell out of me, even though I knew it was rubbish. On another page, there was a different picture, this one of a spectacled, balding, bar-owning bigot, making it clear in a sign under a row of bottles on the shelf behind him, who was and who was not welcome in his bar: "Fagots — stay out," spelling faggots with only one "g," of course. If they approached any nice-looking guy and tried to do any recruiting, he'd have them shot. Who cared about them, anyway?

I was so enraged by this travesty of journalism that I immediately wrote a letter of protest to the managing editor of *Life*, someone called George P. Hunt — How could I forget a name that sounded so solid and respectable? — but, sad to say, I never sent it. I should have, but the fear of losing my job at Mason if all this became public outweighed the anger I felt. The closet doors were still not open, and anyone who read the magazine that week would have had every prejudice confirmed.

Martin, reading it, was not just undeterred, he was positively spurred on. He knew exactly who he was and what he was and had no problem being true to that in any world he inhabited. It was a quality in him I admired, even when it made me fearful.

It was in New York, he told me, that he had an affair with a journalist he picked up in a bar on Christopher Street, whose name he said I would know if he told me, which he didn't. He had then gone on to San Francisco, where he had another affair with an older, distinguished English writer he met in the Castro district, whose identity he would again not reveal. His refusal to do so in both cases surprised me, for Martin had become an inveterate name-dropper by that time.

There followed a San Francisco dalliance with a wealthy corporate executive he had met at a party, someone who wanted to do everything for him and everything to him, but Martin drew the line when Mr. Money Bags wanted to have sex on a large bed covered with one hundred dollar bills and

Martin himself covered in softened chocolate truffles which would be licked off before the big fuck.

After Messrs. Anonymous One and Two and Mr. Trufflelick, he took up residence in London with the great-grandson of a wealthy Victorian shipbuilder, Morley Bryden, someone he had met, at first only casually, on a New York visit, when Morley himself had been there on business. Martin was at no pains to hide the name this time, though it was not a name I knew. He assured me in several letters that the Brydens were distinguished and immensely rich.

A perfect match, he had written, a real English gentleman who adored him and gave him everything. What more could he ask for? His new lover was handsome, smart, rich, and sexy, but not as sexy as I was. I suppose I should have been flattered by such a compliment, but I wondered if this could possibly work, my Martin with a perfect Englishman? The attraction of opposites, maybe.

"You must come to visit us," Martin wrote in early November, 1971, and I realized with a shock that twelve years had gone by since he had come to my rooms to learn about *Comus* and "the sage and serious doctrine of Virginity." He said he had to see me again, and I should make the trip the following summer. They had a flat in London, the Soho area, which couldn't be better for everything — and he meant everything — and they rented a cottage in the country for weekends. I would love it. I had to come, he said.

I replied that I'd think about it. The college was in too precarious a state financially to offer even a modest pay raise that year, and for that I blamed the president. It was enough to make me hope he would backwards stumble his sleepless way, night after night, as far as Leviticus and there get stuck on the infamous bit about not sleeping with another man. He would never have been able to understand the very idea, and no man would want to sleep with him anyway, but that didn't make any difference. There was no money in my bank account. I would have to borrow, yet again; I knew it would be worth it, though my credit rating wasn't so hot. Somehow, if I could, I had to get away from my restrictive environment, escape Mason, escape the pull of the baths. Everywhere I looked in the world, I saw problems, and every sort of structure — political, social, racial, religious — seemed to reflect the mess and uncertainty of my private life.

Five years after the article in *Life*, hundreds of gays had rioted at the Stonewall Inn, a Greenwich Village gay bar that had been raided by nine New York cops. It happened the day after Judy Garland had been buried, which may not have been a coincidence, because she had long been a recognized symbol for those who had endured abuse and would do so no longer. On June 27, 1969 — when you were not quite twenty-four yourself but must have been aware of all this — the feeling spread that even gays who lived across the border would one day overcome. The bill that Pierre Elliott Trudeau brought in, as Minister of Justice, declaring that "the state has no place in the bedrooms of the nation," was already the law in Canada, but everywhere in the country there were dangers still to be faced.

On one dark and terrible Palm Sunday in 1970, my father in Stratford did something that made local headlines. My mother, more distressed than I had ever heard her on the phone, said she would have to send me the clipping, because she could hardly bear to speak of it.

"Both Christians and humanists delude themselves with images of light," he said in a sermon that morning, when his church was full of the righteous sitting below their stained glass windows. He no longer believed the stone would be rolled away. He stepped down from the pulpit, without a thought of Easter, threw his vestments onto the floor, and walked down the centre aisle, out into his own private darkness.

When I learned the story, I realized my father had been too close to God to be close to me, but removed from God, he went even further away.

The FLQ crisis flared in October that same year, precipitating genuine debate among civil libertarians because of the way Trudeau dealt with it. Not just my father, but the whole country seemed now to be approaching a precipice, with dangers everywhere. I felt more strongly than ever that I had to get away, see Martin again, meet Morley: there had to be other worlds. But it wasn't until the next year that I had enough money to arrange for a flight the year after that. Time passed as it always does, with all the usual distractions of life and teaching, not to mention my overnight visits to Toronto, and I arrived in London on schedule in mid-June of 1972.

Ahead of time, I learned that Morley would be out of the country when I arrived, which only increased my excitement at the thought of going to bed with Martin right away. He was, however, teaching school in London and surprised me by insisting that I visit his classroom immediately upon my arrival. I puzzled over why he was making me wait for what I presumed he too would want immediately. I certainly wanted him, despite a night without sleep in the plane's economy section, where it had been my misfortune to be squeezed into the middle of three seats. His apparent indifference puzzled me, but later I understood. The weekend that followed in the rented country cottage explained a great deal.

The old section of the school where he taught, not far from Kilburn Park, was formidable in appearance — red brick, heavy doors, stone stairwells with long protective bars running vertically through a three-storey height. The whole effect that of a cell-block. The class Martin taught had demolished seven previous teachers in succession. His immediate predecessor had lasted three days before having a nervous breakdown.

My heart sank when I saw the place. I wondered how he withstood the pressure, and how long he would continue to do so. For now, he was very much in control — strong, aggressive, cheerful. He taught all subjects, it seemed, but each only for as long as his students' attention would hold. Sex was the unifying theme, the adhesive he used to bind the class together. He would read from an economics textbook and make it sound lascivious, so that in a short space of time the law of diminishing returns became equated with multiple orgasms.

He introduced me to the boys as his "tutor from Canada," whereupon they all chorused, like the well-trained English schoolboys they really weren't: "Good morning, sir!"

Martin had told me on our way to the school that he let them say whatever they liked, because they were a reasonably bright lot and not at all inhibited. It seemed best to allow them some free rein. They usually read a few pages of something together and then branched off; he announced they would start that morning with "The Clerk's Tale," then go on to *Major Barbara*. There were no concessions to luxury in this room, I noted. Old desks, marked, initialled, a print or two on the wall, maps and charts, French Impressionists, faded.

Sammy, bespectacled and spotty with adolescence, began the lines from Chaucer in modern English I knew from my university days:

> A marquis once was lord of all that land ...
> Discreet enough to lead his nation, he,
> Save in some things wherein he was to blame,
> And Walter was this young lord's Christian name ...

Martin interrupted. They had to decide about Walter. They already knew the story, how he tested his wife. But was he, in fact, sadistic, making her swear total obedience before he even married her? Was that a perverted social instinct? Did this mean that Griselda was a masochist? She, after all, liked taking what he had to give her. Was this not, in fact, a balanced relationship? Were there any comments?

"What colour were her socks?" said a boy.

Was he confusing her with the Wife of Bath, Martin asked. *Her* socks were red. That was a sign she was full-blooded and sexy. When the boys laughed, I remembered something, as did Martin. Blue was the colour for love, he continued, asking how many were wearing blue socks that morning, or should he just assume they were all wearing red ones? More laughter at that.

Obviously, Martin was enjoying himself, and was aware that I, too, was in his audience. His comments about Walter and Griselda seemed his way of telling me that he now knew what sado-masochism entailed, which I later learned was true. By that time he had met Derek, and had discovered a new world in the old world — another room in his house.

The boys pleaded to hear about the Marquis de Sade, only to have Martin move on to *Major Barbara*, where followed further pleadings that he tell them what an "experience" meeting was. Young bodies without experience believed in only one kind: orgy, orgy. Flames raced higher now, with everyone talking and laughing, and only I noticed the fat boy in the back row whose hand was groping the erection of the pimply boy sitting next to him. All was now at such a height that Martin shouted at them to shut up. It was time for their sex-education test, and with that he wrote on the board: OVARIES, TESTICLES, ORGASM, NIPPLES, CONDOM, FAIRY.

Someone asked, without getting an answer, what kind of fairy he meant. Was it the fairy in the woods or the other kind of fairy?

The other kind of fairy? Is that what Martin was? It's a loathsome word, taken over that way, cruelly used to wound, when it was meant originally to conjure an image of lightness and grace. I was sometimes called a fairy in school, and it always cut deep. Martin's own Canadian brother-in-law, married to his twin sister, Jane, had called him that on more than one occasion.

Chuck had once invited Martin and Morley to go for a drive in his large forest-green Oldsmobile, with its fake leather seats and Kewpie doll suspended from the back window.

"I expect you two will want to sit in the back and hold hands like a couple of fairies, so go to it. I won't look," he had said. He was Chuck to his friends: "Attaboy, Chuck," they would say admiringly when he talked of cheating on his wife and screwing his favourite broad "for a flat fifty bucks, and she does everything, I mean everything." He worked for an engineering firm, designing elevators for buildings over twenty storeys high. "I know how to get 'em up and bring 'em down," he would say, amused by his own ribald sense of the crude double-entendre. His offices in Montreal were in the Place Ville Marie. "Christ, no, I don't speak French. Let the frogs learn English," was his attitude to bilingualism.

Martin endured Chuck's company for the sake of his sister, and was happy when they divorced. Had lust been Chuck's only experience, I wondered, and was mine now so very different? What had happened to love? Where was Shelley's baby?

Back at the Soho flat, Martin said what I wanted to hear. He asked if I remembered the night he had come to me for the very first time, after that lecture on *Comus*. I remained his one fixed star and I should believe that. Watched over, at last, by a baby who had been seized by a poet, we went to bed.

Three days later Morley returned from his business trip to Colombo, and the day after that the three of us left for a weekend in the country. Meeting Morley for the first time, I was able to see his relationship with Martin as sensibly balanced. He brought wealth, social position, sensibility, and high intelligence, while Martin supplied exuberance and flair, the sheer fun of expressing himself unreservedly in a restrictive and conventional world. Since my only experience of sex with an Englishman had been with Clifford, I suppose part of my anxiety had been that Morley might resemble him in some way. He didn't. Not at all.

Martin and Morley had been lovers only at the beginning of their relationship, and had soon stopped sharing the same bed, which confirmed my intuition about the sort of open relationship they would probably have. They agreed that sexual passion should, for the most part, be placed outside their particular bond, devising, however, a mutually acceptable rule: extra-curricular indulgence would be only allowed on neutral territory. For Morley that meant the Far East on his frequent travels, especially Indonesia where boys with flashing teeth and coffee-coloured skin reminded him beautifully and regretfully of what he had lost in Martin. For Martin it meant the pubs of London, the steam-baths of Berlin, the streets of Amsterdam, and any other easily cruised area. It was a challenge, I confess, for me to come to terms with all that, but I was no example of celibacy myself.

"Derek will be arriving soon," Martin announced, once we had reached the Gloucestershire cottage. I was assured that I'd like him. Most people thought he was a tough cockney, but he was really half Welsh. He was running a restaurant for someone else — a front for a pimping agency — but he hoped to open a real one of his own before long.

Before he was due to arrive, I had time to look around and get my bearings. The cottage that Comus took the Lady to was described as "low but loyal," and this one seemed rather like that. Built of Cotswold stone, it was tucked away in the corner of a large estate.

Approaching it from the main house, the road sloped between two barns and then dipped suddenly into a hollow which obscured the cottage until that point. The dirt track continued in a curve to the left, past the cottage, dipped even lower where it crossed the stream, then, rising and curving, sharply to the left, ran through an area thick with trees, branches hanging low over the puddle-marked road until it joined a wide avenue, lined with laburnums, which went from the highway to the main house. The empty barn, where Martin and Derek were to play out their fantasies, was a scant seventy-five yards from the front door of the cottage.

A small dining room and kitchen were to the right of the front door, living-room to the left, and through it stairs, built like a cupboard in the wall, to three bedrooms and bathroom above. Furniture, pictures, books, and *objets d'art* all reflected Morley's taste, intelligence, and wealth, but had been combined and arranged with Martin's characteristic flair. There was, everywhere in the small rooms, a striking mixture of the modern and the old. Victorian bric-a-brac was set against contemporary lampshades and stuffed chairs. Eighteenth century silver sat next to enamel plates on a Regency table. The whole place had about it an air of comfort and elegance, as well as declaring itself a bit of a joke.

Before the late night encounter Martin and Derek were to have in the barn, dinner was held in the dining room where a round mahogany table was set with four big Georgian chairs. On the eighteenth century sideboard, a number of glasses, decanters, and bottles of whisky, brandy, and port had been pre-selected and arranged. On the walls I had noticed a coloured print of *Joseph Interpreting Pharaoh's Dream*, and of course I remembered a particular sermon of my father's about the lean kine in Egypt and the lean years that lay ahead for everyone, if they didn't prepare for the future. I wondered at the time if the sermon was directed at me.

Next to the print was a sampler, full of dark forebodings, embroidered in 1825 by a ten-year-old child, who could not have understood the words she stitched about the fall of Adam, and how the vengeance of the Lord had fixed His everlasting hatred "betwixt the woman's seed" and Satan.

Two other pictures in that room were in sharp contrast to each other. One was a photograph with a Victorian naval theme — "Handy afloat, handy ashore." A handsome young naval officer stood with a distinguished, equally handsome military commander, making me wonder if they were meant to represent Martin and Morley. The other picture was a contemporary lithograph depicting four gangster-like figures in black coats converging on a fifth seated at a small table with a red chequered cloth. A sixth grey-blue figure, obviously dead, was stretched in the right foreground against a large irregular rectangle of white. But who were the gangsters? Who were they threatening? What had happened to the figure in grey and blue?

Another Victorian sampler on an opposite wall — this one by Ann Drinkwater — provided an optimistic counter to the gloomy prognostications of ten-year-old Mary Patrick:

> Enrich me with thy heavenly grace
> Endue me with thy spirit and
> Let my soul when hence it goes
> Eternal Life Inherit.

But eternal life? Life that goes on forever? Who really wants that? Surely one life is enough. I think often of that grey-blue figure on a rectangle of white. Let that be all.

I found Derek attractive in unexpected ways. His fair hair, cut short, was curly. His blue eyes were bright and alert, even friendly, but his mouth was tightly drawn, and his lips so thin as to be almost not in evidence. It was unlikely he trusted anyone. Only occasionally were there hints of his cockney accent. For the most part, he spoke with a slight drawl, wishing, no doubt, that he had been to Eton. Martin had picked him up in a Soho pub on Frith Street and later had invited him to meet his friends, including me. On all the country weekends that followed, he and Derek would go off late at night to the deserted barn, dressed alike in torn, tight-fitting jeans, black leather jackets unbuttoned, chests exposed, linked chain belts around each waist, armed with ropes, tit-clamps, and paddles, faces masked. Neither of them wore blue socks.

Physically, Derek was trim and well proportioned. The lilt in his voice made the quality of his speech engaging. When his lips parted in a smile, I noticed a slight gap between his two front teeth, a sure medieval sign for someone highly sexed. The Wife of Bath was gap-toothed, in addition to being red-stockinged, wasn't she? Clearly Derek was a man of action and a man for action, with no tales of mastery to tell, no debate about the battle of the sexes. One sex only for him. Mutual punishments given and taken. Limits respected. The cardinal rule. Probably a good match for Martin, anxious to extend his sexual range and visit more rooms in his great house of dreams than I knew of myself. For a few weekends, anyway.

I confess I had some difficulty with the whole thing. Pain is not on my wish-list. I have never been able to endure it easily, and I find it hard to understand why anyone would seek it out. The idea might titillate, but only the idea. Yet, I was not prepared to talk to Martin about it or raise any protest when it was put in front of me so blatantly. Was that yet another failure on my part?

Morley set the conversational tone that evening. It was evident that his cultural and intellectual background was far beyond what Derek, the Welsh-cockney intruder, could comprehend. To my embarrassment, Martin was flaunting Derek as his latest sexual partner, but Morley's outward demeanour betrayed nothing. No one was to see beyond his own protective layers. There must be no suggestion of his own humiliation.

He had been educated at Winchester and Trinity College, Cambridge, and, at thirty-nine, epitomized the English gentleman at his finest. Martin had been right about that. His distinguished profile, with a hint of Jewish ancestry in the nose, was worthy of kingly imprint on a national coin. He was impeccably mannered, sartorially elegant, naturally intelligent, and rich. His family had been shipbuilders since the early nineteenth century, and the Bryden Shipping Line between Liverpool and Cape Town had been particularly profitable. He was well-travelled and unemotional, trained never to show his feelings. English public schoolboys were, after all, expected to act like men. How else would the Empire have been built? Clifford would have agreed.

I could sense that Morley disapproved of Derek, but he said nothing about it, any more than I did. Shopping for provisions in the nearby village that morning, he was like a young Sir Roger de Coverley, greeting everyone, extending the right patronage, going the familiar round as though nothing were wrong — cheese and eggs at the market; wines from Mr. Jenkins, the wine-merchant; bread from old Mrs. Peabody from the little shop on the corner; and meat from Mr. Sloan, the butcher. He went his way charmingly, graciously, pleasing all, a justification for Winchester and Cambridge. His brown hair waved and curled down his neck, his sideburns were bushy at the ears, his eyes were clear blue, and his smile was a genuine flash of warmth. His speech was unruffled perfection, each syllable clearly articulated.

I asked him, when we stopped for a pint at The Crown and Feathers, if he had ever done any acting, and he said yes, in his old prep school, when he was a very small boy indeed. That's where he got his big break at the age of nine. He was in two plays: *The Merchant of Venice* and *A Midsummer Night's Dream*. He told me to guess what roles he played.

I suggested first the Prince of Morocco, and after that Nerissa, both of which were wrong. The first role had been Jessica, and after that, he had played Titania. As Jessica, he had to wear a very unsatisfactory black wig, which was rather Jewish-looking; but as Titania, he wore a long blonde wig, which was extraordinarily beautiful, especially with him in it. He had gone to Winchester next, where there was no proper drama group, only a couple of organizations with dull names like "The Player's Club" and "The School Thespians." Neither was there a real theatre or decent stage. It had been a bad situation all round until one day he and some of his friends decided to produce something themselves. They found a frightfully clever young master who said he would sponsor them, provided they did all the work. As a consequence, Morley was put in charge. The group decided they might as well aim for the top and do *Hamlet*, which Morley took upon himself to cut by forty percent. In retrospect, he thought it had all been rather appalling, but at least he had played the Prince, and did not have to wear a wig. He had also played Olivia once when he was in the navy, a production in which everyone spoke Russian. He was sure that was all rather bad, too, though they thought they were terribly clever speaking it in another language, especially a Slavic one.

I was pretty impressed by all this, I must say. Assured that Morley could deal with any situation that might arise without showing distress, I went with him to the local butcher, encountering there another layer of snobbery which so much amused him. The shop was just off the main street, cramped and ill lit. One had to stoop a little to enter, but there, immediately in front, was Mrs. Sloan, the wife, preserved forever in her very own glass booth in the family poulterer's shop, keeping her accounts as she always had, fumbling to find the correct change in a darkened drawer, the recesses of which must yet have contained old shillings and pence, groping to secure more and more receipts on old nails which could no longer hold the bulk. There, too, was Mr. Sloan, a model of proper deference, who recognized a gentleman when he saw one.

"Good morning, Mr. Bryden. A very nice bit of rabbit today, Mr. Bryden. I think you'll like this, Mr. Bryden. It'll make a very good stew. Oh, it's a boisterous wind today, Mr. Bryden."

If Morley moved as easily in this particular context as he did in a graceful, sophisticated world, it was because he was trained to it and knew the duties of his station. It must have been just that way, I thought, with William Pound, an eighteenth century porter, at the opposite end of the social scale in Christ Church, Oxford. There's a tablet on the wall in the small cloisters of Killcanon, which I used to stop to look at every day when I walked through to Meadow buildings, words I learned by heart because I liked them so much, attesting to virtues similar to Morley's. They commemorated this porter who "by an exemplary Life and Behaviour and an honest attention to the Duties of his Station deserved and obtained the approbation and esteem of the whole Society." Everyone in his hierarchical place. How English can you get? Morley was assured of his position at the top of society, whereas Derek was only on his way up. He would never make it.

How different from what we know in Canada! Your parents were pretty well-off, you said, unlike mine, but that in itself didn't guarantee anything. You still had to work to get where you are, but rich young men in England didn't always have to do that. Edward Troy-Jeffers certainly didn't have to fend for himself. But as in most things, Morley proved the exception. He knew he was at the top, but he also knew he had to justify his being there, and he did.

The meal that night began at ten o'clock after many drinks on the small terrace, which ran the width of the cottage. There, under a clear evening sky, Morley began to recite a poem of Auden's about looking up at the stars. He said that he wasn't sure he could finish it unless he concentrated very hard, which he did. He gave special emphasis to the couplet about equal affection: if it was not to be, then he would claim the more loving role. Blue socks for Morley, red for Martin. I glanced at Derek who appeared not to understand the poem. His association with Martin and Morley was part of his self-improvement scheme, bringing social dividends beyond sexual pleasure, even when he couldn't keep pace.

At dinner we ate off white enamel plates, the current vogue, set with exquisite silver and crystal goblets. After a first course of caviar and chopped eggs, Morley ladled onto each plate very small portions of the rabbit stew he had made from Mr. Sloan's best offerings. The emphasis was rather more on drink, with Morley also pouring the wine, telling us always to keep our glasses on the table when he refilled them. The supply was endless, and he got progressively drunker, more so than the rest of us.

Morley wouldn't allow any music during a meal; Martin had turned off the stereo, which had been playing a new recording of music and songs from *The Graduate*.

It really was rather curious, Morley told us: one could like and appreciate music and yet be insensitive to all the other arts and even, as a person, quite lacking in understanding. This insensitivity seemed to be a condition peculiar to music and musicians. He had not observed that other forms of art affected people in quite the same way. Had any of us ever noticed that?

Martin insisted, of course, that before they met, Morley really didn't know anything much about music and didn't even like it. He certainly never went to any concerts, and he hated opera. Morley only agreed that that proved what he was saying. Literature and painting and sculpture and architecture had been his first loves. Music came later, and he was glad it did.

"Something has to be done to separate the sheep from the goats" was Derek's sudden contribution, thrilled to be able to participate in talk he considered pretty high-level. Anxious to hold his own, he went on that he never knew why, in the Bible, there was so much talk about separating the sheep from the goats, when it seemed to him that there was no possibility of getting them muddled. Then someone had told him that in the Middle East they were very much alike, which explained the whole thing. It really did take some sorting after all.

He looked triumphant when he got to the end, slightly flushed by his own exegesis of a question no one had asked. Morley, scarcely acknowledging that Derek had spoken at all, steered the same topic in a different direction.

"I know you won't believe this," he began, pouring some more wine into his own glass and sinking a little lower into his high-back Georgian chair, "but I had an aunt who was an authority on goats. The greatest living authority in England, in fact."

He went on to tell us that she'd written a book on goats and published all sorts of goat articles. What her reputation was in Lebanon or Syria, he had no idea. But who was it who talked of separating the sheep from the goats in the first place, as though the sheep were all good and the goats were all bad? It sounded like Saint Paul, didn't it? Yes, it must have been Saint Paul. But then he was such a bore, the arch-bore of all time. Obviously he didn't know anything about goats. Morley's conclusion to all this was that if he had to choose in some afterlife which he'd like to be, he'd say not a sheep, please, but a goat. Goats had a far more interesting time.

I asked him which he thought we were equivalent to in this life.

"What are we all? Why goats, of course. We are the outcasts, the rejects. It's not possible for homosexuals to be anything other than goats. But everyone wants to make us into nice well-adjusted sheep."

From the caviar with chopped onions and hard-boiled eggs, washed down with iced vodka, to Mr. Sloan's very nice bit of rabbit, to salad and cheese and fruit, the meal progressed. Empty bottles were replaced with full ones.

It was very interesting, Morley continued, he had decided to be a sort of volunteer-witness for a couple of researchers at the University of Sussex who were making a study of homosexuality. One of them was a woman who asked him what he had against the female sex and if he hated his father and identified with his mother, and all that sort of psychological shit, which is how he referred to it. He said he surprised the woman by stating that he admired and liked his father very much and had nothing at all against women. He just didn't want to go to bed with them. When she kept on asking him why, he had to say quite frankly that he found the whole business aesthetically displeasing and deeply boring. She shut up then, but he expected he would be called back to see her again quite soon, since most of the people they got for such studies were either stupid or socially maladjusted.

Martin interrupted to ask if Morley remembered the man they met at the Wilsons' party who asked all those awful questions.

"Good God, yes! How could I forget?"

"Tell us about him," said Derek, recognizing by now how little he had to contribute.

Morley said he thought the man very gross indeed. He hardly knew him, but there he was, after a few drinks, right in front of him, saying he'd heard Morley didn't like women.

His first instinct had been not to answer, but he thought better of it and said that wasn't quite true, that he liked some women very much; indeed, he had a number of women friends but had never gone to bed with a woman and never would. The drunken party-goer, leering at him further, had asked if he was a queer. Morley told him he preferred the word homosexual, a perfectly good word which he was not ashamed to use, though his interrogator might also try the word gay if he wanted to be up-to-date. The man asked if that meant Morley liked men, to which Morley responded, "Some men, yes." The boor came really close and asked if Morley would like to go to bed with him, since he was a man. He got a memorable and stunning reply when Morley made it perfectly clear that the whole idea was far more repellent to him than it was to his questioner, who had even thought it possible.

By now, Morley himself was beginning to slur his words. The reminder of his boorish interrogator both amused and depressed him. He was drinking large amounts of brandy. He looked at Martin and Derek, knowing their plans for the night, and moved further into his own deep personal despair, brooding, on a level where none could reach him. I confess I never even tried. All my uneasy feelings I kept to myself.

It was Martin who took over, trying to save this part of the evening.

"Morley is so clever. I must tell you ..."

"Oh, darling, do shut up," was Morley's response.

"No, I must tell them about the time we came on the ship from America, and you recited a Russian poem."

"Must you?"

Martin was not to be stopped. He explained that Morley knew Russian, had studied it for two years, and still spoke it fluently. He really was most awfully good at languages.

There had been a gala night on board, and various people had been asked to do something in the way of entertainment. Morley had a volume of Yevtushenko's poems with him, and he agreed to recite one. He spent three days writing and polishing an English translation, as well as learning the original in Russian. When the gala evening came about, and he got up to recite, there was total silence in the ship's ballroom. People were genuinely surprised when Morley said he would recite the poem in both languages, which he did, quietly but firmly in his lovely voice. It was a poem about waiting, just waiting, which was all very Russian. People had tears in their eyes when he finished.

He stopped his narrative at this point so that he could urge Morley to recite the poem again, beginning with the original, but Morley was by now very drunk and deeper in depression. He looked across at Martin, angry to have been given a build-up which, in his condition, he knew he could not match with a comparable performance. His words came out with surprising bite and clarity:

"That's unfair of you. You really must give me proper warning. No, I cannot remember any of it. I will not say one line."

"Then, I'll begin it," Martin said.

No, Morley countered, he would not have it. He would not have Martin spoil his story. It really was unfair. With that, he started up from his chair, unsteadily. Martin went over to him, sure-footed, well practised, expertly supporting him, his left arm around Morley's waist, Morley's right arm held high around his own neck. The two of them moved towards the doorway. There, Morley turned with his summary of the evening, still drunk, infinitely sad, mind still working:

"There's nothing but nothingness in this cottage, and if you had my half-sister and a limp, you'd be as Byronic as I am."

Martin took him up to bed, and we all retired soon after that. Martin and Derek went in one direction, I in another. But it was not long before I heard the door to my room being quietly opened. I shut my eyes and pretended to be asleep.

Martin entered, moved towards my bed, bent down, and kissed me, but I didn't respond. He went to the cupboard that stood against the far wall and took something from it. I heard the rattling of chains and partly opened my eyes. In the half-light I could see that he was dressed in his costume. Were it not for the kiss, I might have thought him a burglar.

I knew that Derek was waiting for him downstairs, even as I remembered my own first night with Martin. I tried to understand, but in the pit of my stomach I felt sick. Should I have tried to stop him? I look back on my own behaviour now, what I did or didn't do, how I did or didn't react, and am surprised.

Maybe it's someone else I've been telling you about.

X

Although it was Martin who had urged me to make the trip to England in the first place, it was the nothingness in that cottage that had sent me back to Canada. This became the pattern for what I could almost call my yo-yo travel over the rest of that decade. Always I took myself with me whenever I crossed the Atlantic in either direction and always returned to square one.

With a selective memory that's capable of blotting out unwanted images, I was able to remove Derek from the chemistry of my brain before he became fixed there forever. Besides, Martin wrote to assure me that Derek had not long remained at the top of his hit parade, and he was moving on to other rooms, taking me with him. His love for me remained, and whatever happened, I would try to understand, wouldn't I? I was, of course, ready to believe him, as I always was.

Early the following year, he wrote to tell me that he and Morley were no longer going to rent the cottage with its barn so full of ghosts, and that they planned to build a much larger house of their own on land they had bought nearby. Naturally, they had hired only the best architects — he wanted me to know that — and the place was going to get written up in *Country and Living* when it was finished. No one would mention that they were gay, of course. "Partners," they would be called. He reminded me that they slept in the same bed sometimes, but that was about all. They were going to have separate bedrooms in the new house, and when I visited, I could share his bed, if I wanted to, provided no one else was in it.

Unable to resist, I booked a ticket as soon as I got the letter, and added yet more to my bank loan. The thought of Martin's bed was enough. I would settle for being at the top of his hit parade, no matter how many others were on the chart, because there had also been others on mine, bathhouse pick-ups and lonely boys who hang about in donut shops at midnight and are never faithful. It was, after all, only 1974, and the world was full of attractive men.

The remodelled house was only a mile outside the same village but stood in splendid isolation, high on its own ridge, but settled snugly in its context of trees and fields. It was a brilliant architectural blending of medieval foundations, eighteenth century walls, and new extensions of glass and steel on two levels, achieving unlikely harmony in the unspoiled Gloucestershire countryside.

The upstairs, brown-carpeted drawing room, an extension of the original house, was forty feet long and half as wide, sparingly furnished but to glorious effect. Three new walls were made entirely of glass, and nothing but old oak trees immediately outside obscured the view of pastoral Gloucestershire. Contemporary black leather chairs, low-slung and armless, were positioned next to an exquisite mahogany Chippendale chest, on top of which stood an eighteenth century clock, brought from the cottage, and a porcelain jug filled with dried sheaves of wheat.

A few large cushions scattered on the floor, a couple of white plastic end tables, low mushroom-shaped floor lamps, and tall free-standing glass shelves for modern and antique *objets d'art*, were the main features of the decor, except for one large hanging of weathered wood on which one could read the word MISTS in letters sixteen inches high. Martin explained that the hanging was just half of an old sign from a CHEMISTS shop, something he had discovered in a second-hand junk place when driving through Banbury one day. It amused him to turn it into what others might be tempted to think of as art.

There was a single gesture to pop art in a silvered Coke bottle with a straw stuck in it, but nowhere was there a sign of gloomy little Mary Patrick's Victorian sampler. Ann Drinkwater was in evidence, however, and it was her prayer that I hoped would be fulfilled in this new place: "Enrich me with thy heavenly grace / Endue me with thy spirit."

Martin was still youthful in his early thirties, his thick black hair a mass of curls. He greeted me this time, unlike the last, with genuine warmth and passion, and we went to bed immediately.

"Have a bath," he said to me, twenty minutes later. "You're all fucked out. That'll relax you."

He led me from his bed to the louvered doors across one wall that opened into his tiled bathroom, where everything chrome was polished to a high gleam, and glass shelves were stacked with only the most expensive toiletries for men. He kissed me and left me alone, closing the louvered doors behind him, though I was aware he had gone back to bed and was waiting for me there.

Reclining in the bath, I thought again about the mysterious

force that kept our relationship together, a love that was so passionate and so detached at the same time, and I decided it was because of the quiet confidence we shared in each other, rather like the way I seem to be sharing things with you now, so instinctively. But who can tell how these things really work? Martin and I just knew where we stood on all the basic issues, loyalty being high on the list, approval being low. You don't have to approve of everything someone does to go on loving them, provided you know that a core of devotion remains. I had to believe this.

Martin was by now seriously into drugs — mostly amphetamines, not much cocaine — but he combined them with alcohol, and I feared the mix was deadly. He tried to deny this and said I wasn't to fuss about it. He was a big boy and I, of all people, ought to know that. He claimed to know exactly what it was he was doing, but that, of course, was untrue.

Morley, on the other hand, continued his own heavy drinking. They shared their city lives, Martin in his school, where discipline was always a problem, Morley in his family business, where larger shipping conglomerates were threatening to take over. But they escaped for weekends in the country, and continued to put their sexual lives in separate compartments. The only change from their earlier behaviour was that now they tried to follow their own rules.

We reached our zenith that August, and though we took note of the larger world, it didn't really affect us. We were too busy having a good time. Besides, the news was always bad, so why not avoid it? When I say that now, it must make us seem rather shallow. But when I started to tell you all this, I vowed not to gloss over anything.

Nixon was on television, an overwhelming spectacle of self-deceit, exercising its evil fascination, compelling us to watch. But still we went about our lives as though Watergate were happening on one of the moons of Jupiter. There were stories on television, closer to home, which cast a shadow, such as the Irish mother, cruelly interviewed after a shooting the night before, her voice robbed of emotion until she came to the climax: "I heard my husband screaming as he ran down the hill: 'Paddy's shot dead; he's lying down there in the meadow.'" While the scream she let out was loud enough for all the mothers in the world to hear, we continued to live in our untouched world, aware of suffering, but keeping it at bay.

Happy to be together again, Martin, Morley and I had a race with Time. In London we went to the National Theatre to see *Spring Awakening*, written in 1891 in Germany by Frank Wedekind, but banned in Britain by the Lord Chamberlain until the abolition of censorship in 1968. It was an unflinching exposé of sexual taboos in a world of hypocrisy, much like our own. Characters as real as ourselves told of their sexual awakening as adolescents, with one pregnant girl dying and a boy committing suicide. We watched one boy kiss another with tenderness beyond imagining, while others, sent to a house of correction, sat in a circle and masturbated together, each hoping that his ejaculating spurt would be the first to hit a coin placed in the centre. We watched a world of parents and adults and teachers who understood nothing of a young person's pain. Our own childhoods were on stage and we were moved to tears.

There were parties in London and parties in the country, an endless flow of good wine and an endless flow of visitors.

For me there was also someone special, Hugh Norton, a friend of Morley's and Martin's and an invited guest for my last weekend. Martin said I might even fall in love with him, he was so attractive, but Martin was like that when he was well, always direct and always prompted by a generosity of heart difficult to match.

We travelled by back roads until we got to Oxford where the sight of Tom Tower, even viewed over factory tops, rekindled a hundred moments of wonder, joy, passion, and grief. From Oxford, we continued along the Woodstock Road as far as the Trout Inn, where we stopped for lunch, its idyllic setting spoiled neither by the centuries nor the ravages of tourism.

Despite all the cars in the car park, the pub itself was uncrowded. Patrons sat in the sunshine, eating their sandwiches, drinking their beer, while tame peacocks strutted about in the open, nibbling any bits of food thrown in their direction. Fish gathered in quiet waters below the wall. The ruins of Godstow Nunnery crumbled across the river. The arched wooden bridge looked like it was made out of matchsticks and appeared just about as safe. Yet still, for me, there was a desiccated sound from a corner of the terrace - Clifford's voice.

He and I had cycled from Meadows one day in spring, through the traffic at Carfax, along the Cornmarket to the Woodstock road, arriving at the Trout just when it opened. Although the air was cool for sitting outside, we had taken our beers to a quiet table near the river's edge, there to continue our everlasting debate on personal pleasure versus public duty. For Clifford, there was no question: our private goals were less important than our country's good. But I, aware of my obsessive need for him, pleaded the opposite, summoning all the ghosts of that place to help me.

It's the all-important issue, isn't it? How can anyone properly live if he hasn't discovered the depth and passion of love? This is one of the things Shelley's baby must have known before he came into the world but had obviously forgotten. This is what we have to find out. Where do we stand when it comes to love?

What we feel is unimportant, Clifford had said that day, leaving me in disbelief; but I was now hearing more clearly the whispered message from Angus: "We have to learn to love."

It was on to Woodstock then and Banbury, by another circuitous route, there to await the arrival of Morley and Hugh Norton on the five o'clock train from Paddington. "You'll love him," Martin had said, and he was right.

Hugh Norton looked about twenty but was actually thirty, slight of build, fair complexion, his hair soft and gently curling, a full sensuous mouth, evenly spaced teeth, and blue eyes, the whole image the work of some inspired artist. It was later that weekend that he said of himself, and pretty accurately, too, that he had always wanted to be compared to Caravaggio's *Bacchus* in the Villa Borghese, who was slightly round-faced and florid and sensuously beautiful. He hadn't good bone structure, and he had the weakest chin in Christendom, but he still wished he were like that Caravaggio.

In truth, however, he was as beautiful as he longed to be, and intelligent and witty. Like Angus, he had been educated first in Scotland, but unlike Angus, he had gone on to London for post-graduate work in English on the lesser-known novels of nineteenth century England. He'd read them all, novels that no one had even heard of, but he didn't like it much, so he gave it up and went into business. Now he was a stockbroker and made just enough money to do what he liked. His boss was incredibly rich. He kept a yacht in Malta that had a crew of four and could sleep ten. He had been on it for two weeks only the previous month. That's why he was all brown. Couldn't get brown in England very well. But on the yacht they all sun-bathed in the nude. It was glorious, absolutely glorious.

His conversation was always amusing, learned without any sign of pedantry, and his fooling an inspired kind of nonsense. While in quieter moments he sat reading Trollope's *Phineas Redux*, he came to life before and after meals, spurred on, of course, by drinks that flowed unceasingly from mid-morning to very late at night all weekend until, at last, we all returned to London, immensely hung over.

Between us and various visitors, invited and unannounced, we consumed several dozen bottles of white wine, red wine, champagne, sherry, vodka, gin, and brandy. The supply was endless, the joy un-ceasing. Throughout it all there was music, broadcast from speakers upstairs and down: the BBC Third Programme, Proms from the Albert Hall, symphonies, concerti, choirs, and recordings on the stereo, John Ogden, Janet Baker, Scott Joplin — the insistent beat, the sheer exhilaration pushing all of us to dance, which I did one night with Hugh, for half an hour after dinner, running and tapping the length of the great brown-carpeted, glass-walled living room, circling, weaving, laughing, embracing, running

and quick-stepping to a rhythm that demanded total surrender, until we fell happily onto the cushions and looked
across darkened Gloucestershire fields to a crescent moon
that hung over ancient trees.

Hard to imagine all that sitting here with you in this
restaurant in Toronto, all these years later. Well, only seven
years later, I guess; but as with everything else, it seems a
lifetime ago. What would have happened if I had met you
then, I wonder?

In any case, we danced that night like the children of
Bacchus we were. Only it was I who held the Caravaggio in
my arms and kept him all that night in my bed, comforted
once more by the words of Angus that still sang in my heart.

The parade of visitors seemed unceasing, the greatest
number having been invited to drink white wine on Sunday
at noon. From the village came Bernard Saunders, a charming man in his early forties, with his wife, Marilyn, a big
well-draped pregnant blonde. By profession he thought
himself an artist but was, in fact, a London restaurant owner.
Martin had referred to him as a "Sunday painter," adding
that he had stopped painting long enough on one particular
Sunday afternoon to get him into his bed.

"I didn't mean to get into the restaurant business,"
Bernard explained. It had just happened. An accident almost.
Marilyn had a little money, and he wasn't making much as
an artist, so he just started in a small way. Now the money
rolled in. Almost more than one wanted really or knew what
to do with. Still, there it was, and with that, he arranged to
brush his body close against Martin, as he manœuvered his
wife to a chair.

The handsome Robert MacDonald was there with his

equally beautiful Irish wife, who had a near unpronounce-able name — Anashuya, right out of Yeats. And there was Matthew, Robert's ambiguously attractive brother, a man in his early thirties, darkly good looking and wearing a white cheesecloth shirt opened half way down his chest, which was covered with fine black hair. His smile was teasingly inviting, his warmth provocative to the point of flirtation. With him was his five-year-old daughter, Amanda, the only child in this group of adults, who comported herself with perfect aplomb for two hours and then, for no accountable reason, fell crying across the big black leather chair, no longer able to cope with the world she was witnessing.

There was a thickset, somewhat lumpish fellow with very heavy hair who declared himself a pest control officer with ten thousand pounds to invest and did anyone have any ideas, and his slender girlfriend with an equally messy mass of black curly hair which fell all over her face and down her back. Tidied up she might have been beautiful, with her enormous black eyes, but as it was, she could only look sluttish.

"I'm Margaret from New York," she announced, and when I asked what brought her to England, her answer was that she sold erotic photographs. Not of herself, mind you, and she didn't create them either. She just peddled them, found people to buy them, arranged stuff for magazines and "all that jazz." It was not pornography either. Just pictures of naked women posing in every possible way. Erotica. Too bad it wasn't men, I thought.

Two boys from nearby Milner House completed the party. One, called Carl, had just finished school at Bryanston and was about to go up to Cambridge to read English. At eighteen, he was extremely assured and sophisticated, full of grace and charm, and very much at ease in any group. Paul, his brother, was a year older, lightly bearded, quiet, and shy, with dark eyes that were infinite pools of sadness, an observer of mankind, I felt sure, and I was drawn to him at once.

"You can have him, I know," Martin whispered when he saw me looking past Hugh Norton at this other possibility.

"I will be faithful, in my fashion," I replied, and made no overtures beyond the formal introduction. It was not hard to convince myself that the Caravaggio I had in my bed was enough for any man.

Continuously the guests circled about the room, sometimes standing, sometimes lying on cushions in shifting arrangements of two, three, four, or five. The sun shone. Scott Joplin played. Hugh and I looked at each other, recalling the previous night's revelry in the same spot, our feet held now in check, our passions sated for the moment.

Martin and Matthew joined us, Martin declaring that Matthew also liked to dance at parties. In fact, he usually took off all his clothes. He was known for it. Just the previous year, in this very room, Matthew had stripped and they had danced together, absolutely starkers. It had been marvellous fun. Too bad everyone was now so inhibited. It was then that Matthew's daughter fell sobbing across the chair. He went over to her.

"What's wrong, darling? Tell Matthew. Tell Daddy."

Wrapped in her childhood grief, deep, unknowable, Amanda was beyond consolation. Matthew took her in his arms and carried her from the room, accompanied by Robert and Anashuya. The darkening shadow became a cue for Margaret also to leave, linking arms with her lumpish boyfriend. Carl and Paul followed, even as Paul looked back at me.

By four o'clock it was raining, a fine soft drizzle at first, but not enough to dampen the party mood. Lunch had come in the interim, and with it more white wine. Whatever Amanda's distress, there was no need for the remaining adults to sober up.

"We must go swimming," Hugh announced, after Bernard had taken Marilyn home to rest. We should go over to Milner House, where Morley's cousins lived. The invitation was open anytime. Besides, that's where Carl and Paul were staying, and we might see them again. I thought it a good idea myself.

Rain or no rain, the fifteen mile drive to Milner House took us on narrow roads and lanes further into Gloucester-shire and the Cotswolds, through fields and villages which might have been a model for Constable, unchanged by progress. In the honey-coloured village, we drove directly to the house. The pool was situated in a quiet corner of the garden, removed from public sight. I had swum there before, but that was nothing like this — four men, all slightly drunk, swimming nude in the rain, in a pool of Grecian mosaic design, in an English garden surrounded with flowers, and over all, just above the trees across the road, the pinnacled tower of the sixteenth century parish church.

Morley's cousin, Sheila, came from the main house when the rain let up a little, but too late to see us swimming in the nude, which had been her hope. On previous visits she had always come to watch, saying on one occasion how much she liked men. She didn't like women much. She liked the look of men. She liked their bodies, their hard legs and their buttocks. But on this particular afternoon, Sheila had arrived too late to indulge her admitted, though innocent voyeurism. Clearly she was disappointed that we all had our trousers on by the time she stepped under the shelter of the little Greek portico; all, that is, except Hugh.

Rubbed dry, we retired to the house, through the conservatory and into the drawing room, where all of Sheila's house guests, including Carl and Paul, sat about in varying states of languid recovery. Paul tried not to look at me: was he afraid of something? Sheila remarked to Martin how much she liked Hugh, to which Martin replied that, yes, we all did: we had all been to bed with him at one time or another. He was the most marvellous weekend guest, and didn't she think he was beautiful?

Indeed, she did, for she had glimpsed, as not all her guests had done, the total Caravaggio by the Grecian pool on that wet Sunday afternoon in summer.

For the return journey, Morley took the wheel of what Martin called their "clever little Renault," endeavouring to steer it soberly back to base, while Martin proceeded to demonstrate to Hugh its cleverness by collapsing the small back seat even as they sat on it. This required a gymnastic dexterity, which would have been impossible had Martin and Hugh been sober. As it was, they clung to the sides and roof of the very small car in contortions hard even for me to have anticipated, despite the intimate knowledge I had long possessed of Martin's agility in a confined space.

Difficulties notwithstanding, the seat was eventually flattened into an area not quite four feet square, while Morley continued to drive the clever French car through

English rain on back country roads. Encouraged by this success, laughing and singing, the backseat passengers proceeded to remove every stitch of their clothing and then to simulate a series of coital positions worthy of illustration in a sex manual, none of which Morley could view satisfactorily in the rear-view mirror, and which I could glimpse only in part by turning in a way that gave a crick in the neck.

Mission accomplished and journey over, a naked Caravaggio leapt from the car to pursue an equally naked Arab Boy through the rain into the house. Later that evening, four still-inebriated men found their way to what they hoped were their appropriate rooms, though I woke in the morning to find everyone in bed with me. They had not been there all night they claimed.

Black clouds and white clouds continued to pass through a blue sky until late that morning, but by two o'clock it was clear that lunch could later be taken outdoors. By this time, the sun had moved from the terrace, so we carried the black plastic outdoor table a few feet further to what was not lawn, not field, but a place where the grasses stood four feet high and the tops of thistles blew in the wind. Martin picked from an adjacent area, untangling them from the thicket, long strands of columbine, which he wove together as a garland and placed on a circular centrepiece, the white flowers glistening from the rain on the shiny black tabletop.

Morley maintained they didn't want a lawn. Much too boring. But if they did, the way to keep grass cut was perfectly simple. They would just get a couple of ewes who were with lamb and turn them loose in the field. Give a few bottles of whisky to their local farmer at Christmas, and he would look after the rest. Sheep were immensely stupid, of course, not at all like goats. They eat so much they finally explode. So the farmer takes the wool, gives you the meat, and then you look for more ewes the following year. But who wanted to bother with all that? Morley and Martin liked the grasses four feet high.

Enough sherry and gin had been consumed before lunch was started at four o'clock to guarantee its success, and the sun continued to shine. With Morley fluent in French, Italian, German, and Russian, Martin with a passing knowledge of the first three, and Hugh reasonably conversant in several, much of the small talk, especially about food, went on in a language other than English.

Throughout the meal there was, certainly, a consciousness of language, a demonstrated level of wit, and an awareness that took us far beyond the little patch of weeds and thistles where we drank and ate at an elegantly set table under an English sky. I thought of Coriolanus, banished from Rome: "There is a world elsewhere." Back in Canada, back in Mason College, I cherished that line.

Morley told us that he and Martin had once arranged a little competition between themselves, but they had kept it a secret from guests who were present. It was to see which one of them could most easily and naturally drop the words *palimpsest* and *tatterdemalion* into the conversation.

Martin told everyone that he had awakened the previous morning feeling more palimpsest than any of them could possibly imagine, and chattered endlessly about concealed tatterdemalions under the lintels of all Cotswold houses and the measures that should be taken to eliminate them. In the meantime, there Morley was, at the other end of the room, constructing the most elaborate sentences, his syntax of an ingenuity hard to equal, winding his careful way towards what he considered a deeply boring but, nonetheless, technically correct, discussion of medieval palimpsests, with a brief digression on the sort of tatterdemalion scholar who indulged those appalling pursuits, all the while having to listen to Martin babbling away about tatterdemalion ink-stands of the eighteenth century and a greedy palimpsest he once had the misfortune to encounter in Canada.

Martin had won hands down, of course, for he made absolutely no effort to use the words correctly. He was perfectly sure no one else knew what they meant either. "One should put a premium on honesty," Morley concluded.

More wine followed, more and more, and the sun moved further west, slanting through the blown tops of the purple flowered thistles.

"Had we but world enough and time," Hugh began to recite, going through the whole poem flawlessly in his fine Scottish accent, adding lilt to the lines in a way I had not heard them before. "But at my back I always hear / Time's wingéd chariot hurrying near." Marvell was newly illuminated, and I looked at Martin to see if he would catch the echoes of another day and *Comus*. He assured me with a nod that he did.

Hugh claimed, when he had finished, that he knew only one other poem in the English language, but that was a distinct untruth; before the end of the day, he had gone through several others, including Herrick, whose rosebuds we had been gathering without invitation, Milton, whose twenty-third birthday we had long surpassed, despite the subtle thief of youth, and Hopkins, who strove with us "to keep / Back beauty, keep it, beauty, beauty, beauty, ... from vanishing away." Nowhere were there hints that night, except in that one poem, briefly, of tombs and worms and tumbling to decay. In no way were we beginning to despair or even to think it possible.

Declaring that all their guests were not as charming and agreeable as Hugh was, Morley told of a weekend he had spent with some people who thought him neither agreeable nor charming, and who ended up cordially disliking him.

He had gone to stay with some people, friends, he thought, who were tremendously interested in amateur theatricals, though why he couldn't imagine, for the local group was worse than any of us might have thought possible and was presided over by a lesbian director who always wore hats with broad brims — even to bed he was told, though he wasn't quite ready to believe that one. These friends had insisted he go with them to a benefit performance for the blind, held in the church hall, and this he dutifully did.

The whole thing was excruciating and carried off with the maximum amount of bad taste. The actors were unsure of their lines and the costumes didn't fit and all the women looked as though they were wearing clothes long ago discarded by the Queen Mother. The upholstered look. He sat through all this until, at the end, a blind man came onto the stage, led by his dog, to thank everyone for supporting the local effort. He spoke well enough, as Morley remembered, and was even quite touching when he quoted Milton, the bit about not being so wretched to be blind as to be incapable of enduring blindness. But then, building to his climax, he said it was not just bad enough for him to have lost his sight and for his friends to have lost theirs also, but his dog was blind as well. That did it. It was too much for

Morley, altogether too much. He simply fell about laughing.

"I was doubled up in my seat," he said. The very idea of a blind dog. The blind leading the blind. It was hysterical. He couldn't control himself. But when he looked over at his hosts, they were just sitting there, stony-faced, and definitely not amused. He fled the scene without even saying goodbye, and took the very next train to London, adding that he never heard from the people again. He supposed he had been terribly rude.

Hugh declared Morley had not been so rude as he had once been. It concerned a perfectly dreadful man called Lewis Lubbock who was a professor of English at London University and just happened to be his supervisor. Lubbock was the supreme academic bore, someone who knew all about such deeply obscure and unimportant topics as the decasyllabic couplets in the unsuccessful poetry of Matthew Prior. Hugh was sitting next to Lewis Lubbock at a party for graduate students at the end of the year, which was all frightfully grand, and everyone drank a great deal of champagne. Late in the evening, Hugh turned to this absolutely appalling man and said: "To find myself sitting next to you on this occasion is positively absurd. In three whole years, you made absolutely no contribution to my education, none whatsoever, and what you ought to be doing right now is sitting over there in that empty corner, eating your own shit." With that, he stood up and departed, making a very unsteady exit into the quad.

We agreed that Hugh should win the prize, for by this time we were on to the cheeses — Boursin, Camembert, Stilton, Double Gloucester — and more bottles of red wine, all of us increasingly inebriated and finding any joke amusing, any story worth telling.

Martin asked Morley if he remembered the story his mother used to tell about the waiter taking around liqueurs after dinner and saying to a very proper lady, "Liqueurs, madam?" and her snappy reply, "Lick your own and bugger off."

"Yes, and the cheese one. The religious fanatic who went up to a man who happened to be French and said, 'Do you like Jesus?' and the man's reply: 'Camembert, *oui*, Roquefort, *oui, mais* ... your dried up English cheeses, *non!*'"

Shrieks of laughter greeted these not very funny stories, but who cared? As outcast goats, we were in a world of our own, doing what we liked, saying what we liked, aware only of the unbreakable bonds between us. There were no shadows present, except the very real, lengthening ones of the long grasses at our feet.

The sound of the church bell in the village summoning the faithful to evensong prompted Morley to tell yet another of his stories, and it was years later I realized this was his way of keeping out the darkness he felt gathering around him.

When he was at school, he began, chapel was compulsory and a dreary bore. Day after day the students found themselves singing hymns and saying prayers, but without any of it having any effect. Not on Morley, and not on anyone else either, including the masters, one of whom, a Mr. Ayckbourn, in a burst of daring decided to set them an essay on the topic of chapel-going.

The topic was "Animadversions on Compulsory Chapel",

so Morley believed, quite naturally, that honesty was expected. He, therefore, wrote honestly, saying, in effect, that he thought chapel services were a lot of rubbish. The Bible itself had some good bits in it but was mostly stodge. There was a fearful hullabaloo from Mr. Ayckbourn when he got the essay. He was a mouldy old bugger, an absolutely appalling man, a cricketer and all that was bad. The House-master summoned Morley, and he got the most frightful dressing-down. He was told he had caused Mr. Ayckbourn deep hurt, that he had wounded his sensibilities and mocked the values he held sacred. He was, however, prepared to forget. He would simply try to forget the whole thing.

"Prepared to forget?" Morley cried. He could have understood it if the man had ripped his essay apart, criticized his grammar, ridiculed his feeble attempts at style, and pointed out a fault in his logic here and there. But no, the poor man was only hurt.

Martin took the last piece of Stilton and popped it in his mouth, prompting Hugh to say, slightly slurring his words, there should be no more trouble with mice. All Martin needed to do was to breathe heavily at a mouse and it would come running at him. He could wait for it, in fact, with baited breath.

"Baited breath" reminded Martin of a Christmas they once had in Rome, and he proceeded to tell his own story, not to be outdone by Morley and Hugh. They had agreed to meet a friend of theirs from New York called Robert who was a curator at the Frick, a funny little man with teeny-weeny feet and manicured hands, and the three of them checked in at a fancy hotel in the Piazza Navona.

The Italians had an extraordinary custom — he didn't

know where they got it — of celebrating Christ's birth by soaking panettone in champagne and then eating it. It was the most boring cake in the world, so it had to be soaked in something. They soaked it all morning and right on into the afternoon, and became rather soaked themselves, while they waited. Finally, they grabbed the panettone and started throwing it around at anything they saw, just for the hell of it: pictures on the wall, mirrors, furniture, each other, getting the whole place quickly into the most frightful mess. Morley went in to take a shower, and Robert went back to his own room to change his shirt, leaving Martin who, of course, immediately ordered more champagne. It arrived within two minutes, courtesy of the sexiest Italian waiter imaginable, someone with lots of slicked black hair, flashing teeth, and a tight body. Within seconds, he and Martin were engaged in a passionate Italian kiss.

At that precise moment, Martin heard Robert's little manicured hands fumbling on the jewelled doorknob outside, so he quickly said to the waiter, "Faccia in fretta, apra le tendine," and with that, shoved him behind the massive drapes that hung around the great double bed, causing him to disappear just as Robert entered. Poor little curator! He could hardly reach up to Martin's pectoral muscles, even when standing on tiptoe, but, flushed with champagne, he seized what he thought was his one opportunity for a kiss and, believing that Martin was alone in the room, went dancing over to him, his baby feet now moving seven inches at a time, his thin little arms flying. He threw himself at Martin who saw at once the chance for Beaumarchais farce and responded with a "Quick, get behind the curtain. Morley's coming back."

Not that Morley would have minded. He would have been amused. But Robert went anyway, just as he was told to, with baby steps increased to eight inches in his frenzy, and dived straight into the arms of an already startled waiter behind the velvet curtains.

It was only a matter of seconds before the three of them saw the joke and fell about laughing, joined quickly by Morley who returned from his shower to share in the fun. With so many wild gesticulatings, the whole canopy quickly collapsed on the heads of Robert and the sexy Italian waiter, now trapped under mountains of heavy velvet. By the time they extricated themselves, all four were ready for more champagne, which meant throwing yet more panettone about the room, tripping on the mounds of velvet, laughing, kissing, embracing, and singing whatever snatches of Rossini and Mozart they could remember in their drunken euphoria. They never got to Saint Peter's.

A silly but somehow fitting story with which to end the night. We were trying to outrun Time. We knew it couldn't last. It never does.

The next morning, the clever little Renault carried, through gentle Cotswold villages that were just beginning to wake from their dreams, four men dressed for city life in city suits and city ties. They took the London train. They faced one another in the compartment and read four different newspapers, the *Times*, the *Financial Times*, the *Guardian*, and the *Daily Telegraph*. None of them spoke.

At Paddington Station three of them shook hands with their weekend guest and said goodbye. Soon they were all swallowed up in the London Underground, and two days later, I had to head back to Canada.

XI

I had no idea what I was going to face when I returned to my teaching job. I wondered who would be there and if there would be any new faculty and if they would guess I was gay. I could never be sure what anyone knew, but then I reasoned they, too, could never be sure. Even so, I felt I might be skating for yet another year on thin ice without reliable skates.

Early the following year, something happened which truly alarmed me. Maybe I was overly apprehensive and growing careless about my own security and the closet door, but a new colleague came to my rescue.

We met each other at the reception for all faculty — I had attended seventeen of them since my own arrival in 1958 — given by our gladiolus-growing President, who had gone two years past the normal retirement age of sixty-five and was running out of space for all the mango chutney jars he had collected. By that time, he had also added the books of the apocrypha to the Bible in order to get to sleep, or so it was said.

In the presidential mansion, full of fake Louis IV furniture, there was the usual milling about and examining of each other's stuck on hello-my-name-is tags, everyone assuring everyone else that they had done an immense amount of research throughout July and August, instead of going to their assorted Muskoka cottages, and that the students would surely benefit from all this.

I was aware of someone coming up to me and saying, "Hello, my name is Sybil."

She was older than I — mid-fifties, I thought — life etched in the geography of lines which ran below her eyes and around her mouth. She had a face like Edith Sitwell's. Her voice was low, her eyes penetrating, hawk-like.

I said mine was Peter, pointing to my tag.

There was instant flashback to my first meeting with Clifford in my rooms at Oxford, when introductions had been made in much the same way. I wondered if that was a good or bad sign.

Within minutes of talk, I learned that Dr. Sybil Stone was the new professor of philosophy, brought in to occupy a newly endowed Chair; but later that week, I learned how truly distinguished she was. She had written a well-respected book on Schopenhauer without absorbing any of his personal pessimism and darkness. In fact, she radiated light, as only genuine scholars do, and exercised compassion, as would-be scholars do not. All learning for her was ongoing, both in her study and in life. She proved her mettle when Bob Fletcher, always the sociologist, waved in front of us the current issue of *Time* magazine, September 8, 1975. On its cover was a head and shoulders photograph of an American Air Force sergeant, the name "Matlovich" shown clearly on his tag and four rows of striped ribbon medals over his heart. In contrast with the red border of *Time*'s cover, and against the sergeant's white shirt, were the starkly printed words: "I Am a Homosexual — The Gay Drive for Acceptance."

I had not seen it. Was this a trap? It was eleven years after the article in *Life*, but dangers still lurked. When Bob asked what I thought of it, I said I hadn't read it, trying not to sound self-defensive.

Sybil, who seemed to want to take the pressure off me, moved quickly to confront the spanking historian, who had just joined us. Stuffing more anchovy-egg canapés into his mouth than anyone should at one time — except he knew they were free — Tom Burton was on a rampage against gay men everywhere, military types lumped in with priests, doctors, lawyers, teachers, the works. It didn't matter. They all made him sick to his stomach, which might have been the exact cue Sybil was waiting for. She marshalled her wits and went on the attack, demolishing his bigotry with her own cool logic, causing him to flee.

This rout of the historian led Bob to believe the ball was once more in his court. He seized the magazine from Dennis, who had been reading it in a corner to catch up on his psychological research, and endeavoured to impress us with his ability to read intelligently that magazine's classic prose.

The article discussed whether or not gays should be teachers, declaring it a volatile issue among parents. A father in the Bronx said that all gays were deviants and they were to be kept apart from children. Another couple stated categorically that homosexuals who were teachers deserved no protection from the law, and their conduct was never to be condoned.

Very pertinently, Sybil asked why homosexuals shouldn't

teach. It was nonsense to think otherwise. She'd known lots of homosexuals who were wonderful teachers, and they were not to be muddled up with pederasts and child molesters. Only the ignorant thought that. We probably had our share of homosexuals right there in Mason College, whether people knew it or not. She asked what I thought, and I said I agreed.

Joe Gaudry, who had listened to the whole debate without saying a word, asked if any of us remembered a story that had appeared the previous year in the *Globe and Mail*. It was about a man who had hanged his dog and then himself when his wife found out he was gay. Looking deeply distressed, he added: "He was a teacher, *n'est ce pas?*"

"He was. *Oui*. Yes," I answered, fumbling for words, for I had read the story, too. I made no further comment to Joseph, who continued to look upset.

"Makes you think, doesn't it?" said Dennis.

"I should hope so," said Sybil, as we all made a move to leave.

Later that evening, when I asked her to go with me to the Paper Doll Café, where Rachel still held elegant sway, Sybil said to me very directly: "You're gay, aren't you?"

Was I that obvious? I asked her.

She said no, I was not a stereotype, but she could always tell.

"Thank God and thank *you*," I said, meaning it, and asked, without any build-up to the topic, if she thought two men who loved each other could ever live happily together in this world.

I was beginning to wonder if I was, after all, like the baby Shelley had grabbed, someone who knew more in an earlier life, but had forgotten how everything was supposed to work.

Her answer was wonderfully straightforward, though it made my heart skip a beat: "Why not? What's wrong with it?"

"Most people ..." I began, my voice trailing off.

"Most people! What do most people know about it? Nothing, nothing at all. They're ignorant. Count on people to be afraid of things they don't know anything about."

I argued that she was the exception, she had to be the exception.

Well, she wouldn't be the exception forever, she said. People could grow. People could learn. It might take a long time, but it was possible. All religions were narrow and small, yet they were the ones who were always making such a fuss. Christians, Muslims, Hindus, it didn't matter. If any one of us had been God, could we possibly have conceived of one religion having all the answers? They were all small, and if we aspired to be like God, we had to be a hell of a lot bigger.

In Sybil I had found another friend, and I wish you could meet her. Maybe you will one day. She would be a kindred spirit. Much later I learned that her husband, a doctor who had cured others, was unable to cure himself of prostate cancer and had died some ten years earlier. But Sybil had carried on somehow, convinced that twenty-two years of loving another person, of whatever sex, were better than no years at all, and she had been blessed. She wanted never to forget that, and she valued being alive to say so.

For the next two years I had no money to cross the Atlantic, and only letters written by Martin and occasionally by Morley told the story of Martin's ill health. He was in hospital, Morley wrote, and not in good shape. The doctors wouldn't give any sort of prognosis. They made it clear, however, that he was not to drink. His liver was starting to go and his digestive tract was shot to hell because he wasn't eating properly.

Martin, of course, countered that I should pay no attention to whatever Morley may have written and he was getting on just fine. Nothing that a single glass of red wine wouldn't cure, and he would soon be well again.

Not long afterwards, though, Morley informed me that Martin had undergone surgery for cancer of the colon. The doctors thought they'd got it all, but couldn't be totally sure. It was terribly unpleasant for Martin because he had to wear a colostomy bag for a time, but his spirits were good.

Martin wrote a few days later to say he was going to beat the cancer. There was only one thing he wanted stuck up his ass, and it wasn't whatever it was they had up there at the moment.

A postcard from Morley followed, to the effect that Martin had been out of the hospital for three weeks. The doctors declared it a miracle. Next, a cablegram from Martin, saying I should come for a visit in May. It was the Queen's Jubilee. We would celebrate. I had to say yes.

Of course I said yes, but I also heard my far-distant voice: "Chastity suggests temperance, the proper use of the body," — I had not been temperate myself — and Martin's equally distant reply: "What is chastity anyway?"

I was still finding out after eighteen years. The yo-yo string had been yanked again, and off I went, as soon as the term was over.

XII

At thirty-five thousand feet, I found myself looking down on a cold Atlantic once again, remembering the painful voyage after my Oxford finals, returning to Canada, seasick to the point of desiring death, my heart shattered by what had happened and not happened with Clifford. The old anguish I felt was mixed now with a new sorrow, the sorrow for Martin. My mind was racing to get control of all these disparate elements. The past and the present became one. Gander, Prestwick, and then London. There were glimpses of Gloucestershire as the plane came through cloud patches over Heathrow, and I tried to guess what lay ahead. I wondered how Martin would look and behave and for how long he could survive and if the situation were really serious.

Such thoughts were interrupted by the practical struggle with suitcases and parcels and the self-important minor officials spawned in airports by bureaucracy and business. There was an elderly woman there, very British, with her grey hair shingle cut, who seemed less able to cope than anyone else when she encountered a surly woman attendant, a real Cerberus, at the bus entrance. She was trying to sort out her baggage in order to get at her purse when the watchdog snarled at her and she snapped back, saying the girl was overpaid and underworked and shouldn't be so rude to taxpayers. She did an about-face, and hailed a taxi, leaving me in the underworld. "Single to Reading," I said to Cerberus and boarded the bus.

In Reading, I would have to wait for a train to take me to Gloucestershire, but I would also be obliged to change at Oxford, that city of spires and dreams, so heavy with memories of Clifford. Married now, he was probably comfortable in his life as a civil servant and maybe it would be a mistake to see him again, as if anything could be settled after a nineteen-year gap, especially with his wife around. He wrote every year at Christmastime in his fine, cramped hand, but the letter was always a travelogue. Never a hint of feeling about anything, and what's the point of writing a letter, if you don't say what you're feeling? Who wants to hear a string of facts about where you went and what you did and what you ate and what the weather was like?

He and his wife Marion were pleased to tell me they had been to the continent. Always Europe. Never North America. The trains had been on time in Germany, as they were in Hitler's day, though they shouldn't be making comparisons. Everything worked, including the plumbing. They had been to the south of France. They loved Avignon. The food was superb. Had I ever tasted *La Daube de Boeuf Provençale*?

Now I was on a train that was taking me to some new destiny, my heart forever pounding. In front of me was the Thames valley, achingly green, the river a haven for boats, some moored against a grassy edge, others cutting a swath through brown water, cattle and sheep in the fields beyond, the even clicking of wheels on a smooth track. Then the dreaming spires of Oxford, a muddled silhouette of medieval wonder and modern squalor from the railroad station, with Tom Tower looking squat and Wolsey's great guzzling hall hidden in scaffolding. Past all this and deeper into Cotswold country, the hills closing in, everything suffused in the soft May light.

When the train stopped, I was aware of the station clinging to the track like a paper clip, hardly there at all, but given weight by the figures on the platform, among them my Arab Boy. But not only had the train stopped. So had time. Martin at thirty-six had changed not at all. Had I fixed his age at half of that forever? He gave me a hug, kissed me on both cheeks, took my arm, and led me to the car, saying, "What did I tell you? I'm perfectly all right, and I still want you to fuck me." It was pretty obvious he was better, and we went off to the pub to meet Morley who gave me a hug himself.

Just as he had done in the classroom, Martin introduced me to the locals at The Crown and Feathers as his "tutor from Canada," the person who had taught him all he needed to know. There was ambiguous laughter at this, naturally, but I knew now the universe was unfolding as it should. There was ceremony and order and laughter and light, and I was happy. A joyous country weekend had been planned for my arrival, with all of us together again: Hugh, Martin, Morley and myself.

Even as Martin gulped down three double gins before lunch, he told me that Hugh now drank a great deal, giving me details as we drove back to the station where he was to arrive on a later train. The last time he'd been with them, he had behaved so badly that they considered never inviting him back. But my visit was special, and they'd told him how much I was looking forward to it. He was to be on his best behaviour.

Indeed, when I saw my Caravaggio again, he more than lived up to my memory. The model of elegance and beauty, golden hair softly waved and curling, complexion flawless, bright eyes, dazzling smile, mouth as sensuous as ever, suit impeccably tailored, pin-stripe shirt with white collar, hands fine and graceful, and on the third finger of his right hand a very large, hand-crafted silver ring. We embraced each other warmly on the little station platform, while others around us were shaking hands.

Initial greetings over, there followed throughout the weekend those small familiar rituals which were the stuff of previous visits — shopping in the village for supplies, with Mistress Sloan still behind glass in the butcher's shop, more drinks at The Crown and Feathers, the usual flow of friends for drinks at the house, and short expeditions to other friends' houses, as always, for drinks.

Even the acidulous American schoolteacher, Helen Morris, among locals in the pub on that first day, came over to talk to me. Martin had described her in a letter as "short, dumpy, sexless, and intellectual." She lived alone in the village and was generally misanthropic, endearing herself to no one. Once a month she went by herself to London, there to see plays and exhibitions. No one in the village stimulated her, she said, and she hated the children she taught.

For two years, Helen had, in her own perverse way, been in love with Martin, giving him little presents and telephoning him on occasion. But any effort she made to disport herself sartorially proved more pathetic than provocative.

She would dress, Martin told me, in form-fitting clothes, and wear only the colours in current fashion, which that year meant all shades of pink. Her nail polish matched her fuchsia coloured blouse.

Helen seemed to warm to me at once because of my interest in the theatre, and was ready both to question me about what I wanted to see in London and to make recommendations for my benefit. Martin said later he had rarely seen her so outgoing, and he might be prepared to fuck her if she were always like that.

For the little time I talked to Helen Morris, however, she blossomed as though she knew only a balanced world of sunshine and rain. Her one testy comment came in relation to the Derek Jarman film *Sebastiane*, which I had just seen at a private screening in Toronto and she had just seen at a public cinema in London. That it was obviously a homosexual film bothered her not at all. She tore it to pieces on other grounds, describing it as risible. It was all faked and not at all true to history. Could I understand anything at all? And that wrestling scene on the rocks. It must have been frightfully uncomfortable for the poor boys. She knew Sebastian had been shot to death by arrows, but surely not like that. She supposed it was meant to be symbolic, the penetrating phallus and so on. The love-wish and death-wish all mixed up, but it was pure nonsense, in her view. Quite, quite risible. She granted there were a lot of beautiful naked men around, but you couldn't get by on that.

Maybe you can't, I thought, but lots can and do. My own view of the film was that that was all it did get by on, but it seemed the wiser part of discretion to pursue the subject no further. She polished off her drink and went home. She was, after all, a schoolteacher and had lessons to prepare, traps to set for children.

By contrast, I realized what a genuine teacher Martin was, and not just with his students in school. He wanted to show me as many rooms in his house as he could, and I was prepared to learn. He announced that before going on to planned celebrations that evening, I had to go with him to meet a wonderful woman called Elizabeth Salter, the real chatelaine of the village, who had become a dear friend.

We set off immediately and arrived at her house in heavy rain, but were greeted with such grace and style that the weather became irrelevant. We were led into a charmingly formal but small drawing-room, full of paintings and books and comfortable furniture, including a few Sheraton chairs, an exquisite small Regency desk, and a larger writing table. Her husband had been a publisher and author of several novels, but for those in the know, his reputation as a writer of elegant prose rested securely on the discreetly anonymous editorials he wrote for the *Times*. She had mingled, therefore, with all the literary and political figures of consequence, and their names fell naturally into her conversation without any appearance of snobbery on her part.

"My husband knew Lord David Cecil," she said, when I happened to mention that I had sat, quite literally, at his feet in the overcrowded dining hall at New College when I was an Oxford undergraduate. "Such a dear man, and such a funny man!" Most academics and scholars weren't a bit creative, but he was. Didn't I agree?

I had in my mind at that moment a single yet multiple image of all too many academics everywhere, including some at Mason College, who were tenured, complacent, and humourless, pedants and non-teachers, who publish their trivia in irrelevant journals for other pedants and non-teachers to read. She went on to talk of the critics Desmond MacCarthy and Bernard Levin, and of politicians past and present. She almost persuaded me she was on intimate terms with Palmerston, Gladstone, and Disraeli, so detailed were her comments, before she passed on to Harold Wilson and Marcia, the new Lady Falkender.

"Of course he was frightened of her. She was the real power behind the scenes." But a man had to have that, didn't I think? All the Prime Ministers had had someone. That was the trouble with Edward Heath, of course. He had no one behind him of either sex, so far as anyone could make out, and that's why he failed. A man couldn't do these things alone. He had to have someone to talk to.

She was right. We need someone to talk to. Gerald and Sybil were in my life, but I was still alone, even when I was in bed with someone else. What do you say to a one-night stand? What did I have to say, for example, to Thomas Alexander Spence, who so obsessed me? Nothing, nothing of any consequence. Going once to Vancouver, courtesy of a travel grant, for meetings I rarely attended of the learned societies, I stayed at the downtown "Y", where I met a young man from Nanaimo, standing at the Coke machine in the lobby.

"How does this thing work?" he asked, pretending he didn't know.

He had a lot of fair hair, a low forehead, and eyes that were too close together, but his blue jeans and too-tight shirt, with most of the buttons undone, revealed a compact body, splendidly endowed, the result, I felt sure, of spending more time in the weight room than the library. But that didn't matter just then. I wasn't looking for Socrates.

"Want some change?"

"Thanks."

In those few seconds, we had managed to size each other up, and I went to his room for the night. We did everything there was to do, a mechanical routine that left nothing in the body either untouched or unentered. But when we parted in the morning, there was nothing we had to say to each other except, "See you around." And even that was untrue. It was yet another sterile encounter. Could life offer nothing more?

There are advantages to solitude, and a single person can also be whole, but there are hazards. Without personal commitment to another, there often comes detachment, the growing capacity, even the desire, to watch from the outside, always observing, never being lavish with the heart. Never allowing for humiliation and what it teaches. Never, in fact, learning.

I needed someone — I know that — and I still do. In the past, it wasn't Clifford, it couldn't be Hugh, and it was no longer Martin. I have come to realize I need to look ahead for someone else, if I can, though it's hard to do that. But surely somewhere he exists.

At Elizabeth Salter's, we drank the gin and tonic, and the rain continued to fall. It was a visit I will always remember, as she expressed herself forthrightly on every possible topic except sex and religion. I could see why Martin was drawn to her and she to him, forbidden topics notwithstanding.

Martin had told me he would give the signal for our departure when the time was right. No one stayed too long at Elizabeth Salter's; if they did, they were never invited back. Acting as stage manager, Martin announced we had to see the garden, even if we had to walk under umbrellas, and I accepted this as our cue. It was a perfect English garden, he went on, and I mustn't miss it. We could all go out in the rain. Though he was insistently loquacious after the double gin he had managed to pour for himself, Elizabeth was all charm in granting a request which, I felt sure, she had hoped we would make. Her garden was an obvious source of pride. She pointed out the architectural features of the house, the main building of 1690, the addition made a century later, and her own contemporary improvements.

What did I think of Pevsner's book on Gloucestershire? she asked me. Very dull, like all the rest, didn't I think? But full of information. Much of it quite wrong, but what Englishman would want to write a book about all the shires of England? It had to be a German, of course, and a German couldn't very well get it right, now could he? I said I supposed not, acquiescing in her settled judgement as we proceeded along a path towards the main perennial bed and, beyond that, to an arch that framed a vista of the distant hills. Everything was in its place, masterfully planned, worthy of the best eighteenth century landscape gardener, with daffodils and bright blue squills along a patterned path, just like those in Amy Lowell's poem.

Unexpectedly, I was filled with the old anger, the old anguish, my heart pounding at the memory of Clifford and the emotional gulf fixed between us forever. Is that what some people were destined to do all their lives, stay on patterned garden paths and never escape? But even as I heard the scream inside my head — "Christ! What are patterns for?" — I said goodbye to this highly cultivated woman and thanked her for the visit. She closed the doors of her house very quietly behind her and went to the window to watch us drive off in the rain to the Jubilee Fête in the village. She would go back to her housekeeper and her two servants and her garden and the memory of a husband in a wheelchair and a sister recently committed. But, most of all, she would go back to her patterned garden paths, while I remained in mine.

The Jubilee Fête in the village park was of an entirely different order, and although Martin grabbed drinks whenever and wherever he could, he remained in control, and I could see no serious signs of his physical disintegration. Egged on by Sarah Nisbitt, the socially pretentious wife of the local doctor, everyone in the village had turned out to honour the Queen, some, I thought, in the same clothes they must have been wearing twenty-five years previously, so little were they conscious of the changing fashions of London.

Entering the grounds of the old school hall, we were greeted by Bill Jones — chairman of The Little Compton Great Bell Rope Fund and other similarly lost causes — with a complimentary glass of sangria. It was filthy stuff, but, joined by Morley and Hugh, we all gushed our thanks and walked in the drizzle and ever-increasing cold of the evening to a clearing at the back, drawn by the warmth of five barbecue fires burning in petrol drums cut length-wise in half for the celebration.

"Don't you think he's attractive," Martin said, pointing out the town constable, whose name happened to be Angel. Could I believe it? Constable Angel. Could any policeman anywhere possibly improve on that? He had clearly given extra attention to his uniform that day, trousers creased, buttons polished, looking ready for some sort of action. Martin said, "I know he's available."

"Will you never stop?" was Morley's good-natured comment before telling me that Martin thought everyone was available, given the right circumstances. But it was Hugh who grabbed the sangria just then from Martin's hand and drank it in one gulp, having finished his own. So, we all went for more, complaining all along how truly awful it was.

There was a general shuffling into place for the fancy dress parade, supervised by Constable Angel, all contestants circling about in understandable, though cheerful, self-consciousness. As one might have guessed, the costumes reflected the collective imagination of the village — one Ann Boleyn, two Queen Victorias, one Prince Albert with a Groucho Marx moustache, a Morris Dancer, an executioner, a village idiot, a belly dancer, one man dressed as galloping inflation (a Union Jack on his back) and his wife as current affairs (in a costume that had currants stuck all over it), and a couple of Arab Sheiks, one with face exposed, the other covered up to his eyes.

Music came from the Victrola inside the schoolhouse; a local grey-bearded worthy proposed the loyal toast to the Queen, and beneath the willow trees, under a threatening sky, while cows and sheep looked on from the adjoining field, Queen Victoria and the executioner — odd bedfellows — were unanimously declared the winners, though Martin himself made it clear that he favoured the sexy young Morris Dancer whom he claimed to have bedded on some earlier occasion, and I believed him.

The Arab Sheik, whose face was almost totally obscured, moved towards Martin, affecting a bad Saudi accent at first, but then speaking in his normal voice, revealing himself as the local vicar. After I was introduced, Martin whispered something to him and left us together. There, in the midst of Jubilee celebrations in the park, surrounded by solid village characters and badly costumed contestants from the parade, the local vicar, disguised as an Arab, told me his story.

He had been in the village for only three years, and he had been married. He had two children, aged eleven and nine. But then, I should understand, he was also gay. His superiors in the church knew all about it from the beginning, and he also told his wife. Of course, she didn't believe him at first. Then she became very bitter. Things went from bad to worse, so he went to see the Bishop.

"Sounds like my father," I said, blurting it out, but not explaining further. His circumstances were quite different was all I added, even as I apologized for interrupting.

Continuing with his story, he told me he had gone to see the Bishop, and, with his wife's agreement, was then sent on to a counsellor. His wife said she would abide by whatever the counsellor said, but then the counsellor himself turned out to be gay, and the vicar thought the match-making Bishop must have known that, which is why he was sent to him in the first place. A divorce had followed, and now he was living with the counsellor. Things just happened sometimes. He was really quite happy. His wife, of course, was still upset about it, but he could see the children whenever he wanted. Things were easier that way, in the long run, and he said the congregation had been absolutely splendid. He was glad he didn't have to hide any more. But what had happened to my father? He wasn't gay, too, was he?

I said no, he wasn't gay. Not in any sense of the word. He had just decided he didn't believe in any of it. Not one word.

"What frightfully bad luck!" was the Arab vicar's frightfully English response. He was so sorry. Maybe he could help.

Before I could answer, Sarah Nisbitt, faux chatelaine, playing very much the lady of the manor in the absence of Elizabeth Salter, came swooping over to guess the identity of the Arab Sheik.

"You're not going to fool me, you naughty man," she said. "I know perfectly well who you are," and she snatched at the headdress, which came away in her hands. This thoroughly rattled her, and her apologies to the vicar were overwhelming and profuse. She was so sorry. She'd been appallingly rude. She had no idea, and so on, as she ticked off a list worthy of any catechism.

Pretending he wasn't upset, the vicar introduced me as Peter Lindley, a friend of Martin's, visiting from Canada.

"Oh," she said, still fumbling through her sins, "I feel all flustered. Not the best way to meet someone. Now, do tell me where you live."

"Near Toronto," I answered, wondering how she would deal with that bit of challenging information.

She met it, however, head-on with: "I have some friends in Calgary. I wonder if you know them. Is that near you, by any chance?"

I said it wasn't.

Or maybe it was Kitchener, she thought. She knew it began with a "K." Her muddled mind began fluttering through the alphabet, while she pressed the vicar's head-piece to her bosom.

Her extended, chattering apology gave me the chance to slip away to the school hall where dancing had already started and where I could stand alone for a few minutes, pondering the extraordinary story I had just heard. The vicar called out that he would look for me again. I hoped not.

The old schoolroom was decorated with tatty little flags hung from cross-ceilinged bars. Probably they had been there since 1952, positioned by an optimist who believed in silver jubilees. Small electric heaters were also positioned high up on the walls where their slight heating capacities were further diminished. The only other wall hangings were two cross-section charts put there years earlier by a biology teacher with misplaced zeal for what life really offered: "The Excitement of the Pond." Tadpoles would grow up to be frogs.

The walls were lined with chairs taken, largely, by the older folk. Four women in a row, wearing raincoats, bundled themselves against the cold of an English summer, their hair severely done (two of them with braided curls on each side, reminiscent of a younger Queen Victoria, though it was not her jubilee they were celebrating), their dresses austerely plain, where they could be seen beneath layers of coats, their shoes sturdy. The men sat nearer the table which contained Hook Norton ale, stout men in caps, leaning on their sticks, sucking on their pipes. One of them, gnarled face blackened from the weather, sat totally alone, staring at the dancers, unable to believe that once upon a time he, too, had been very young.

I watched Martin dance "The Gay Gordon" with a young girl he selected at random from the passive onlookers, while the non-clergyman Arab danced with Queen Victoria, no executioner in sight. The master of ceremonies called for silence, and a bearded young man with a guitar sang a ballad about the poacher of Eynsham, with a chorus in which everyone joined — "Laddie-i-o, Laddie-i-o." Looking at Martin, I thought he would never change. He was, indeed, the everlastingness of youth. But it was someone else I had with me then.

At the end of the evening, the four of us drove back to our country heaven-haven through waving fields of mustard and villages of yellow stone. Once there, and Morley and Martin had retired for the night, I asked Hugh if he would sleep with me again, and I didn't mean just sleep.

"Why aren't you in love with me?" I said.

"I am, I am, the same way you're in love with me. I can be constant for a time."

He was right about that; we were not in love with each other. We only went to bed together, a replicating one-night stand, happy in its own inconstancy.

We had gone upstairs to the great glass-walled living room where, through the windows, hung the slenderest crescent of a new moon, faintly luminous in the twilight.

"Quick," Hugh said, "if you have money in your pocket, turn it over," adding that if I did that whenever I saw a new moon through glass, I would get my wish.

But would he get his, I asked.

"Of course. Because I'm young and pretty."

Indeed he was, but that's not always enough, is it?

XIII

Sunday began well enough, Hugh and me breakfasting in bed together on soft-boiled duck's eggs and very thin slices of toast with gooseberry jam. Martin fussed around us, pretending to be a Mexican waiter but wearing nothing more than the large straw hat he had bought on an earlier trip to Acapulco and playing Ricard Strauss so loudly on the stereo that Morley threatened to "throw the bloody thing out the window." Everything, in other words, seemed normal.

Summer was already upon us, despite the cold rain of the day before, and the sun shone gloriously by mid-morning. We sun-bathed in the nude on the rooftop, Hugh, Martin and I, while Morley, after two strong vodkas, wandered off happily to do some gardening.

"I'm in a bamboo forest full of Chinese singing birds," he called up to us from the field of long grasses just outside the house, and then proceeded to plant scarlet runner beans in a circle round a lilac bush, ignoring the carefully printed instructions on the package of seeds. He telescoped all seasons into one half hour, tilling in the autumn, manuring in the winter, and planting in the spring, assured already that summer was there.

Hugh declared that we couldn't possibly have lunch outside, because it was so windy, and even the lettuce leaves would be blown out of our very mouths. But that's exactly what we eventually did, setting the glossy black table as much as we could in the lee of the house, in order to frustrate his prophecy.

Lunch started with several seagulls' eggs apiece, rare and delicate, brought by Hugh from London as a special gift. But coming, as they did, after that day's breakfast, I wondered if there were ever any ordinary eggs from chickens in the house and would ostrich eggs follow for dinner? Veal Marengo did, as it turned out, but, even so, food took always second place to drink: the wine cellar was never seen to be empty, even when the bread supply was low.

There followed an afternoon of unending stories, with all of us moving, after lunch, back into the house where we could more easily get at the good bottles of wine stored in the cellar. Morley had purchased them in London from their wine-merchant, who had brought to their flat, only a few months earlier, all the Gewürztraminer, St. Emilion, and Spätlese we were now consuming so appreciatively. There were frequent toasts to Herr Schmidt, the punctilious German who knew his wines better than Herr Pevsner knew the shires of England.

For the next two hours Hugh gave every appearance of being in control, even of the conversation, deftly steering it at one point towards the splendours of the National Gallery. He had taken the opportunity the previous week, during one of his lunch breaks, to see a new acquisition, Claude's *Enchanted Castle*, a remarkable work he recommended to all of us. The theme was love, its quirkiness, moodiness, jealousies, mysteries, and triumphs, and all of us might learn something from it.

Morley said he had seen it, which should have been no surprise to us, and he'd seen the film presentation as well. But this didn't deter Hugh from explaining the myth of Cupid and Psyche to Martin and me.

Claude's painting, he told us, gave only part of the story. In the foreground, you saw Psyche sitting disconsolately on a grassy bank, with the magical palace, an architectural mishmash, behind her. One window was open to show where Cupid had made an exit. But there was more to the situation than that. It had all been a frightful muddle. Psyche had been one of three sisters, and she was so beautiful that Venus, the goddess of love, was jealous of her and decided to punish her by marrying her off to some truly awful creature. So a message was sent via Cupid, who did a very naughty thing by falling in love with her himself. This complicated things enormously because Cupid wouldn't allow Psyche either to see him or talk to him.

Psyche appeared not to mind the secrecy, until one day her wicked sisters came to see her and persuaded her that all this wafting about by unseen beings was a lot of non-sense and told her to take a lamp and go and have a good look at her lover when he was lying there some night, exhausted from sex. She did this, but the silly thing let a drop of oil spill on Cupid who woke up and was terribly cross and flew away without saying a single word. Naturally, Psyche was very upset and sat about a great deal on the grass outside the palace, feeling sorry for herself. That's what Claude had given us in the painting.

In the myth's happy conclusion, Cupid was persuaded that Psyche really did love him, so they went along to Zeus to plead their case. When he approved, they had a perfectly enormous party to celebrate their marriage and ordered lots of good wine, no doubt from Herr Schmidt. It was from this marriage that pleasure was born. The end.

"Then, it's to pleasure!" I said and lifted my glass.

"To fucking!" said Martin who ran from the house.

"To spirits!" said Hugh who downed three stiff vodkas in quick succession, none of them with ice.

Morley was still happy with his wine. I started to clear the table.

Ten minutes later, Hugh announced in belligerent tones that he wasn't going back to London that night, only to have Morley, who had not really noticed his condition, say he bloody well was. We were all going back. No, said Hugh, he and Martin were staying right there, weren't they?

Martin, who had gone to pee in the long grasses, had returned at that moment and asked, "Weren't we what?"

Hugh made a slurring sound like, "Shstaaying here."

"I've no idea," Martin said. He had just been in the bamboo forest, peeing on the runner beans. It was good for them. They would grow even faster.

"Fuck the running harlots," Hugh shouted. He lay down on the floor.

Morley, annoyed, said not to be ridiculous, we all had a train to catch, and he must get up. He moved to Hugh's right side, motioning me to the left. We got him first onto his feet and into a chair, where he slumped and immediately passed out.

"What a bore!" Morley exclaimed. Just like the last time. They should never have invited him back. I asked if they had invited him just because of me and Morley assured me I was not to blame. Hugh was now an alcoholic. Our immediate problem was to get him onto the train.

I offered to help, but Martin simply stood, watching. Then he broke into song, an aria from *Pagliacci*: "Vesti la giubba."

"I said help, not sing," Morley snapped.

"What do you want me to do?"

"Pack. We've got a train to catch."

Leaving Hugh in his stupor, the three of us dispersed to collect our things, scurrying about from room to room, quickly clearing up the kitchen en route. We returned some twenty minutes later to gather up Hugh and, with difficulty, get him into the clever little Renault, where he came to sufficiently to ask if we were off to see the Queen and were we celebrating her Jubilee.

With Morley at the wheel, me beside him, and Martin and Hugh in the back, we drove to the country station along the route that was mercifully familiar; any surprises in the topography, and the chauffeur might not have been able to cope. Martin, considering himself no longer under a restrictive silence, announced that he was going to sing a solo.

"Must you?" said the driver.

"Yes," came the reply. It would be fun. It was a marvellous evening. He would sing about the gloaming. He broke into a baritone rendition of old nineteenth century favourites about gloaming and roaming and taking lovers home, at the end of which there was no applause, just shrieks of laughter from the singer.

Silence from Morley. Silence from me. Silence, too, I thought, from Hugh, but just at that point we arrived at the small station parking lot where Hugh jumped up and stood with his head through the open roof of the clever little car, shouting: "Fuck me, Jesus, fuck me with your holy rod."

Morley told him to shut up and turned in his seat to make a grab at Hugh, at the precise moment that Martin did the same thing from his position at the back. The incongruous and unexpected result was that Hugh's trousers, insecurely done up at the waist, were pulled to his knees.

"Mary, Queen of Fucking Heaven," Hugh continued. "I'm getting it already. Jesus! That was quick."

It was a ludicrous and potentially embarrassing moment, but all the would-be passengers were already inside the station. Greater embarrassment was to come.

Hugh was somehow extracted from the car by the three of us who, despite the control we showed, were not entirely sober ourselves. Once inside the station, however, the real performance began for the questionable benefit of those who had paid for tickets to London and not for a travelling side-show done in bad taste.

Morley and I had managed to get Hugh seated on one small bench, Martin beside him, while we sat opposite against another wall. There had been a silence when we first entered the constricted space, as seven waiting passengers did what the English do best, looking askance even while pretending not to notice. But any pretence at indifference was shattered when Hugh pushed Martin onto the floor and then knelt beside him, arranging somehow, as he did so, to put a scarf over his head and pretend to be Cleopatra. His voice rang out with surprising clarity, considering how drunk he was, his memory for those great speeches unimpaired. Even for him, in those circumstances, the lines were truly memorable:

Come hither, come! come, come, and take a Queen
Worth many babes and beggars! ...
Sir, I will eat no meat, I'll not drink, sir; ...
I'll not sleep neither ...
Lay me stark naked, and let the water-flies
Blow me into abhorring!

At that, he threw himself back against the bench, twisting
his body at the same time, so that his crotch was thrust
straight into Martin's face, low on the floor.

"Blow me, blow me," he cried. "Lay me, lay me stark
naked ... blow me, blow me."

In another context, the drunken spectacle might have
amused. In this particular English railway station, it drew
only stares and silence. As luck would have it, a whistle was
heard just then, and all the passengers outdid each other in
a stampede to get onto the platform and into the train when
it stopped. Hugh was picked up somehow by the three of us
and got into a compartment already occupied by a middle-
aged man with his wife, who sat opposite each other, not
smiling, not speaking.

Hugh immediately passed out in his corner and started
to snore. Morley, in the opposite corner, shut his eyes and
pretended to sleep, while Martin and I found ourselves
opposite each other in the centre seats, wife on my left,
husband on Martin's right. The train made the usual quick
get-away. I prayed that nothing more would happen.

I tried looking out the window, but a kick from Martin got
my attention, and a series of gestures followed. He let his
eyes fall to my lap, he moistened his lips with his tongue and

began to writhe in his seat. The wife noticed, but this was not enough to deter Martin. The lewd gestures continued. He pulled his shirt off one shoulder, cupped his crotch in his hands, shut his eyes, opened them, looked at me again, and moaned slightly.

The wife, shocked but also titillated in full view of a husband who obviously paid her no attention at any time — he went on reading his newspaper — squirmed a little, crossed her legs, and tried to look the other way.

Morley, sensing that something was happening but also pretending not to notice, simply picked up his book and started to read. He was determined to reread all of Proust that summer, not in translation, and he was now at *Sodome et Gomorrhe*. Martin began to breathe more heavily, counterpointed by Hugh's loud snorings; after some minutes, he mimed an orgasmic climax, and sank back into his seat, smiling and looking relieved, as, indeed, did the wife. More appalled than amused by this grotesquerie, I tried again to look out the window.

Morley had seen it all over the top of his book, which he put down and innocently asked if I had had a good day. I had been to Oxford, hadn't I? He thought I said I was to spend the day in Oxford, so had I had a good day? It was only then I realized he was making an effort to restore normalcy in the train compartment, where no one else was speaking, by fabricating an on-the-spot story and involving me in it.

There followed an exchange between us, not unlike a tennis match, which would have brought the crowd to its feet if the husband and wife had understood the game we were playing. Morley would serve a wicked sentence at me, and I would have to answer back. He could put a spin on a word so it bounced off me in a way I never expected. He could lob an idea across the space between us, even without a net, which had me running for a response. I said yes, I had had a very good day thank you.

Persisting in the charade and questioning me further, he asked if I had walked about The Parks. Yes, I had. No, I had not gone as far as Parson's Pleasure. Yes, Blackwell's was the place for books. Yes, I had been to evensong at Christ Church. No, it was not the regular choir. Yes, there were more women in it than boys. Yes, that was a pity. No, I mean yes. Because it took only minutes to trounce me in what Morley must have thought a successful game with a purpose, he went back to his book, looking in Proust for all things lost, while I focussed exclusively on the view out the window until the train pulled into Paddington.

Hugh woke and suddenly asked where the fuck we were. "Paddington Station," I answered. This was the stop. We were in London, cue enough for the silent husband to push his frustrated wife into the corridor for a quick exit, while Morley leaned from the window to open the other door with its inconvenient outside handle. Hugh, on his feet by now, almost fell onto the platform and rushed straight for the front of the taxi queue, even though we were not taking a taxi and upsetting all those who were. We forcibly moved him from his position, with muttered apologies to everyone, and headed for the Underground. There he leered at all the boys and dropped more profanities into his speech than a New York construction worker. At Oxford Circus tube station, he protested his fare to the ticket collector, and yet managed to walk with us several blocks into Soho.

It was there on a corner of Charlotte Street, outside a

pub, ironically named The Rising Sun, that he said he would go for a nightcap and wanted to be alone. It was there I said goodbye to my Caravaggio, never to see him again.

"Bacchus with the weakest chin in Christendom," he had pronounced, and maybe he was right. He never again tried to communicate, and I never wrote. He had said: "I can be constant for a time." That was also true of me.

I had asked Martin when we first met, "Who are you?" It seemed to be taking a lifetime to get a definitive answer. But maybe there isn't any such thing as a definitive answer, and it's always foolish to expect one. None of us can be reduced to simple statements that truthfully reflect what we are, for when we say we are one thing, another is left out, and always we are more. When I declare I'm gay, I'm telling the truth about myself, but only a partial truth, for I am always more than that, and so are you. Always we are more, much, much more than can be said of us or we can say about ourselves. Hugh was an alcoholic. I knew that. But I was forced to wonder if that defined the essence of the man. My Carvaggio an alcoholic? Is that all that could be said of him? Truly he was more than that, much, much more.

It was three years later that Morley wrote to tell me Hugh had lost his job, and was quite out of control. He went out every night to discotheques and clubs and bars, dancing and drinking heavily until dawn, and brought home a different body each time. He picked up boys in public urinals, sucked off any man who would shove his cock through a glory hole, insulted strangers on the street, had been beaten and now had a cracked tooth in addition to his bruises. He had been thrown out of a restaurant the week before by two black bouncers because he couldn't pay his bill and was now cadging, or trying to, from all his friends. He was on a course of auto-destruction and could be dead in no time. His blood count was dangerously low, and his future looked grim. There were signs, also, of increasing mental derangement. No one knew how long he could last. He really looked quite dreadful.

I put the letter down, aware now of a darkening world. But life for eternity? This life? Surely not even Hugh would want that. He was more than what he had become.

But I've jumped ahead of myself in telling what happened to Hugh. Like every story, mine has interlocking threads and tangents, and I must go back to '77, because something else happened that summer.

XIV

This has to do with Gloria, Martin's niece, who came from Canada to stay with her uncle the week after I arrived. She immediately settled into the flat, which was never designed for four people, for what she obviously decided would be a holiday of decent length. I could hardly believe, when I first met her, that she was only eighteen, because she gave every appearance of sophistication as she smoked and drank and threw her blonde hair around and talked of the life she intended to have as an actress. She was small-faced, fair, and pretty. She struck poses constantly as though providing photo opportunities for a crush of waiting photographers: she framed herself in doorways, sat only on the arms of chairs, and stole lingering glances at herself whenever she passed the full-length mirror in the hall.

Martin embarrassed her by saying how much more beautiful she was than her older sister, Miranda. The year previously, Miranda married the attractive Greg, and they had travelled to the Far East, just two of the thousands who wander the world in search of peace and the good life. But five peripatetic months had been enough for Miranda, and she returned to Canada, leaving the sexy Greg lying on a beach in Bali, dreaming of serenity in a world of moral chaos. This left Martin free to fantasize about having Greg for himself. Inappropriately, he also thought it obligated Gloria to seek aggressively the experiences her sister lacked. She was so beautiful, she should have no trouble.

"I'm going to be an actress," she announced on arrival, running her hands through her long tresses, fluffed and wavy. She was going to star in *West Side Story* at her school, where she had already been in *The Crucible* and several other plays. "I just love the theatre," she kept saying. You know the type. A sophisticated little girl, poised and worldly, I thought, but also vulnerable.

Martin kept saying in her presence: "Gloria is so beautiful. Don't you think my niece is beautiful?" My reply was always vaguely muttered, for I didn't think her beautiful, merely pretty. I did not, in fact, much care for her, but realizing she was eighteen — the same age Martin was when I met him — I felt protective.

What Gloria needed now was experience, despite her mother's claim that what she needed was a holiday. She'd been depressed and had to be looked after. She should meet people. She shouldn't be hiding her light under a bushel. She was much too beautiful for that. There were lots of attractive young men around, and he would have to introduce her. He would even buy her peacock eggs mixed with fish oil, the best aphrodisiac you could get, just to help her along. Experience counted. She had to have experience — Martin went on and on — and she had to make up for Miranda's failure. Anyone as beautiful as she was simply had to have experience. She could come and go as she pleased, and we would pay no attention, so long as she didn't come home a virgin.

One part of me may have admired the directness of Martin's speech, but I was surprised and distressed by its tone. I hardly knew what to say to Gloria who then, rather obviously flushed, turned on her high heels and left the room. I could see, however, that she still acknowledged the mirror in the hall as she went by.

I asked Martin if he thought that was an appropriate way to speak to someone who was just eighteen, only to have him remind me that he had been eighteen when I met him, and so what? But she was his niece, I told him, which made a difference, and she was depressed.

Adolescent histrionics, was how he described it. There'd been a car accident, and her boyfriend was killed. She was upset and had tried to slash her wrists, which was the most theatrical thing she could do. She made sure she wasn't successful, so it couldn't have been all that bad. Our job — well, his job, if I wouldn't help him — was to pull her out of her mess. Find another man. That's what she needed, a good hard man, and he knew exactly what was meant by that. He was, in fact, the very uncle to help her find one. His own uncle had given him money but had done nothing to advance his sex life. Gloria was lucky to have him help her with hers. She would survive.

Silenced by his arguments, I poured myself a drink and retreated to my own room where I could weigh what I had heard. Was this really the person I had christened my Arab Boy, and was this part of his dream house with its many rooms ? I wanted to believe, believe in something more than man's smudge in a bent world. But Gloria would have to survive without help from above.

A whole week passed without incident, but events seemed crammed like a tightened spring in a box, ready to break out. Martin went back to his teaching, Morley to his shipping line business, and I to my desultory life as a visitor, contenting myself with museums and book shops by day and concerts and theatres by night.

Oh! Calcutta! was still running — everyone was by now used to the nudity — and *A Chorus Line*, having conquered Broadway, was doing the same in London. There was a new play by David Edgar, called *Destiny*, which I found boring — all politics and no passion — though the comment it made on the National Front Party in Britain was shocking. There was a West End farce, aptly enough called *Donkey's Years*, a foolish piece which might have been funny but wasn't, especially in a theatre that was half empty. But mostly, there was Gloria, our aspiring actress from Canada, who came and went, as Martin had encouraged her to do, striking poses whenever and wherever she could. None of us really kept track of her, except to note that she was invariably out after midnight.

I began to think I had fussed unnecessarily. She was perfectly capable of looking after herself. Indeed, my reassessment seemed confirmed at the end of that week when she insisted that I join her for lunch in a nearby pub. It happened to be The Rising Sun, where Hugh had gone for his nightcap after our embarrassing train journey; but this time the auspices were different and, I believed, happier.

Gloria settled for traditional pub food — bangers and mash with a pint of bitter — and I did the same. Her purpose in asking me to join her was to tell me of the experiences she had had in the previous five days with five different men, relaying this story to me, no doubt, so that I might voluntarily pass the information on to Martin. In that way, she hoped to escape his closer attentions, having followed his prescription with such conspicuous success. She encouraged me to believe that she had slept with all five. One a day seemed, indeed, an impressive score.

There was Tony, the boy she had met in this same pub; Mark, the boy she had met on her trans-Atlantic flight; Scott, the married man she had met on a train; Guy, a music student she had met when purchasing an Angel recording; and, for contrast, Rob, another boy from the pub, a cockney who was there again that day, a tall well-built youth with lots of dark hair and smouldering eyes. Indeed, I thought him pretty sexy myself, with noticeable power in his crotch, and said as much to Gloria, who seemed amused at the thought and feigned a little jealousy.

"Oh, I can be a real bitch when I want to be," she said. "I get what I want, and I know how to fight. In fact, I'm a dirty fighter. I fight with my nails. Look!" She showed me how long and sharp the nails were on her right hand.

It had been agreed that Morley would go with me to see a new Sam Shepard play and that Martin would take Gloria out for dinner, all of this amicably arranged, including a later Charlotte Street rendezvous. Before the evening began, however, it was obvious that Martin had had an exhausting day at school.

"The little fuckers," he said as soon as he came in. Some days he thought he'd like to fuck them with the biggest dildo in the world just to let them see how it felt. Only they might like it too much. He said he had witnessed one boy bending down to pick up a piece of paper and another boy came up behind him and gave him such a shove against the concrete wall that he smashed his head in. There was blood all over the place, and the poor bastard had to have four stitches, which served him right, because Martin was sure he was the one who had written "fruit" and "pansy" all over the board one morning before he arrived.

I had a vivid memory of seeing those same words on little bits of paper, tucked into my schoolbag when I was a boy — Sissy. Fruit. Pansy. Fifi — and of my mother trying to comfort me. She said that boys who aimed such language at others might never find love, but someday I might. I wondered if that would ever be.

Martin poured himself a large vodka and went to the privacy of his room where he first took speed to help him face the evening and then another double vodka after his bath. Morley and I, in the meantime, had left for the theatre, reminding Gloria that we would join her and Martin after the play.

The bleak metaphors in *Curse of the Starving Class*, with family life in disarray, were appropriate enough for what followed. Martin and Gloria had gone to a small Greek restaurant called Patris, a particular haunt for the young, where everyone sang and danced a great deal more than they ate. After the play we had seen, Morley and I were not, however, in the mood for such aggressive jollity. We got to Charlotte Street, as planned, but Morley refused to go with me into the noisy, crowded space, preferring instead to wait outside while I went in to tell Martin and Gloria that we favoured a quieter restaurant in the next block.

I fought my way to the back, where I found them drinking

retsina, their moussaka and salad pushed aside. Martin was obviously drunk, Gloria tense and restless.

"Excuse me," she said as soon as I reached their table, adding, "I'll be right back." Whereupon she headed for the washroom.

When I asked if anything was wrong, Martin spat out that she was a bitch. When I opened my mouth to protest his language, he cut me off, saying he didn't need any lecture from me.

Nothing at all had happened, was his line, and that was just the point. He had brought her there for a good time, and what had she done? Nothing. He wanted her to dance, get up and have fun, but she said she didn't know anyone, as if that mattered. There were lots of beautiful boys around with tight crotches and willing asses just waiting for a fuck, and she could have any of them, if she put her mind to it.

I said that wasn't true, and he should know it. She'd been having a great time all week. She'd told me so herself. She'd been out with all sorts of boys. Slept with them, as well. Isn't that what he wanted her to do?

No, he didn't believe her. She was a cockteaser, a real cockteaser, and he would bet she was still a virgin. She was just a spoiled, silly bitch who got in the way, and if she wasn't going to appreciate what he was doing for her, then ...

Trying to hold back my fury and sense of outrage, I said I wasn't going to stand there and listen to his rantings. But at that point, Gloria returned.

"Oh, darling," said Martin, switching his tone, "would you go outside and tell Morley that Peter will be right along? He has just been telling me about the play. We're almost done, but Morley hates waiting around."

Gloria left again, saying nothing, while I wondered how it was possible for Martin to talk coherently when he was as drunk as I knew him to be. Yet, he went right on. He was not going to stand it any longer. We couldn't do anything when she was around. He wanted me to fuck him right then and there.

Angry by now, I told him to fuck himself. I left him.

Hastening after Gloria, I got to her before she reached the door. Martin was in a filthy mood, I told her. He must have had a really bad day in school. Did she want to leave and come home with us? No, she replied in a constrained voice. She was a fighter. She could look after herself. She would stay. I knew just then that the coiled spring was tightly packed in its box, but I couldn't tell if her eyes were watering because of the smoke-filled room or out of repressed rage. She pushed back her blonde hair with the hand that had the long nails and went back to Martin's table. I rejoined Morley and, over dinner, told him what had happened.

Now it was my turn not to eat. The encounter at the restaurant had left me with a sense of foreboding, but my rationalizing instincts took over. Gloria was not my niece. She was in a public place. She said she was a fighter. Martin would come to his senses. I must regain my own perspective. I really must keep out of it. So began the self-deluding, self-protecting tricks of the mind which, writ large, can deny even the holocaust.

Morley seemed emotionally detached from what I told him. He said to pay no attention. He had seen it all before. Martin would get tired or upset or depressed and he would take a drink and another and another and lose control and do a few bad things or say something frightfully rude and then it would all be over. It never amounted to much, and the next day he could never remember a thing. His mind would be a total blank, and he would be sorry. That was exactly the way all this would turn out, so I should stop worrying and eat some food. Food always helped.

When I told him I still didn't understand, he asked if I wanted to account for everything, because that was impossible. It wasn't that exactly, I answered, but I wanted to know. Well, that was different from understanding, was his reply. Lots of people knew much but understood nothing, and maybe he didn't understand it either: he only knew what he saw. In that case, did he know about Gloria? Did she really try to slash her wrists? Yes, her mother had written to them about it, and it was a long letter.

Morley had finished his meal, but I was still unable to eat mine. He told me Gloria and her boyfriend, Nick, had been driving from Calgary through the Rockies back to Vancouver. Gloria was at the wheel, and it was Nick's car, which may have meant she wasn't really used to it. They had also been drinking — not much, it seems, but enough. They came to one of those bad curves you get in the mountains, and there was a bloody great lorry coming from the other direction. She panicked and overcompensated. She pulled way over too far to the right, having failed to notice a giant boulder that protruded almost onto the highway. The boulder was on the passenger side, and Nick was killed. Not outright, though. He lingered a few days on life support systems, which made things worse. She blamed herself. In her mind, it was her fault, though it could have happened to anyone.

I said I knew there'd been an accident, but I hadn't known

Gloria was responsible. Morley told me about how she had gone to pieces, and after her suicide attempt had to have psychiatric help. She was much better, as I should be able to see for myself, and the trip to England was supposed to finish off her therapy. Obviously she was still insecure and pretty vulnerable behind all that blonde hair and all those photographic poses, and she was understandably nervous about getting involved with other men, but she would come round. She needed time.

I remained silent and looked at my plate. If I wasn't going to eat, Morley told me, I should at least finish my drink so we could go, which is what we did.

Back at the flat, I said goodnight and went immediately to my room, where I tried to sleep but couldn't. Instead, I wrestled with all the questions I couldn't solve. At three in the morning, there are never any answers for anything. Certainly not for Martin's conduct, boorish beyond the telling. Not even for my own conduct, weak and self-protective in my failure to deal with the situation. If I loved him simply because he was my Arab Boy, that was surely not to excuse his behaviour. My amateur psychologizing left me in doubt about my own motives and reactions. I heard a door slam and an argument begin that soon threatened violence.

"I'm going to bed," I heard Gloria say, whereupon Martin called her pretty fucking rude to want to do that as soon as they got home. She should stay up and talk to him. He didn't care if she was tired. He was tired, too. He worked his ass off entertaining her, and she wasn't even grateful. He had spent a lot of money, taking her out, and she ought to be more polite. She said that she wanted to be left alone, and I heard her move from the hallway into her own room, next to mine. Martin followed her. He'd leave her alone all right. But first she had to listen to him. This was his fucking apartment, and she was goddamned lucky to be there.

She pleaded with him to go away, but he must have made a grab for her, because I heard her scream: "Don't touch me!"

He spat out his words. He wouldn't hit her. He'd never hit a professional virgin, because that's what she was, a professional virgin. She wanted to get fucked but she didn't want to get fucked. She was a regular cockteaser. What she bloody well ought to do now was to go out and get fucked. Just go out and get fucking well fucked by someone with a big cock.

"Please, please, leave me alone," she pleaded.

I was in agony, and yet I didn't act. Had it been a public square outside my private room, would I still have abnegated my responsibility? I feared I might. Morley will wake up, I thought. He will know what to do.

I heard Martin leave the room, but, in less than a minute, he returned, still belligerent. She was just a spoiled, silly girl. Who cared about her depression? She should fucking well grow up. She had ruined everything by being there when I was there. She had ruined my entire visit.

Once more, there was her cry to be left alone. She hadn't wanted to spoil his visit with me. It was none of her business what we did. She didn't care. She just pleaded with him to leave her alone. But his crude barrage continued: "Fuck you. Fuck yourself. Go out and get fucked. That's what you want. Just do it. Get fucked. Go on!"

She warned him not to come near, to stay away, stay away, but he would not be stopped, and I heard the slap as he struck her across the face. "You bitch. Serves you right." She screamed in response to that. She must also have sprung to the attack just as I shot out of my room, galvanized at last, no longer the victim of my too refined and pusillanimous scruples. By the time Morley and I reached them — he, too, had heard and responded — they were struggling on the floor.

Despite the sharpness of his verbal attack, Martin's drunkenness put him at a physical disadvantage. Gloria had obviously caught him off-balance, and her own uncoiled springs provided an adrenalin rush which had knocked him over. She was on top of him, screaming obscenities, lashing out, scratching his face and neck with her long nails. He had become curiously passive. He had, in fact, passed out. We pulled her away and managed to sit her on the edge of the bed.

"It's over now. There, there, it's all right. It's over," I said. She should lie down now. Nothing more was going to happen. She was quite safe.

Several minutes went by before I could get her to do that, but once the task was accomplished, I helped Morley carry Martin to his own bed where, fully clothed, he spent the rest of the night in untroubled sleep, ignorant of what he had done.

Returning to Gloria's room, I found her huddled with two pillows in one corner of the bed, knees drawn up under her chin, her arms around her legs. Her fair hair was dishevelled, her face a mask of pain, and she still sobbed convulsively. I took her in my arms, holding her as I would a child, this little slip of a girl.

"Let me hold you now until you get to sleep," I said, then added words that floated to the surface of my memory from some long forgotten dream: "You won't be alone any more." Her sobs were her answer.

The next morning, after Martin had somehow got himself together for school and Morley had left for the office, Gloria packed her things to leave. She didn't know where she would go, but thought she would stay with the cockney boy, Robbie, who had wanted her to meet his mother. She gave me then her version of the evening, and I never tried to stop her as it all came pouring out.

The essence was that she couldn't stay. That her uncle would call her a beautiful but stupid virgin in a restaurant full of strangers who heard everything was something she could never forgive him for. She admitted she'd lied about sleeping with lots of boys, but she'd only done it hoping I'd pass the word on to Martin and make him stop trying to set her up all the time. Her boyfriend had been killed, and it was her fault. They'd never been to bed together, which made her feel terrible, because she was in love with him. He had wanted it, but she thought she wasn't ready. At eighteen, she knew she was a woman, but she was still confused about sex and love, and now Martin had made everything worse.

True to her word, she packed her things and went to stay with Robbie and his mother. Twice she returned to the flat, when she knew only I would be there, to collect forgotten things or to make phone calls. "No, I've not forgiven him yet," she said the last time she appeared, before going back to Canada. She wished I were her uncle instead of Martin.

I had, of course, long since confronted Martin, who could remember nothing about the restaurant or the fight. He had taken speed to get through the evening because of the bad time he had had at school. He couldn't talk about it just then. He was too tired. He needed a few days. He had to recover.

I said we all had to recover and walked out of the room.

Morley was in his own room and called out to me as I went by: "I'm sorry you were dragged into that particularly unpleasant scene. For my part, I was hoping to stay out of it."

XV

You probably understand why the whole incident with Gloria left me unsettled. I'd witnessed something ugly but I'd been as reluctant as Morley to get involved. I deplored Martin's conduct but at the same time questioned my own. I found myself moving like a somnambulist in a territory I didn't know.

Not only had there been this particularly unpleasant scene with Martin and Gloria, but there had been Hugh the week before, which gave me genuine cause to worry now about the future. Martin's health was at risk, but he didn't care. Morley was surviving emotionally with the help of alcohol, but appeared detached. As for me, I had been a passive witness, forced into action only after a violent confrontation and after most of the damage had been done.

I wondered then if there was another cause for my distress. Some claim that we carry within us unfathomed, even unfathomable, wells of pain, and dive into them more deeply than we need when pushed by something else, even by something quite small. When that happens, we experience again all the old unresolved grief which, in turn, accentuates the new sorrow. My distress for Martin was genuine enough, and yet I thought it might be linked to something else, and would only go away if that something else were faced.

I thought of Clifford and how my failed relationship with him had haunted me for all my adult life. This might be the year to exorcise his ghost. I had not seen him for nineteen years, and realized now I had to face him and meet his wife. Because we had communicated every year at Christmas, if superficial sentences from me and lengthy travelogues from him could be called communication, the way was open for a phone call, at least, and I made that immediately.

Clifford invited me for lunch the very next day. I could take the 11:40 from Waterloo, he said, and he would meet me at Guildford. Yes, I assured Martin, I would be back in time to go to the theatre; and yes, *Salomé* with Lindsay Kemp was what I wanted to see, and could he make the reservations.

Any misgivings I had were confirmed as soon as I reached my destination. Clifford — or someone who looked enough like the Clifford I once knew to satisfy me it *was* Clifford — moved towards me with outstretched hand, guiding his "too short" wife, as she later described herself, along with him.

"Peter, how wonderful! Is it really you? I can't believe it. What a surprise! After all these years! Darling, this is Peter. At last you can meet Peter."

Those actual words convey nothing of their tone, and I didn't know if they indicated genuine pleasure, or if they were covering up something. I responded that I was happy to be there, though I really wasn't so sure. I had to remember that I had invited myself.

"Clifford's told me all about you. Well, not everything, I expect, but a great deal," Marion said.

Yes, I thought, I bet he has, but certainly not everything, not the important thing.

They were so glad I could come for a visit, but it was awfully short notice after so many years. Why hadn't I let them know earlier? They could have done something special. But it was a lovely day, and the three of us could still have lunch in the garden.

Marion's chattering gave me a chance to look at her husband. Could I believe she had the knowledge I had of his body? Did she ever take him in her mouth? Had she followed every curve and line with finger and hand?

They were parked just outside the station. Their house wasn't far away. Marion said that England must still seem very quaint to me; it did to her, even though she lived there. She shouldn't say she lived there, should she? She should say they lived there. She was from Scotland, near Brechin, though that was pretty quaint, too, when you thought about it. Maybe I didn't know Brechin. It was rather a small place, even a little severe, but certainly quaint.

Beyond Clifford's initial greeting and my brief reply, we had not said anything to each other. Could he be recalling one particular night when I knelt beside his bed, as I so often did after that first time when love's labours were lost? I had been once again the suppliant lover, my right hand making its familiar journey underneath the covers, from his chest, across his abdomen, and down to where this time, unlike all other times, he had placed over his cock the protective hard covering of a pouch for cricketers, fortress against my invasion. He said nothing when my hand stopped at the barrier, and I said nothing when I got up and walked away. But back in my own room, I cried the cry of defeat, embarrassment, and shame. What he had allowed and even encouraged after our truce seemed sordid now. Yet, it made no difference. The truce was broken over and over again by both of us.

There was no stopping Marion, who went on and on, never slipping off the surface, unaware of what was going on and on below that, in my mind. She assured me that I wouldn't think too much of their little house, which had in it only one bedroom, but they liked it, and she knew I was not going to be staying for the night. How much did they like it, I wondered. What did they do there and how often did they do it. Did they do it at all? They had, she said, an extensive and beautiful garden. Clifford did all the heavy work, but she did the rest. A lot of things she couldn't quite reach because she was so short, too short, really. No, no, I thought, you can reach. You can reach if you want to. Height doesn't matter when you're in bed. You should know that. I wondered then if she could have been reading my mind, correcting my thoughts, when she added that she was too short when it came to pruning? Pruning, oh yes, and was I supposed to believe that one? But Clifford was a dear, a real dear. I must know that already, of course, because she understood that we were such good friends.

All this time I had been looking directly at Clifford who was looking at Marion who was looking straight ahead as she walked; but when Marion said, in a slightly louder voice, that I must know he was a dear, my eyes met Clifford's for the first significant time. It was only for a moment, but the moment held, and I looked past William Pound and the Trout Inn and the patterned garden paths of Merton College to a quiet, interior place where he and I at first touched hands and sang and all the world was green again and full of grace. Then the moment was over, not to be repeated. Paradise glimpsed and gone. It had always been that way. Love's labours forever lost, seen only as disgusting.

The reality was that Clifford had changed. His thick eyebrows, a marked feature in his youth, were still thick, but now, at fifty, his black hair had thinned to almost nothing on top and gone to grey on the sides. He remained lean, but walked with a slight limp.

Marion went on, unabated, as a social columnist might do. Maybe she wrote for the local paper. I never found out. Clifford had injured his knee playing cricket the summer before. He really shouldn't have been playing, not at his age, but there it was! I might remember that he was always a little deaf in the right ear, ever since he was a child. Now he was deaf in both ears. I would have to speak up, as she did herself just then, announcing to Clifford that she was just telling me he was a little deaf, but still they got along, didn't they?

Better never to go back. I had always known that. But I had no choice. I had to go back. This is what I had to face. And there was more to come. Already I felt the exorcism working. Already Martin to me appeared in a different light — foolish at times, flawed like the rest of us, wayward, difficult, even reprehensible, but, when he was well, passionately and generously alive. Surely that was better than this.

Lunch was to be served in the garden, the neatest garden I had ever seen, where everything grew in ordered rows, exactly where it should, according to predetermined plan. I admired the delphinium especially, which seemed, for some disconnected reason, to be Marion's cue to produce the lunch — a cold salad plate, with chives from this very garden. I noticed that the chives were planted next to the delphinium. Marion said they helped with the bugs, then she disappeared, leaving Clifford and me alone for the first time in nineteen years.

"Do you remember that day in the Master's Garden?" I began, after a prolonged and awkward silence. I strove for the noncommittal, but thought only of Clifford's bed.

He didn't hear me, and I had to repeat the question, reminding him that we used to go there to read when the weather was decent. The truth is I never could read when he sat beside me, both of us propped against the same tree, and I wonder how much he read. If the sexual current between us had been harnessed to a generator, it might have lit up Toronto. But, as it was, we sat in darkness in the sunlight. I was still in darkness after nineteen years, wondering what in hell he was thinking.

His next question provided the answer: "What's the weather like in Canada?"

The weather, for God's sake! Was he asking about snow in Yellowknife, droughts in Manitoba, fog in the Bay of Fundy, only because he couldn't ask if I did the same disgusting things he so much enjoyed? Maybe I was looking for something that was never there.

Fortunately, Marion returned just at that point with the salad plates, and the three of us sat to eat. Under the table, my knee touched his — accidentally, I assure you — but I didn't take it away. Neither did he move his, but I now felt nothing, nothing at all. It was just a knee under a table that happened to touch mine. It could have been attached to anyone's body.

I said to Marion that I was just telling Clifford about Canada, and she replied that she'd like to go, but he never would. She was sure of that.

"Too much to see in Europe," Clifford said. What was the point of seeing new places when you hadn't seen the old ones? Besides, they liked their comforts. Wasn't Canada rather a crude place? With all due respect, what did we do for culture?

The level of my speaking was notched up several decibels when I practically shouted: "We've two cultures. English and French. They're the main ones, but we've others, too. We're rich. Not that we always know it, but we're rich."

Well, he didn't think he'd want his cultures and his races all mixed up. When he and Marion went to France, they went to France and left England behind. He had told me in a letter about their trip to Avignon, hadn't he? Should he remind me we had also been there? Did I remember the Palace of the Popes? Fourteenth century, but more of a fortress than a palace and spread over three acres. Luxurious too. Seven Popes had lived there at one time or another. They had their catamites, he was told. Pretty disgusting, that was. But the food was good. Had I ever eaten *La Daube de Boeuf Provençale*? Just a fancy name for stew, really. He had been telling Marion about the little place we had stayed in and where we had to share a bed — *il n'y a qu'un lit.*

"I expect you've forgotten all that. It was a funny night, really. You slept like a log."

Very funny, yes, I thought to myself, though I remembered it differently, remembered the weight of his left leg over mine, remembered how silently I took myself in hand, remembered how my heart almost stopped, as it was threatening to do again. I was ready to be carried out on a stretcher, after so much denial, when Marion brought me back to life's surface with her trivial injunction that I help myself to mayonnaise.

"And Ireland. Remember Connemara? That's where I made you promise ... Still, that was a long time ago," said Clifford. Maybe he shouldn't go into all that again. He was sure I had changed.

"Into all what?" Marion asked.

"Just our little secret," he told her.

Just a blade of grass, I thought.

But no, he would never want to go to Canada. What was so special about Niagara Falls, anyway? Just a lot of water falling over a cliff, and a lot of tourists taking pictures. Mostly Japanese, he was told. No, he'd rather go to Africa. See Victoria Falls. Besides, Canada was too cold. "Now, tell me ..." he began to say.

Tell you what? Tell you I was sick and now am better? Tell you that I had to lose myself to find myself? Tell you that the search is everything? Tell you that failure is sometimes triumph? Tell you that all things end, even when nothing is ever lost? Tell you what you would never understand?

I helped myself to mayonnaise, and thank you very much for the trifle, it was delicious, and no I still didn't have a girlfriend, and no I would never marry, and yes I am very happy, thank you, knowing there is an exterior world and an interior world, and it's the latter place that interests me and, oh I'm sorry how the time has simply flown, and I really should be leaving for the train, if you'd be good enough to chauffeur me again, thank you, and yes do write to me at Christmas, and don't forget to send the recipe for that stew.

They said they were sorry I had to run.

They hoped I would come again.

They took me to the station.

Clifford even shook my hand.

Settled in my compartment which I didn't have to share with anyone, I watched the landscape go by, image after image, pushed behind me and left there. What I had seen I had now to leave behind. I saw him. I heard him. I felt his knee under the table. But nothing meant anything any more. I'd lost what was never there in the first place, and I didn't feel sad about it either.

When I got into a taxi at Waterloo Station, I was even smiling a little to myself, and at the door of the flat, I volunteered an answer to the question Martin didn't ask. "Yes, you'll always be my Arab Boy." I kissed him rather more passionately than I would otherwise have done.

"Obviously you need a drink," he said. "I've already started. I had a truly frightful day at school."

As he led the way to the liquor cupboard in the kitchen, I noticed how smartly he was dressed for our theatre date in the new white trousers he had said he was going to buy, worn now with a blue silk shirt and black jacket. I noticed also how he added a double shot of vodka to his own glass before handing me the scotch and soda, which was my usual. It was only then that he asked about my visit with Clifford.

It wasn't easy, I told him, but it was over. At last I knew I was free from that particular pain. Martin said that made the two of us pretty special. To have lasted. To have come through. Still feeling something. Still caring. He did care, he assured me. No matter what I thought, he cared about me. He cared about Morley, too, and he cared about Gloria. He had never planned to hurt her. She would recover because she was tough, but he found it hard that she wouldn't speak to him. After all, he was her uncle.

I suggested that he give her time, which doesn't always heal, but usually does. He moved over to the window and looked down on the London traffic. Gloria was down there somewhere.

"Maybe Robbie's mother is looking after her," he said quietly.

It was only a short sentence, directed more to himself than to me. He stood in silence for some time before he spoke again, asking if time had sorted things out with Clifford.

"Yes, in a way," I answered, adding that I didn't feel anything any more, at least nothing compared with what I remembered. We had been speaking a different language, and mine might just as well have been Cantonese.

"I thought he knew Chinese," Martin replied.

Not the Chinese I speak, I told him. But then I was always meeting people who are painted into a landscape quite foreign to me, their words encased in bubbles of sound impossible to translate. You know the kind. Pick up any paper any day and there they are — bankers, politicians, top executives of companies, even university presidents — surrounded with graphs and statistics, believing only in what can be measured.

Quite pointedly, Martin asked if I could forgive Clifford, and it was only then I knew my answer to be yes. No other answer, in fact, was possible. I had to forgive him, if I wanted him to forgive me. It was not his fault he couldn't speak my language, though I could also not speak his.

XVI

My conversation with Martin made both of us forget we were supposed to be getting ready for the theatre, and had invited Old Bill for a drink beforehand. Martin said he would go and fetch him, because he'd never make the stairs on his own. Thoughts of Clifford were pushed aside, overtaken by the rush of new events.

Old Bill, for I never heard him referred to in any other way, and Old Dr. Pat, likewise, occupied the two other flats in the four-storey building where my Arab Boy lived with Morley, with Old Bill above and Old Dr. Pat below, while on the ground floor, a small Italian restaurant co-existed uneasily beside a very English pub.

There was a bohemian charm about the unfashionable locale which had long appealed to Martin and Morley, secure and comfortable in their elegantly appointed oasis. Coming in from street level, however, one also encountered the less attractive, unblended odours of pungent tomato sauces and stale beer from the pub next door, made worse late at night by the strong smell of urine from those who had stepped inside the ground-floor darkened entrance, adjacent to the pub, mistaking it for something else.

Old Dr. Pat was a medical man of nearly eighty, who still practised in an inept kind of way, despite being an alcoholic.

He was someone lost in the vast bureaucracy of Britain's unwieldy and failing health service, never to be caught in the safety net for standards. Each day he would go to the pub at noon and be brought back at closing time by his drunken cronies. It was a situation straight out of Sean O'Casey, with little of the saving humour.

These were the same drunks, rejects, dope addicts, and n'er-do-wells that Dr. Pat would minister to when he was sober enough. Up and down the lower flight of stairs would come a daily parade of sadly disreputable characters, bringing their urine in little jam jars with insecure tops, sometimes leaving samples of themselves more naturally in the entrance, lending yet another flavour to those who used the same space late at night.

Martin and Morley attempted to have a reluctant and penny-pinching management put an effective lock on the outer door; they had planned, on this particular evening, to brief Old Bill, over a drink, on the absurdly contentious negotiations.

I had met Old Bill, a faded music hall queen of uncertain vintage, on two occasions in the pub, where he always sat in the same corner, talking nostalgically about the glory of the music halls and surrounding himself with a generation of young listeners who had, of course, no memory of what they never knew, but egged him on just the same, an easy figure of fun. He plucked his eyebrows, dabbed on always a little rouge, complained about his figure as much as he did about the coming of films, and ended all his drinking sessions with a rendition of "Pack Up Your Troubles in Your Old Kit Bag," at which point he was led upstairs to bed by any friends more sober than he.

Martin had visited him often in his meticulous flat, where every newspaper he had bought during his years as a performer had been carefully kept and piled in one corner of his bedroom, all the way to the ceiling. But Martin had also observed tea stains on the carpet, which Old Bill had tried to clean, without success. Because Old Bill no longer had any boyfriends, Martin had become a caring substitute. He cared for him very differently from the way he treated Gloria. He had even gone there one day with a scrubbing brush.

I heard the two of them negotiating the narrow stairs when suddenly there was a crash. I rushed to open the door, the same door that Martin had come through with Gloria so unhappily the previous week. Old Bill had fallen headfirst down the stairs, had slithered around the curve, and lay motionless, with a great deal of blood starting to gush from an open wound on the top of his bald head. Martin was quick to leap over the body, but turned immediately to cradle Old Bill in his arms.

"Poor Bill! Poor Bill!" he said, blood now covering his new white trousers. "There! There! We'll fix you up. You're going to be all right. You're quite safe. I'll hold you now. Poor, poor Bill! Don't you worry. You're not alone."

I had little time to reflect on the irony of these being almost the same words I had spoken to Gloria, holding her in my arms and trying to comfort her, before Martin roused me with firmly spoken orders to call the police, but first the ambulance.

I must have hesitated. The sight of blood has always unnerved me. After my father chopped the head off that chicken when I was six years old, following my sister's death,

I clearly remember refusing to eat flesh of any kind for some time after. A long recurring nightmare featured bloodless scenes of execution — human beings strapped into electric chairs, tied onto gurneys, led into gas chambers, and sprung through trap doors — but changed always to the guillotine. A continuing aversion to the sight of blood, even as an adult, has made it impossible for me, without fainting, ever to donate any of my own at Red Cross clinics set up for the purpose. I simply stared transfixed at the bleeding head and at Martin's trousers, with their ever-increasing stain.

Shouting at me, he said I should not just stand there. I had to help lift this slight old man into the flat and prop him up in an armchair. I got water and a towel from the kitchen, and Martin bathed the open cut. That accomplished, he ran downstairs for Dr. Pat, while Old Bill, moaning, dabbed at his face with a handkerchief, smearing it with blood, rouge and mascara. Martin was quick to return, fulminating, because there was a sign on Dr. Pat's door that read, "Back in 10 minutes." But who knew when Dr. Pat had put it up? The stupid old fucker! He was probably down in the pub, getting drunk, as usual.

Seizing his unfinished drink with one hand, Martin grabbed the telephone with the other to summon an ambulance, all the while trying to comfort Old Bill who was worried about who would feed his cat, Gigi, and water his plants if he ended up having to stay in the hospital. Gigi was a special cat: she made little "mirping" sounds when she wanted to be fed, and had an extra treat of tuna fish on Sunday nights at eight o'clock when the news was on. Old Bill started to shed tears at the thought of leaving her for even a day and a night.

"Cats can look after themselves. They're not like dogs," Martin said, feeling the pressure of circumstances, but attempting brisk efficiency in getting through to the hospital. I marvelled that he could be so unerring in handling such a situation, providing sympathy and a practical solution at the same time. I marvelled even more when I realized later that he had been snorting coke.

"No point fussing and clucking and wringing your hands. You've got to act," he said, as we waited for the ambulance to arrive. Sympathy was worthless without action, sympathy was just words. He continued to wipe blood from Old Bill's face, softly calling his name, until the ambulance men arrived and took him away on a stretcher. All the while, Old Bill dabbed at his mascara, saying he must look a mess and reminded us to look after Gigi.

He was out the door by then, and that particular incident was over, but not the night to come. It had all taken a great deal of time, and, anxious to get to the theatre, I was further on edge. So was Martin, on whom the effects of alcohol and drugs were becoming more pronounced. Morley was nowhere to be seen; he had not yet returned from a long day at the office.

Martin told me to go on ahead and not wait. He would follow a bit later. He had to change his bloodstained trousers. I argued the point and said I would wait, which I did, but none of this was a good prelude for the theatre.

If the biggest disappointments in life come from anticipating that others will act in the way we determine for them, believing that we would act in that way ourselves in parallel circumstances, then I was in for a major disappointment with Martin. I had constructed for him what was, in effect, a scenario for myself, and he was refusing to play the part. I felt increasingly anxious, as he changed into another outfit — slowly.

"Be an angel," he said sweetly, "and pour me a quick vodka." He was exhausted and really needed a drink. But I refused to be an angel, telling him he had quite enough. So he poured it for himself, a big one, probably four ounces.

Valuable minutes were lost before he was ready, and it was a long ride in the Underground to the theatre near Fulham Broadway. It seemed even longer because we didn't speak. I knew Martin was no longer interested in going to the play and was positively unconcerned about the time. I, on the other hand, was obsessive about punctuality, and didn't want to miss the opening. As we neared our destination, I told him he didn't have to come.

His disobliging answer came quickly enough: "I'm here, aren't I?"

Nothing further was said until we reached the out-of-the-way theatre, which looked like a converted warehouse. A strong smell of incense — or was it dope? — overwhelmed us as soon as we entered the already darkened space and stumbled into our seats, led there by a disobliging usher.

"Fuck, I can't see," Martin said in a too-loud voice.

I told him to sit down, and the other patrons in the immediate area made sshhing sounds, for the play was ready to start. Had we come in one minute later, no one would have heard us over the loudly blaring music which served as an introduction to this evening of "total" theatre, with Lindsay Kemp himself performing in *Salomé*. This same company had been responsible for the scenes of phallic worship at the beginning of *Sebastiane*, and I wondered if Helen Morris might dismiss this, too, as "risible". For my part, I was rivetted by the imaginative exploitation of colour and sound and movement.

Lurid stage lights revealed voluptuous scenes of near-naked men in Herod's palace — the Young Syrian, the Page of Herodias, the soldiers, Tigellinus, and glistening black oil-covered Nubians with bodies designed for sex. There was Herodias herself, who condemned all those who looked too long on the moon, and Herod, the Tetrarch, who heard in the air "something that is like the beating of wings, like the beating of vast wings" — those marvellous lines that stay forever in the mind. There was Salomé in ecstasy, untempted by the promise of "beautiful white peacocks that walk in the garden between the myrtles and the tall cypress trees," unmoved at the thought of "chrysolites and beryls and chrysoprases and rubies, sardonyx and hyacinth stones and stones of chalcedony," insisting only on the head of John the Baptist in a silver charger. And there was Jokanaan himself, not just an offstage voice but a naked body suspended from a high theatre grid, strapped into a harness, like some great heavenly dove, with feathered wings that spread themselves immensely over an erotic, incense-saturated court.

It became evident before very long that, no matter what Oscar Wilde and Helen might have thought, Martin was in no mood for any of it. In less than ten minutes, he had slumped in his seat and closed his eyes. Fearing that he might snore, I gave him a nudge, at which he quickly woke up and announced that he was going to leave.

Whispering, I tried to tell him that we couldn't leave: we had only just got there. But he said he had to pee, and said it so loudly that others around could hear.

"Pee if you must, but do shut up," said the lady next to him, who was very much focussed on the naked John the Baptist.

Martin thanked her profusely for giving him permission. He flashed the lady a dazzling smile, although her attention was now fixed on the sexy, oil-slicked Nubians, and was quickly out of the theatre, leaving me both embarrassed and annoyed. My first thought was to follow him, but since I had come a long way to see this spectacle, I decided to remain. Besides, Martin might change his mind and return. Yes, I had to stay. Furthermore, if art mirrored life, what strange concatenation of circumstances had led me to Oscar Wilde on this particular night after my particular day, my day with Clifford, and Martin and Old Bill lying in a pool of blood?

Three quarters of an hour passed without Martin's returning, each minute increasing my fears, adding to the pain I felt for what had happened and what I sensed was yet to come. Then, just as the play neared its climax, Martin came back to his seat. Within minutes, Salomé, daughter of Herodias, Princess of Judaea, was dead.

The applause was thunderous as all the actors crowded onto the stage for a well-choreographed curtain call. John the Baptist, who had been taken up into the flies, was again let down, but this time all the way to the floor. Salomé was held in the embrace of his extended wings, and Herod and Herodias smiled at this bit of revisionist history, while all the naked Nubians danced together in a circle under coloured lights. More incense was wafted everywhere by some hard-working special effects assistant, and music continued to blare through loudspeakers from every corner of the theatre.

Martin sprang to his feet, seemingly on cue, shouting, "Rubbish! Rubbish! You're awful! Rubbish! Shame!" I tried to grab him from one side to make him sit down, while the lady on his other side, who had encouraged him to go for a pee, told him in no uncertain terms to shut up.

"I won't shut up," he answered her. It was balls, a cheat, rubbish, disgusting rubbish, plain bloody rot.

"You didn't see any of it," said the Nubian-loving lady.

"I saw enough," he shot back.

I had managed to pull him down into his seat by this point, but again he stood up and shouted: "Shit! It's unadulterated shit. That's what it is." Although most of the actors were leaving the stage by now, Naaman, the executioner, not prominently placed for his curtain call, and other similarly neglected soldiers, who had spent the entire play waiting for their opportunity to crush Salomé beneath their shields, all moved in solid phalanx towards the front edge of the playing area, threatening now to quell the audience disturbance which Martin had started. Other audience members were crowding in, with enough shouts and shoves to rival the riot in the Abbey Theatre at the opening of *The Playboy of the Western World*. I had to get Martin out of there.

"For Christ's sake," I said, and seized him from behind with both arms and pushed him ahead of me, telling him to move and hurry up about it. If I had reacted slowly to Old Bill on the staircase, my strength was now apparent.

I was angry and upset. All at once, I thought of Miranda and her odyssey, her search for the shy dove of peace. I remembered Gloria and Hugh and Clifford and Morley and Angus, even the vicar disguised as an Arab, and my own apostate father brooding in a darkened room in Stratford, while my mother wondered how she would manage the accounts. Such are the disparate thoughts that occupy the mind, flashing in and out of focus, when all seems turned to dust.

Once outside the theatre, I let go of Martin and walked a whole block before I looked back. He waited where I had left him, but as soon as he saw me turn, crossed the street and entered what must have been the same pub he had retired to during the performance. I hesitated for a moment, but then crossed the street myself and followed him in.

Inside, we had a real altercation, with charges and counter-charges. I said he embarrassed me; he countered that I was too easily embarrassed. I had been embarrassed by Hugh at the train station, and embarrassed by him on the train itself. I should get over it. I said he had created a scene; he replied that the actors had created the scene, and he was only responding to it. It was rubbish, absolute rubbish.

I told him he hadn't seen ninety percent of it, so how could he judge? He'd seen all he wanted to see and still thought it shit. He placed a five-pound note on the counter, and said to the barman, "Double vodka." He turned to me and said, "You'll have one, won't you?" He didn't wait for my answer. "Make it two. One for my friend here, and if he won't drink it, I will." He then began a speech which, despite the slurring of words and crudity of thought, was surprisingly coherent. I almost wish I could forget it, but I can't:

"Want a real experience? Just go over there and ask for the fuck-dove. You'll find him in his harness all ready for you. Sit down and spread your legs. There's lots of room.

He'll come right away. And I mean come. So will you. Tickle your ass with a feather while he's about it. And when you're finished, you'll slither about in all the fucking mess of feathers and come and watch Salomé shit herself blind when she kisses your severed prick instead of John the Baptist's mouth."

I could stand it no more. This was what I had been waiting for, the ultimate outrage. I made a lunge for the glass Martin now held in his right hand, but I tripped on the leg of my own stool and fell forward against him, knocking him onto the floor. He managed to hold onto the glass even as he fell. It broke against the edge of the bar and came down on my left arm, jagged edge first. For the second time that night, I looked at the spurting of blood.

"You bastard," I said, bending over him, "Now see what you've done."

My arm was bleeding profusely from a gash just below the elbow, on the inside.

"Quick," said an anonymous woman, coming forward. "Hand me a towel," this directed to the publican behind the counter, who quickly complied. She proceeded to wrap it around my arm, just above the cut, as an impromptu tourniquet.

Others in the pub crowded around Martin, someone noting, rather obviously, that he had passed out and should be given water. Another got the water, amidst this shuffling and noisy talk, bent down, and tried to pour some between Martin's lips.

"He'll be all right. Give him a minute," said the woman who was ministering to me but seemed also to be in charge of the total operation. "Is that better, love? It's a nasty cut.

You'd better see a doctor. I can only do so much."

I thanked her for being so kind. She said she worked for the Red Cross, in the blood clinic, so she was used to it. She knew what to do. I must have a great heart, she told me, the way it was pumping out the blood. I was obviously very strong. Did I ever give blood at a clinic?

I had difficulty responding, as my mind went to crucifixions and chickens with their heads chopped off and the blood-red wine in communion cups, so she said never mind. Probably she shouldn't have asked — it was hardly the best time — but someone, somewhere was always needing blood. She advised me to get going since my friend seemed to be coming to.

Telling a man beside her to hail a cab, this anonymous Florence Nightingale took me gently by my good arm and led me outside, while her friends propelled Martin to the sidewalk just in time for the cab that appeared almost immediately.

I tried to thank her, as I fumbled with one hand to get my wallet from a back pocket, but she would have none of it. "Things work out. Remember that," was her parting benediction.

My emotions were in such turmoil now, apart from any physical discomfort I felt, that I did not insist. I thanked her yet again and settled with Martin in the backseat of the taxi. It was a long ride back to the flat, and I had plenty of time to think. Mostly I felt rage, mixed with embarrassment, even shame that I was caught up in anything so sordid. As for my arm, if Dr. Pat was not in the building, I would go to the hospital in the next block.

Martin was on a path of self-destruction, fuelled by alcohol and drugs, which were no cure for cancer. Even if this was the Queen's Jubilee, it was still not a year to celebrate, and I wanted no continuing part of it. The play I had seen that night had in it a special line for me: "I am sad tonight. Yes; I am passing sad tonight."

I determined then to leave my Arab Boy. My garden of doves and silver lilies had vanished. I would return to Canada sooner than planned. That would be sensible.

"I'm going home tomorrow," I said to Martin the next day when he was sober enough to take it in. I had got him home and put him to bed with Morley's help, after which I was able to arouse Old Dr. Pat, who proved surprisingly competent in bandaging my arm.

"The usual, I see," Morley had said. He had seen it all before and betrayed no emotion. Together we had got Martin up the carpeted, urine-soaked stairs and into his own room, where we bid each other only "Good night," nothing more. It was, however, a pointless adjuration, for it had not been a good night, and I slept little as a result.

When daylight broke, I remained firm in my resolve to leave Martin and get on with my own life in Canada. This had been my final throw: I had staked all and lost all. I would occupy myself, when I got back, in looking for a new job, something as far removed from the academic world as possible. Every aspect of my life had grown weary and emotionally unprofitable. I definitely needed a change and couldn't wait another day to make it. Yes, Air Canada had said, surprising me with their co-operation, my ticket allowed a change of date. The flight was not fully booked, and I could return to Toronto the following morning.

Of course Martin remembered almost nothing about the

night before, though he did think to ask how Old Bill was.

"It's not Old Bill I'm worried about. It's you," I told him.

"Why me? Why are you worried about me?" he asked.

When I challenged him to look at himself, he saw nothing wrong, but I did. Flesh exposed to all the natural ravages of time plus those he had wilfully added himself. Hair unbrushed. Eyes bloodshot. Breath bad. Cheeks puffy. Splotches of red marring his complexion. Deep creases running from each side of his nose to well below the line of his mouth. He was wearing nothing underneath his lightweight dressing gown, which fell open to his navel, showing a smooth white frame in marked contrast to his face. When he crossed his legs, I was still distressingly aware of all the wonder he held between them. "Thy body was a column of ivory." How painfully I remembered! "They say that love hath a bitter taste ... But what of that? What of that?"

"You're unwell," I said harshly, and tore a strip off the Arab Boy I used to take to bed. He was being stupid and wayward and difficult. He drank too much. It made me fucking goddamned bloody angry. How could he possibly go on this way? Drugs, too. Didn't he know it was lethal to put drugs and alcohol together? Was he really that stupid?

He could not have been aware that I was ready to burst into tears because of all we had lost.

He noticed my bandage and asked what was wrong. He seemed to have no recollection of what had happened, and when I answered, he seemed genuinely shocked.

"This can't go on," I concluded.

I crossed to the window. All life was there below me, two floors down on the street and the street beyond it and the street beyond that — Gloria with Robbie, Derek and his pimping agency, Greg returned from Bali, Hugh doing God knows what, Bernard in the restaurant he never meant to have, Margaret with her erotic photographs, Matthew in his cheesecloth shirt, Helen Morris on a trip to London. We were all there, too, Langland's great "field full of folk," all trying to live before we died.

I told him I had to get away, I couldn't stand any more, and he'd be better off if I wasn't around. Maybe I reminded him of too much, too much of what might have been. Maybe we were both in mourning.

When he asked me what for, I said for our past. We were both in mourning for our past.

"Will I always be your Arab Boy?"

I hesitated before saying, "We'll see."

XVII

I left London the day after that painful exchange, and found myself back at Mason College on the Wednesday before Labour Day. The plane had landed in Toronto too late for me to get a bus out of the city, but that meant I could head downtown and straight to the baths, where I could also check my suitcase. Quick sexual relief was what I wanted, needed, and got. I was not in the mood for inviting myself to stay at Gerald's, feeling some guilt that I hadn't written to him in all the time I'd been away.

The topless young man at the front desk who was paid to recognize repeat customers, smiled his vacant pretty smile and was false enough to say he missed me. When I made it clear I had been out of the country, as he could also tell from a look at my airline tags, he fired off his favourite questions: Did I have a good trip? Did I have lots of sex? Yes to the first but no to the second, and that's why I was there. He assured me I wouldn't be disappointed. The place was really hopping. After pushing a towel at me and handing over a locker key, he asked if I would rather have a cubicle, a space of my own where I could receive or reject as many as might pass by. A cubicle, yes, definitely a cubicle. That would cost me an extra four dollars, but it would be worth it. It was in a good locale, and I could expect a lot of visitors. With only a half-folded towel around my middle, I waited for those who came at various intervals throughout the night.

The next day I was thrust precipitately among colleagues who talked of wage increases and inflation and academic standards and how the United Nations should become more pro-active and how bad the weather had been all summer.

A new addition to the faculty asked what I thought of the wave of punk-rock madness gripping London, and if I had seen the record of "God Save the Queen" with its cover depicting the Queen with a safety pin through her nose. I said no, I had not, and didn't care either. My older psychology colleague, with his dark equatorial fantasies, pretended to be shocked at my flippant answer but went right on discussing attendance records with the spanking historian.

Where was Sybil, I wondered?

Students should not be allowed to skip lectures, sang several complainants in chorus, the voice of the commerce instructor alone guaranteeing that most of his students would skip his. Should there not be a new curriculum more in tune with the contemporary world, one that would offer more courses in sociology and experimental psychology? Business administration too, of course, chimed in the off-key voice.

Why wasn't Sybil there? I kept asking myself, looking around to see if she had arrived.

The newly retired professor of classics had died during the summer, but no one remembered exactly when and no one had missed him. Sheila, preparing new library slips, said that was because there were too few women on the faculty, the logic of which escaped me. The library budget for philosophy was to be increased, she added, to provide more copies of Kant in German, whether anyone was able to read them or not, though Mr. Squeaky-Voice assured us that Kant's views on commerce were clear and relevant.

Surely, Sybil would have thought that nonsense.

Samuel Bean, muddle-headed from staying awake when he should have been sleeping, suggested the whole marking system be changed back to real numbers from the letter grades established only the term before, after a committee of five had worked on the matter for twenty-seven months and had produced a two volume report which, again, nobody had read.

"Do any of you know where Sybil is?" I asked.

Carl Hollen, who had been trying unsuccessfully to imitate the rich warbling sound of a purple finch in flight, said that she was in the hospital.

I shot out of the room, jumped into my car and was there in six minutes, faster than any finch.

It was a new hospital, built all on one rambling level, and finished only two years previously, on the edge of the town where it could be set back from the road in a quiet area. Attractive in appearance, built of red sandstone, with a cantilevered roof and panels of glass, it was well run and adequately staffed, but did little to persuade me that a hospital was where I wanted to die.

"Room 7, Ward B," the receptionist said at the front desk, and I hurried along the rubber-tiled floor, past the nurse's station in that wing, to her room.

Entering, I noticed at once that there were no needles stuck into her arms or bits of tubing hanging from above, dripping fluid into her veins. That was a good sign, but no one looks well in hospital light, lying in hospital sheets, and

I must have appeared anxious when I asked her what was
wrong. She dismissed it as nothing very much; she had had
a dizzy spell, that was all. All? I queried. That wouldn't have
been enough to land her in hospital. She admitted only then
that she had fallen on the stairs at home and cracked a rib.
It was still a bit painful, but the doctors didn't know what
caused the dizziness. That's why she was there — for a few
tests.

Assuring me she'd be all right, she insisted that she didn't
believe in getting sick. She'd seen too much of it all her life.
I had to remember she'd been married to a doctor, and had
seen more than her share. Enough was enough. She put her
own ills out of her mind, and I must do the same thing. Her
language was always sensible: "Think positively if you want
to stay well. Nothing else works."

She asked if I had heard about Joe Gaudry, who must
have found it really difficult to think positively, despite
reading Gide.

What about Joe? No one had mentioned anything about
him. Had something happened to Joe Gaudry?

He had committed suicide, she told me, when I was away.
No one really knew why, but he was obviously very lonely.
He had gone home and hanged himself. Sybil had always
thought he was gay.

Immediately I felt guilty, as though I had been his
executioner. I also had suspected he was gay, but made no
effort to talk to him. Neither could language be used as an
excuse. If my French was faulty, his English was not. I might
just as well have supplied the rope. Sybil had learned he was
from New Brunswick, an Acadian. I didn't even know that.
He had left a note, asking to be cremated. He said he

wanted his ashes poured into the Bay of Fundy.

She reminded me what a marvellous place it was. The highest tides in the world. Throughout eternity, he'd be part of all that. Swept over those long beaches. Carried up onto the rocks, then back again to the sands and the tides forever. She might like that herself, when the time came. Wouldn't we all? Though even being part of all that glory would never make up for a lost life.

Would another corruptible body be made glorious that way? Telling her to get better soon, I added, as a poor kind of joke, "I'd rather have you here than in the Bay of Fundy."

I left the hospital, knowing there was still business to attend to at the college that shouldn't wait. I had to move on to worlds elsewhere.

I wrote to Martin a few days later, telling him that I had resigned my position, effective at Christmas, and requested sick leave until then. It was an unusual and radical move, but it had to be made. There was a great deal of consternation in the dean's office, but it had been easier than I thought it would be to get a certificate from my doctor that said I was suffering from stress and there was a suspicion of mononucleosis.

Dean Hilton pressed me to reconsider, but pretending to have the interests of the university at heart I told him that I didn't wish my health to stand in the way of his making a more satisfactory appointment, one that would lend greater academic strength to the department. He thanked me for being so considerate, and the next day wrote a confirming letter, pointing out how all things work together for good. I had not been a productive scholar, had never completed my doctorate, had published only one article in nineteen years, and there was very real doubt that I would ever advance in rank, so maybe it was as well that I eschew a university career. He would always be happy to provide a reference.

I wrote back an equally polite letter, of course, although what I really wanted to say was that I didn't give a fuck, and he could stick the curriculum wherever he liked, as far as I was concerned. At last I was free, and life, or whatever was left of it, would be lived on my own terms.

I returned any unread books to the library, where Sheila Kemp continued her vigilant and unnoticed work, remaining forever on the alert for anyone breaking the rules. But she had had her Andy Warhol fifteen minutes of fame when she had routed the neo-Nazi in our midst and we had all applauded.

Sybil was now out of the hospital, all her tests having come back negative. She strongly supported my move, saying I'd done the right thing, and would be much happier. When I tried to tell her things would have been different from the very beginning if I had been lucky enough to meet more people like her, she said exactly what I might have expected her to say:

"Stop right there. We have what we have as long as we have it, and then go on to something else. That's all there is to it."

Of course, she's absolutely right. She was also categoric when she reminded me that we live in a dangerous world, and that's still true for all of us, isn't it? Constantly there is an edge that threatens to crumble when we walk, and someone can always be found nailing a gay man to a wall, thinking gay means pervert.

I told Martin in my second letter that I didn't know what I was going to do, but would let him know as soon as anything developed. He sent back his reply immediately — a sexy card, a real photograph of a naked Adonis, but more beautiful than anything you would see in life, ready, willing and obviously very able. On it, in boldface print, were the words, "Fuck 'em all."

As far as I've ever been able to tell, misfortune and good luck go hand in hand, linked opposites. I was out of a job, and the economics of that persuaded me to return to live with my parents in Stratford, where my father continued his decline and my mother sought comfort from the religion he had renounced. They lived their diminished lives in a late Victorian yellow-brick house, poorly insulated and darkly furnished with anything they had been able to buy cheaply in their retirement, having lived always in rent-free rectories. They had vague plans for renovations but neither the will nor the money to complete them. The lucky part for me in all of this was that I had now a rent-free place where I could live, and this seemed to please my mother. I made it clear, however, that work might sometimes prevent my coming home at night. I did not confess something else that was lucky for me.

Early in that New Year, I had secured a position in the publicity department — where I still am — at the Stratford Festival, which was growing ever more prosperous in its new home. It's much better than a tent, though it was still designed to look a bit like one, with its scalloped roofline of peaks and its higher gathered point in the centre. And what a great thing that the building still covers the original thrust stage Tanya Moiseiwitsch designed! The whole place is a triumph, and I was happy to be part of it. They had already organized the 1978 season to come and were getting ready to plan the next year, and it suited them to have on their staff someone with an academic background who was able to write with reasonable fluency.

I told them I had written only one scholarly article in the previous nineteen years and it had been specifically designed to get me promoted to the rank of associate professor. It was on "The Place of Weeds in Shakespeare's Pastoral Comedies," and had been thought adequate for promotion, but only to that rank. I confessed that the dean had reminded me I was unlikely ever to go further up the academic ladder because I had published so little — unless, I thought to myself at the time, I moved past weeds to flowers, which would have indicated real progress.

The Festival Manager who hired me seemed to think these were not grave deficiencies and I got the job, without having to jump through any more hoops. There was, furthermore, a fringe benefit quickly found and enjoyed in the person of a young man called Tony, who handled much of the local advertising. Within five days of my being next to him in the same office, it turned out that he was also happy to share a bed, anywhere we could find one, so long as it was not in my parents' house.

He was sexy beyond my most erotic dreams — at forty-six, of course, I found all young men in their twenties sexy — but he was capable of writing only the simplest notes, such as: "Dear Peter. Come with me. xxxx." These he left on my desk to whet an appetite that did not need whetting. Such invitations were at first thrilling but soon limiting, even irritatingly sophomoric, and I couldn't remember ever having written such notes myself. My own note to Angus, inviting him to my Oxford bed so long ago, might have been direct but was, I hoped, more ambiguously phrased. It was he who had reminded me that love, of whatever sex, was always something to be learned, an idea which seemed again elusive. Tony had nothing but sex to share with me, nothing he thought to learn, not about books or art or music or history or much about the universe unfolding around us. Only his cock which, admittedly, he put to good use.

There was, of course, the work we shared in the office, making up ads for the local paper and the *Globe and Mail*, writing blurbs to entice Americans across the border into a town which boasted of swans in a river really called the Avon, just like the real thing somewhere else, and small hotels we were reluctant to rate for obvious reasons, but a theatre unequalled in North America.

Despite finding a sexual outlet, my heart was ill at ease, and I convinced myself I would never learn what Shelley's baby once must have known about love. I was living again with my parents, which is always difficult for an adult child, especially for anyone with a father like mine. There had been so much to understand about him from the very beginning. Rosemarie and I were aware as children that he moved in darkness, unable to smile upon our childish games. We never understood why. This was especially true the day he caught me in my mother's dress. It was only when he was preparing to leave for the war in 1939, just a year after Rosemarie's death, that he told me in detail about his own father and what had happened, believing, I suppose, it was the proper time for me to learn even more about death.

He had been an only boy, the last of three siblings on what was the family farm, twelve miles west of London, Ontario. It was largely a subsistence farm, but one which also produced corn and enough green beans for the local market. The soil, however, was acidic, and my grandfather hadn't a clue how to change it. Still, he managed to teach my father a few basics, such as how to mend fences and mound potatoes and prune raspberry canes for stronger growth the following year, even how to kill chickens humanely, though my father had already shown me the impossibility of that. There had always been enough food for the family, but they nevertheless lived on the edge of poverty.

From the age of six, my father had to get up early to help with the chores before walking a mile and a half to school, and in the late afternoon do the same thing on his return. There were chickens to feed and eggs to collect and cows to milk. There were also stalls to muck out, never a job he liked.

Always he was being told what to do, where to go, how to behave, what to wear, to keep his shoes clean and say his prayers every night. All that sort of thing, and he hated it.

He was a good boy, always a good boy, until one day when he was twelve years old he found his own father dead and thought he was responsible. He had gone to the barn alone that afternoon in late September to collect any eggs that had not been there in the morning. The barn is weathered and its red paint is peeling off — I've seen it: my aunts Fannie and Gertie now run the farm and can't really cope — but it still stands some fifty feet from the house; and to get to it, my father had either to jump over a fence or pull back the long slats of wood that were horizontally notched into uprights for a makeshift gate.

He told me that the sun cast narrow shadows on the floor that particular day, piercing its way through vertical lengths of lumber on the western side of the building where steady driving rains had caused the boards to shrink and pull apart over the years. There were wheelbarrows and buckets and rakes and full sacks of bran leaning together for support, all adding shape and colour to the interior, and pieces of rope coiled and hung on the walls or left lying about in scattered lengths from earlier use. But once inside that space, so full of magical light that afternoon, my father told me how he looked up at the two great supporting crossbeams, before moving to the northeast corner where bales of hay were stacked against each other. With genuine difficulty, he dragged one of the bales to a position immediately below a beam and sat down to plan what had just come into his head.

He was determined to play a game of his own devising, recalling it in vivid detail, as he told me the story. He would get up, stand on the bale, and make a last speech before jumping off, pretending he had a rope around his neck. He wondered if that's the way it was done, and if men died as quickly as women when they were hanged.

He got up on the bale and shouted because he knew that no one could possibly hear, something to the effect that he would keep his shoes on if he wanted to, even if they were muddy, and he wouldn't feed the chickens that day or any other, that his sister Gertie could do it because she was the oldest, and if anyone tried to make him, he would jump with the rope around his neck and they'd be sorry.

He jumped and landed on the floor and laughed at the way he had thwarted everyone. He got up and did it all over again and then he did it a third time. He was tired by then and sat on the bale of hay to rest. At the same time, he picked up from the floor a heavy piece of rope to play with and practise the knots he had learned as a cub scout. You probably remember them yourself if you were ever a cub, which I wasn't.

First he tried the clove hitch which has its two loops, one superimposed on the other, and isn't very difficult to do. But there was nothing immediately accessible to put it around, so he went on to the bowline, which is rather more complicated. He measured this one out on the flat surface of the hay bale, looping one end around the other. He didn't succeed at first, so he tried again. This time he held it out in front of him and repeated the little aid-to-memory story he had learned as a cub: "The rabbit comes out of the hole, goes round the tree and goes back down again." He pushed one end up from behind and through the hole in a shaped figure six, around the stem of the number and brought it back, taking the end to where it had started its journey. It looked a bit like a miniature noose. He tightened it a little and left it there on the bale before he went off to feed the chickens and give bran to the cows. It was six o'clock and time for supper.

When he got to the table, his sister Fannie asked where their father was, because he hadn't appeared for the meal.

My grandmother replied that he had gone next door to the Wilson's farm because he hoped they might be able to help them out.

Gertie asked what they needed help for, but wasn't much interested in any answer, because she was facing her very unfavourite carrot soup instead of the peanut butter sandwiches she always preferred to eat, given the chance. Neither did she understand when my grandmother explained they wanted to use the farm as collateral, a word Gertie had never heard before, and Mr. Wilson might help arrange that, because he was the bank manager. They would all know by the morning what was what.

My father was the first up that next day, as usual, and went to the barn to do his chores. This meant going in a direct line past the area where he had been playing the afternoon before. At first, he hardly noticed when he bumped into something, but then, when he stopped to look, he saw his father's feet at eye level in front of him. Looking up, he saw my grandfather's whole body, perfectly still, head slightly tilted to one side, eyes open and staring at a world which could not be changed, neck broken in a noose made from the same rope my father had been playing with.

He ran screaming from the barn, across the muddy field and into the house, his heart broken, taking the blame himself for having left the bowline on top of the bale, though never as a hint for use. Nothing could comfort him, and from that day on the very mention of a knot was something he couldn't abide.

My grandfather's suicide eventually turned my father to the church, as a salve to conscience. No rational thinking, he claimed, could ever banish the darkness he carried within.

If Clifford's ghost had haunted me for all my adult life, so had my father's, for reasons you might now understand. Having exorcised one, the time had come to try to exorcise the other, now that I was back in Stratford, living with my parents, though many weeks went by before I could screw up my courage. Ridiculous that I found so much difficulty in facing an old man of seventy-eight, but what was true in my childhood still remained true: we had never learned to look at each other. There was only awkwardness when our eyes never quite met, because of the habit my father had of tilting his head forward so that the top rim of his glasses always got in the way of any more direct encounter.

Early photographs of my father show him to have been strikingly handsome, with a head of unusually splendid hair, worthy of a Van Dyck painting if he had let it grow. There is one snapshot in particular, taken in his army uniform at Niagara-on-the-Lake in 1917, but with his hair cut short, when he was only seventeen. He is standing by the edge of Lake Ontario and has obviously scooped up some water in his hands. Several girls are gathered around him, laughing and bending over, ready to drink from his hands. It's an image I remember because I envied the girls. What had happened in the sixty-odd intervening years, I wondered, when, bald now, he still offered me nothing?

The house had a small garden at the back, and a shed with tools and buckets and fertilizer in plastic bags and bits of light rope for tying plants or young trees to stakes so they wouldn't fall down or hang over. It was there, on a late September afternoon, I thought at last to face my father. Would he think, too, the time had come to settle our accounts before some greater reckoning — an obsession with those who grow old — or did he really believe there was nothing to face, either in the garden that afternoon or in the eternal beyond?

He had a folding canvas chair in his favourite spot next to the helenium, its coppery orange, red and yellow tones the only colours left in a faded garden. Beside him, on a small table, was a sherry decanter and one glass, the usual props. There was some warmth left in the sun as he sat with his eyes shut and sweater no longer buttoned up to his thin neck. He even seemed to be smiling a little, which was rare, and encouraged me.

Approaching very softly, I asked if I could get him anything.

"Like what?" said as if he had dragged himself across vast stretches of tundra in order to answer.

Because I really had nothing specific to propose, I just asked if he was warm enough.

"Can't you see I am?" said as if he had now reached some desolate outpost.

God, what a beginning! I felt like a child entering a space for grown-ups only, so I enquired, almost timidly, as a child might, if I could come in, if I could join him.

"Suit yourself."

Two words. Crushed now by two words, and there he sat with his eyes shut.

There was another canvas chair leaning against the wall; I set it at a forty-five degree angle to him, a few feet to the right, so that we could face each other without being confrontational. I ventured another question: what was he thinking about?

"Nothing."

If he was thinking about nothing, I was thinking about much. I was thinking about how much I had longed to please him as a child, please him by writing little notes to accompany my mother's letters when he went into the army as a chaplain, please him when he returned, please him by doing well in school, please him by saying that I would pursue the same career as he had and go into the church, please him by getting the biggest scholarships I could, so that I would be no financial burden. But nothing had ever worked and was again not working.

If he and my mother felt any pleasure in my returning to live with them, it was only my mother who said so. He continued remote and taciturn, and I wondered if, after all, it had been my fault. Whatever was wrong, I had to try again.

I began my next sentence with "Dad", hoping that a word less formal than father might bridge an initial gap, though I never called him Dad and certainly not Daddy, after the still clearly remembered rebuke in that long-ago postscript.

"Dad, I really wish we could talk."

He opened his eyes and said, "Why?"

There was so much to say, I told him. Didn't he want to say anything?

Not really. No. Why should he want to say anything?

Indeed, that had always been true. I had wanted him to tell me things when I was growing up, and he never would. I had wanted him to tell me why he had cut that chicken's head off. I had wanted him to tell me about sex, when my raging hormones started their relentless drive. But he had been silent.

I had searched secretly in his cupboard for hidden books, but the only one I found, called *Married Love*, was no use to me and had no illustrations. I had discovered, however, on the top shelf of the local bookstore a book called *What a Young Boy Ought to Know, The Mystery of Birth Cleanly Told*, the first in an "Up-to-date series for the Boy-Man-Girl-Woman-Wife-Husband," by Sylvanus Stall, Doctor of Divinity, and I read it both avidly and surreptitiously, whenever I could, only to learn that I was guilty of a truly major sin — that of self-abuse, a solitary vice which would lead, inevitably, to the ruin of my nerves and the loss of my hair, to headaches, dizziness, palpitations of the heart, and poor digestion, as well as many other signs and promises of early decline and death. The book had first been printed in 1897. It's laughable, when I think of it now. My digestion is good, and I still have my hair.

I told my father that there were things I wanted to say, even if he didn't.

"Like what?" looking at me, though the rim of his glasses obscured his pupils. But could I bring myself to speak? And about what exactly?

I threw my sentence at him: "Why did you leave the church?"

Nothing, I suppose, in our past history could have prepared him for so direct a question, but I know he remembered the darkness of an earlier Palm Sunday. He poured himself another glass of sherry, not asking if I wanted any — there was, after all, only one glass, and I might have emptied the decanter — and then shut his eyes.

It was very simple, he said. The whole thing was a lie. The virgin birth confused everybody, and not even the Bishop knew how to explain the resurrection. He thought it was nothing physical. As for another life for any of us who might hope to improve our grades elsewhere, he believed that "Into the earth we go, and that's that."

I argued that surely there must be something more, and he asked how could there be? If I lived as long as he had lived, I'd understand that. No doubt about it. None at all. My grandfather had gone first, and he would be next. Then it would be my turn. There had been two world wars in his lifetime, and he had got into both of them. A depression had come in between. There'd never been any money. Death was everywhere. Shouldn't all that be enough for any one man? He was glad to be finished with life.

"But there's got to be more. I want there to be more," I almost shouted at him, I was so upset and even a bit angry.

"Your wanting has nothing to do with it," he said, as if starting another walk across some barren plain. "If your faith is blind, it need not also be stupid."

End of topic. Silence.

"I'm sorry," I said.

"What for?"

"For everything, everything lost."

"Why be sorry?" he asked. Nothing lasts. I should have learned that. After the good years come the lean. That's what growing old means. I had to prepare for it.

I remembered his sermon on Pharoah's dream and how he had chosen to ignore the survivors. Joseph got out of prison, I reminded him. He was not Joseph, he pointed out.

If he was holding out his hands to me, they contained no water. But maybe if I scooped up something from my own reserves of courage, I could say now what I had to say. The time had come. He would have to listen. There was no escape. I would say it right out and I did: "There's something I must tell you. It's important. It's very personal. It's about me. I want you to know."

I could feel blood running up into my head, I was so agitated and tense. I wanted my father to know about me, more than my having blue eyes and a mole on my right arm. I wanted him to know who I truly was, because I was his son. He had to know about me. It was absurd to keep silent.

"It's about the way I am. It's important," my whole self now surging over a vast interior wall.

"Don't tell me."

That's all. Just that.

"Don't tell me."

And he moved to pick up an apple that had fallen nearby. "Look!" he said, holding it out, "there's a worm in it."

I remembered his rage when he caught me in my mother's dress, and I saw his eyes directly now, no rims in the way.

I did not take the apple.

I tried to write this to Martin, tempering my own sadness with ironic amusement where I could. The deepest pain can never be properly shared, but here I am telling you. I did mention to Martin, from time to time, something I heard or read in a play that struck a special chord. The Elephant Man explained why his head was so big: it was full of dreams that could not get out.

Consistently Martin ignored my urgent pleas to let me know about his health. When he was not sending erotic cards of naked men — "Bet you wouldn't kick him out of bed, would you?" — he would write only of events on his social and cultural calendar. At the Ebury Gallery, he had seen a superb exhibition of watercolours. Just nudes and flowers. *Der Rosenkavalier* at Covent Garden had been sheer magic, and he had wept a great deal at the Marschallin's plight, though Morley had said it was only because he was wearing too much cologne. They were just back from the continent. More opera. In Gaeta they heard *The Merry Widow* sung in Italian by the Rumanian Light Opera Company, with everyone wearing costumes left over from the thirties. It was all too ghastly, but Morley had really loved it because he spoke Italian and didn't know much about music.

Occasionally, Martin would mention someone I knew and then only parenthetically, as if it didn't matter. He had heard that Derek had died of something or other. Greg had at last returned from Bali, not to Miranda, who was off with someone else, but to her sister Gloria, if I could believe it. Good for Gloria! She would be fucked at last, though he said he had always rather fancied Greg for himself.

Two years went by, and I still had no clearer idea about Martin's health. I had even written to Morley, asking him directly, but he was similarly evasive. One day, however, he wrote with news of a different kind. His family shipping line had been assigned into bankruptcy, and he had lost most of his wealth. He and Martin would still be able to manage, he said, because they would sell their beautiful country house and give up buying expensive wines from Herr Schmidt. He seemed not as upset as I was.

My own reaction to this news was selfish, and I wrote back to tell of my distress at not being able again to visit that glorious spot, where I had held in my arms a Caravaggio from the Villa Borghese and had thought myself in love for a night. But, please, how was Martin and had he heard from Hugh? Would Morley be so kind as to answer?

Weeks went by, even months. I waited for the letter which never came. I should have known something was wrong, but I did nothing. Instead, I threw myself into my work, and I watched my father die.

His end, when it came, was swift. If he saw, as many do at the point of death, a blinding radiance at the end of a darkening tunnel, he didn't speak of it. He was dead from pneumonia in three days and cremated the day after that. We buried his ashes in a newly consecrated cemetery which was more like an open field. It was a cold, rainy November day, but I couldn't relate to the little urn put into a space that was barely one foot square, any more than I could to the man who had wrestled with God and lost me in the wager. Was that all that was left of my father? Even the God he tried to serve had been against him. My mother wept in my arms, but I was not able to comfort her as she used to comfort me. I was not aware until much later, you see, that she had loved my father.

Later that same afternoon, after the obligatory tea and sandwiches that followed the funeral, I left for Toronto, professing urgent business there, but seeking yet again that place where all my sexual fantasies could be quickly and anonymously indulged. I went from cubicle to cubicle, with only a half-folded towel around me, soliciting partners with eye contact and silent nods and indicating with a gesture what kind of sex I wanted. Never satiated, I looked for the impossible, remembering my father reduced to ashes.

"Into the earth we go, and that's that."

XVIII

My father's death made me wonder more than ever what Shelley's baby knew but couldn't say. Was it simply that love is the secret that lies beyond, the thing we look for in our cave but never find or only partly find? Is it as simple and obvious as that? If my father looked, was it only darkness he saw? And what exactly had I seen in my adult life? Shadows, mostly shadows. The shadow of my obsessive love for Clifford, the shadow of my unbalanced love for Martin, the shadow of my infatuation for Hugh, the dark, dark shadows of a bathhouse world. Nothing real, nothing of substance, nothing that can endure.

I should tell you, though, it wasn't always that way. Once, just once, when I was very much younger, I loved more than a shadow. I loved someone real. His name was Billy, and both of us were sixteen. We lived for a time in a garden full of light, and it's that garden I've been searching for ever since, that place where all of us can grow into whatever we were meant to be. It was a time of innocence for Billy and me, long before we might have been tested in life's crucible. But it was valid, and reached a perfection I've not known since.

My early life in Parkhurst was one I wanted to escape, except for what I am now about to tell you. Never a jock, always a hater of football, though a lover of hockey when it wasn't a brawl, I was, nonetheless, a powerful swimmer, a recreational sport that allowed, even favoured, my not-so-innocent voyeurism in the showers after practice. With no one around to tell me anything, I was able to learn much by observation. Other boys sometimes called me "sissy," "fruit," "pansy," sometimes to my face before they would run away, or write those words on little bits of paper and stuff them in my schoolbag when I wasn't looking, so that I would find them later, when I got home.

My father had been back from the war for three years, but remained as far from me as if he were still in Hong Kong, where he had finished up, trying to help any who had survived that profound horror. I could still not talk to him, and he never asked about anything. He moved around the house like a thin ghost, never saying much, and when he sat, he mostly stared into space. How he managed to get himself together on Sundays and do his sermons, I don't quite know.

Thus pre-occupied, my father never noticed me noticing boys. In the showers one day after swimming, I noticed Billy. Not for the first time, I should add, but I really noticed him, noticed his body. Until that moment, he had been just another boy in my class — Billy Halpert, son of the local druggist, someone who had always smiled at me and never called me names.

Everyone else had left, but the two of us lingered, held there by I don't know what force. He was my age and, like me, tall but better developed. He stood there soaping himself, just soaping himself, first his hair and then his shoulders and abdomen down his legs to his feet, lifting each one to wash between his toes and then up again to his thighs, all soapy now with water dripping down his body, slightly widening his stance, legs apart so he could reach between them to his balls and his cock which was then growing large, and under his balls to the place I longed to go. Turning at that point, he exposed his buttocks to me, still rubbing, still soaping, then turned again to notice my looking. My own cock was erect. He came over and touched me.

Of course I said no I didn't mind when he asked me if I minded, because I didn't mind. Far from it. I was curious. I was excited. I was young. Even in church, I often had difficulty concealing my hard on, when I thought of the things I'd never done but longed for. So it was quite natural for me to say yes when Billy suggested we leave the showers and go some place else. Nothing could have stopped me.

We dressed and went out of the building that housed the civic pool and got into the car his parents allowed him to drive sometimes with his newly acquired license. I asked him where we were going, and he said he would show me a place just past the quarry at St. Mary's.

After parking the car, we crossed the road to a wooded area he obviously knew very well. We quickly undressed and kissed again and put our damp towels on the ground to protect us from any sharp twigs when we lay down. We took turns lying on top of each other, hands exploring erections and curves and crevices, tongues exploring mouths and cocks and buttocks, and though neither of us entered the other that summer afternoon, despite trying, it was my first explosive orgasm with someone I thought I could love. My earlier and lonelier moments would be a thing of the past, I believed. And they were, for a time. Only for a time. Life's usual allowance.

Billy, I soon learned, was a naturally gifted photographer, with a sharp eye. For his fourteenth birthday, his parents had given him a reasonable Kodak camera, complete with the few basics needed for developing black and white film at home: a special red light bulb, trays, frames, printing paper, chemicals, and fixatives.

Thus armed, Billy took me with him into a darkened space improvised in his bedroom cupboard, there to watch the whole magical process, to watch while pictures of me, as well as pictures of him that I had taken, naked in our sylvan setting, would appear first in negative and then on a piece of rectangular white paper immersed in chemical solution. Faint at first, the images under the surface would come clearly into focus, while we spoke in awe of a scientific process we hardly understood.

But all of this was not enough. What Billy really wanted was to learn how to draw and how to paint, how to become an artist in those media. He dreamed and talked of the day when he might go to art school.

"Do you think I'll really get into art school?" he asked one day. "Think I'll really get in?"

I told him of course he would, because it was what he wanted to do, wasn't it? We were lying in our favourite place that summer. The damp towels had been supplanted by a large dark green chenille bedspread I had brought from my bedroom at home, hoping its absence would not be noted.

Half an hour previously, Billy and I had been making love on that bedspread, assured now from practice and so confident in technique that we didn't have to think consciously about who would play what role when and how, because there were no roles to play. We were just ourselves, and there was no one around to tell us it was sinful.

We lay together on that bedspread under the trees in the late sunlight of that warm afternoon, just looking at each other, delighting in each other and kissing each other, my right hand moving down his lower back, my left smoothing his auburn hair, feeling the slight stubble on his face, my fingers gently parting his lips so that he could feel them in his mouth before closing them again and kissing me again, my hand continuing its now familiar journey across his shoulder, down that side of his back, both my hands now near each other, feeling the strength and softness of his buttocks, pressing him in to me, turning him, entering him, changing the world forever.

Like everyone else, you may remember what the first time was like. Not the first entry, which, in our case, had been awkward and I didn't think would work. I mean the very first time you entered someone you believed you loved, as I now loved Billy. No other thought in my head. Just love, pure love. Or was it only sex? No, it was both of these together. That's what made it so special, made us believe the world had just been born and all of it was ours. I knew at last that I was truly alive.

Billy had brought with him his sketchpad and his pencils instead of his camera, and after I assured him that he would really get into art school, he said he wanted to do a nude drawing of me, just as I was, in that place.

I lay there, very still, for half an hour, while his pencil caught the shape of my head, the long line of my back, my arms, my legs, and my penis, now quietly there, privately celebrated. Billy said nothing as he worked. When he handed it over, he said it wasn't very good and didn't do me justice. But it was very good, because he had seen all of me, knew all of me, and accepted all of me, in a way I thought no one else ever would. For all these years, I've kept that drawing as a talisman, a witness to my first innocent love, and it's a youthful work you might like to see one day.

Over and over again that summer, we went to that same sacred spot and for the few short summers that followed, in celebration of a love that now can speak its name, but was then against the law. Billy and I might have been arrested, branded as criminals, shamed in the press and paraded before the courts, our lives in ruins. This was 1949, remember, when you were only four years old, still holding hands with your father when you went for a walk. But even if we had been aware of the law, nothing could have stopped us. We talked of the future, confident it would always be there. Billy would be an artist, and I would be a teacher. The universe would unfold as it should. And it did for a time.

Looking back on it, there was, I think, an omen in a relatively small thing that happened, though it distressed both of us at the time. For his tenth birthday, Billy's father had given him a special present, a classic-looking model electric train, because he could afford for his son the sort of things my father never gave me. That whole railway world remained on an old table painted green, set up in a corner of Billy's bedroom, and it was there he took me to see it the day after he finished my drawing.

The tracks were connected to a small transformer that provided power for everything. There was a gleaming black locomotive trimmed with brass to pull the coal car immediately behind it, followed by the three cream-and-russet passenger cars, all with roofs that could be removed and clipped back on, all cars with little seats, all cars with a light inside, a single bulb, magical to see lit. The last car even had an observation platform, the kind seen in old films, the kind the King and Queen stood on at station stops when they visited Canada in 1939 and had their pictures taken for the history books.

Billy and I crouched that afternoon to watch the passenger coaches click past us at eye level, as if it were night, no royalty on board this time, and we dreamed of what we might be and where we might go. The transformer also provided power for the stationmaster's little white house with red chimney, which stood on the edge of the tracks. There, a reassuring figure would slide in a groove, out through a green door, swinging a lantern as the locomotive rushed by, taking its non-existent passengers only in endless circles on their limited table world. There was also a train station, with an imposing classical facade, where small lead figures of disproportionate size waited endlessly to board a train which would carry them into a future they could never hope to reach, even if the train had been programmed to stop for the eternity it would take to bring them to miraculous life.

On that afternoon, when Billy became again the engineer in charge, the locomotive was made to run faster and faster, as the lever on the transformer was pushed from one to five, so that it went round and round, faster and faster, ever faster, until on one of the curves it jumped the rails, as real trains sometimes do, taking every car with it onto the floor.

Imaginary lives were lost that day and the lonely station-master no longer came from his house to signal that all was well. The scene was desolation, with pieces strewn about the floor and dreams of young men shattered.

An early dream of mine had been to go into the church, in an effort to please my impossible-to-please father, but by now I had given that up as a ploy which wasn't going to work for me any more than it did for him. Much more to my liking, I had decided to do a degree in English at Toronto, as I mentioned earlier, and that was just when Billy got accepted into the fine arts program at Guelph. We would be separated by miles, but we knew we were truly in love, and there would always be weekends and holidays to look forward to.

There came a day, in our first year apart, which began like any other, except for a heavy rainfall and the promise of more to come. It was also the Friday before the long Thanksgiving weekend, and I had an eight-thirty lecture to attend, though how anyone can think clearly at that hour about Boccaccio's influence on Chaucer in the writing of *Troilus and Criseyde* I don't know. Afterwards, I went to the main library to look up a reference the professor had made to *Il Filostrato*, then to Hart House for a quick swim in the pool before lunch in the cafeteria. Billy and I had made no plans yet for Thanksgiving day itself. We tried unenthusiastically to persuade each other over the phone that we really should work for part of it, and we would confer again.

In my residence that early evening, someone shouted down the corridor, "Hey, Peter, it's for you." I ran to the phone booth, expecting to hear Billy's familiar greeting: "Hi, lover boy!" But it was not Billy, it was my mother.

"Is that you, Peter?"

And I knew right away that something was wrong.

"What is it?"

She had just got word from Billy's mother that he had been killed on his motorcycle. He had gone off the road on a bad curve, slippery from all the rain, not far outside Guelph. He had been on his way to see me — a surprise for Thanksgiving.

I was so paralyzed I could only mumble something to the effect that I would take the next bus home. My desolation was beyond tears at that point, but later that evening, alone in a back seat of the bus, rounding that deadly curve before reaching Guelph, I shut my eyes and sobbed uncontrollably.

That bus makes a stop at a convenience store on the edge of town before reaching the terminal, and it was there I got off to meet my mother. Instead of waiting inside, as she should have done, because it was still raining, she was standing outside under my father's large black umbrella with its two broken spokes that cause water to drip unevenly from its edges. From the steps of the bus, I made a hatless dash to the shelter of her arms, the two of us standing there with heavy hearts, mine for sorrow, hers for love of me. She knew there was nothing to be said that had not already been said, nothing that I did not already know about her understanding of me and her acceptance of my relationship with Billy. There are times when language simply won't do, and this was one of them.

I've already told you how my mother spoke of her love for

me on one particular day when I was thirteen and came home upset after school. She spoke of it again a couple of years later when my life was made hell by a number of school bullies who called me Fifi. I tried to hide my distress at home by shutting myself in my room, pretending I was doing homework, but crying a lot of the time into my pillow.

My father never noticed, of course, but my mother always asked what was wrong. I never wanted to tell her, but one day I did. She had come into my room while I was crying, and it was there, sitting on my bed, that she spoke of love.

It was of all kinds, she said, because God had made things that way. "He's not a limited thinker," she assured me. "God's not a limited thinker." We all had to find out what kind of love was best for us. She had to do it on her own, finding love with my father, and I would also have to find it on my own. No one could tell me, and that was both a good thing and a bad thing, because sometimes we all want to be told what to do and we can't be told. The Bible was also unreliable on the subject and could be interpreted in lots of contradictory ways. Looking for the right kind of love was often very painful, but it was important to search, and I should never mind what anyone said, including the boys who called me Fifi. They might never find love, she said, and one day I might. She was right, of course. But with Billy's death, I had lost what I had found.

It was natural, I suppose, though ironic, that my father was asked to take Billy's funeral, knowing nothing of the deceased's relationship to his son. For him it was just another funeral, another body to be made glorious in God's kingdom, which he didn't even believe was there. Another body to go back into the earth, ashes to ashes, dust to dust.

For me, I cannot properly tell you what it was like to be a pallbearer, to be one of six carrying a body I had felt so often on top of mine, underneath mine, a body now cushioned in satin and velvet. At the gravesite, when I threw a handful of soil on the top of his coffin, I knew he was gone forever. I couldn't face going to the Halperts' home afterwards for tea and cookies and hearing everyone say how awful it all was and how much they were going to miss him. No one would ever guess why I would want to go home, get into bed, shut my eyes, and jerk off, which is what I did. You are someone who would understand that, I know. I would have to go on without him, but it was my way of keeping him alive.

XIX

When luck lets go misfortune's hand, it's misfortune that remains, not luck. While I moved past the sorrows of Billy's death in the years that followed, I went on to the frustrations of life with Clifford and the mixed joys of my life with Martin. When he learned of my father's death, he expressed his sympathy in only an off-hand way. We all had to die, he wrote, and even Hamlet lost his dad, so *Strike! drum*.

As for his own health, Martin admitted in a letter that he was once more in quite a lot of pain and his stomach was acting up. But that hadn't stopped him from going to a party at a big country house near Woodstock where there was an ornamental lake on the estate. He got so drunk on all the free booze that he took off in a rowboat and tried to capsize it and drown himself, which he thought might be a good idea. He was thwarted by the people who saved him, which he regretted they had done. I was not to worry, however, because those who talked of suicide did so only to get attention and rarely carried through.

This wasn't Martin's usual chatty letter; it sounded a much more somber note. He had visited all the rooms of his house, and must have thought the party almost over. Maybe he sensed that time was coming to an end. There were matters to settle, things to sort out. No matter how many knots we tie as we go through life, we must make an effort at the end to undo them, uncoil them, and lay them straight on the floor of our minds and memories. It was this realization that sent me back to Martin. I had promised he wouldn't be alone.

Morley, who had written only a few months earlier to tell me of Hugh's decline, seemed to be withdrawing into his own space, where books and art were the only things to sustain him. Martin was so lonely, so far from controlling his own life, that suicide was becoming a palatable option. The world I knew had grown much darker, and I simply had to see Martin again. I made arrangements to fly to London for his birthday, and I hoped the visit might heal any wounds.

I phoned Morley to tell him I was coming and to ask that he keep it as a surprise, then called Gerald to invite myself to stay with him in Toronto the night before my flight. Before leaving Stratford, however, it was important to see my mother, even though I knew there was little point telling her where I was going. She would simply not have been able to take it in. Her health, you see, began to deteriorate soon after my father died, and she made her own decision to enter a nursing home. It was never my wish that she be there, because I knew she would decline quickly.

Like the hospital Sybil had been in, this nursing home is staffed with compassionate nurses and provides my mother with a degree of comfort and security she rarely felt in those last dark years with my father. She has her lucid days, but they are rare. Mostly, she wanders in and out of her memory world, losing her thread, sometimes picking it up again, conveying her random thoughts in minimalist language. Although I recognize that her brain synapses are shutting down, I can only listen in anguish. I have to remind myself that memory flows into featureless seas, and I respond only minimally myself to her questions and her pleas always to go home.

"I didn't mean to live this long ..." was the first thing she said. She went on to say she was in the past tense now, not much in the present. She had "meant to go," as she put it, soon after my father, but she supposed God didn't want it that way. She also couldn't help worrying about little things, like the nurse, and if she'd turn up.

I tried to comfort her, but thought again of Christopher Robin. "Whatever happens, you will understand, won't you?" My childhood had caught up with me. But did I understand? Did my mother understand?

She said she couldn't talk properly any more, but she was clear enough when she asked how I knew she was there. I tried to form a sentence by way of reply, but didn't know how to do that. Who was I talking to? Who was this little figure who had given me my life, lying now on her side, knees drawn up under sheets, dying slowly? She wanted my father to come and get her, to rescue her from being there forever. She drifted from one question to the next, never waiting for the answer she would never be able to grasp, even if it were given. Where did I live now? Who would pay for everything? When would my father get there? What was the name of Mrs. Tomlinson's dog who attacked our cat when I was a child? How did I manage to find her?

Her left hand moved slowly to feel for the bed rail, her fingers so thin that the small diamond on her now loose engagement ring was out of sight, having rotated to an underneath position.

I groped again for language, words getting away from me, and promised her that I would somehow always find her. She was in the nursing home, I told her, aiming for an assured voice.

She replied no, she was in the rectory. That, I realized, could only mean I was there, too, maybe standing on tiptoe, reaching for one of her dresses, the one that felt like the smooth skin of a peach, with the long skirt that caused me to trip when I tried it on. It was only because I knew some happiness in those first few years of my life that I asked her then if she was also happy to be back in the rectory.

"It's lonely," she said.

It was lonely for me, too, especially after Rosemarie was killed. I didn't say that to my mother. I could no longer imagine her in the dresses I remembered. She was dressed now in a pale blue flannelette nightgown imprinted with little roses and gathered at the neck with a piece of faded pink ribbon.

I told her not to worry even as I asked what she was worried about.

"Everything."

Did she mean by that what I meant when my father asked me that day in the garden what I was sorry for, and I had answered, "Everything, everything lost."

I told her she must try to sleep, but she said she wanted the side of the bed down, and I heard the little diamond of her ring scrape against the metal of the bar, which she tried to push against but couldn't. I asked her why she wanted the side of the bed down.

"So I won't be alone when you go. I could get up."

She attempted to lift herself a little, but she couldn't do that either, not on her own. Having raised her right shoulder slightly off the pillow, she fell back again.

I wasn't going to leave her alone, I promised, at which she smiled the blessing that only a mother can give, and whispered:

"I'm not going to leave you alone either."

Our roles were reversed. I was young again, and she was protecting me.

I said we were both lucky in that case, hoping she wouldn't be able to detect the choke in my voice.

What had she liked best about home, I asked her.

"Christmas. Your father at Christmas. I loved your father. Did you know that? I always loved him."

I did not, in fact, know that. I might have guessed at the time of his funeral, but I did not know. A child has little ability to assess the love of one parent for another, and I had remained a child in this.

Did I love him, too? she asked.

What could I say but "I tried, Mother, I tried"?

I reached for her hand, feeling bones under flesh, seeing the little bruises that so easily come to the old, and rotated her ring back to the front. As I moved to kiss her goodbye, brushing aside a few strands of hair on her forehead, I tried to comfort myself as much as I did her when I said that one day she'd be home, and all of us would be there with her, Rosemarie and father and me, and it would be Christmas every day.

She said that would be nice and she hoped God would be there as well. I replied that I hoped so, yes.

"I can't quite picture what God is like, can you?"

I told her not to try. Nobody could. All her life she had tried to imagine what God was like. It was an impossible mystery for her. But suddenly, for me, the answer was there:

"He's like you, Mother. Very much like you."

She was silent for a moment, as if trying to work it out.

"He'll take me home, then?"

"Yes. He'll take you home. That's certain."

I went from that place in tears, walking down the familiar, rubber-tiled corridor, past the few residents capable of wheeling themselves everlastingly up and down those confined spaces, going nowhere. Past the nurse's station, unable to look any of those on duty directly in the eye, making a pretense at blowing my nose, I pushed against the bar-locked door at the end of the hall, releasing myself into a world my mother would never see again, a world of sky and air. It was only then, outside in a garden where everything grew to the light, that I was unaware of decay.

I tried not to show my mood when I got to Gerald's. He's been living for a couple of years now with Ann Gorman. She's a physiotherapist at the Sunnybrook hospital, twelve years younger, and the love of his life. He's appearing these days in reputable literary magazines, and publishers are seriously considering his first manuscript, which makes him even happier. He and Ann live in a modest house, like every other on the street, except for its front garden where a single magnolia tree stands with bugle-weed around it instead of grass. At the back, they have a patio deck, accessed through the kitchen sliding doors. It was there, drink in hand, I told Gerald and Ann why I felt I had to go to London.

I had, of course, noticed what Ann was wearing — slacks and a loose-fitting silk blouse, paisley-patterned in reds and purples — but waited for her or Gerald to give me the news. She had another four months to go. She was well over the first terrible weeks. Couldn't be better. Now she just wanted to sing. Gerald looked as if he could sing, too.

"Have you thought of names?" I asked.

Only if it was a boy, they told me. My name. They liked my name, Peter, *petros*, a rock. They thought it a strong name.

When I protested that I hadn't been strong, Gerald reminded me that, although all sorts of things had happened to me, I was still in one piece. It was possible for the years to strengthen rather than weaken, and I should remember that. He had seen me go up and down all sorts of mountains on foot for twenty-three years, carrying lots of baggage, and it wasn't over yet.

What if their dear little baby boy turned out to be gay? I asked. Gerald's answer was, what if their dear little baby boy turned out to be heterosexual? It hardly mattered, did it, so long as he was human and didn't go about his life destroying things.

"My feelings, too," said Ann, and changed the subject to tell us the meal was ready. Gerald opened another bottle of Riesling and we sat to a dinner of porcini mushrooms with asiago cheese, stuffed tomatoes, and a tarragon-roasted capon. "You should cook for Air Canada," I said, thinking ahead to what I would probably not want to eat twenty-four hours later, when I would be higher above the ocean than the tip of Mount Everest.

In conversation, we touched on all the usual topics — the weather, mutual friends, movies, the Mayor of Toronto. Ten years ago, there was a Gay Day Picnic at Hanlan's Point to raise money to send activists to Ottawa for a march, but the Mayor of Toronto had denied permission for a Pride Week march on Yonge Street just two years after that. Earlier this year, Metro Police raided a number of bathhouses and arrested four hundred men. I wasn't one of them, thank God, but I could've been, because I'd been there just the previous weekend. The police humiliated the found-ins by herding them into the street to be *processed*, when they were clad only in their towels. The state may have been out of our bedrooms for years, but anyone in a bathhouse was considered fair game. Despite all this evidence to the contrary, things were slowly getting better, Gerald insisted, and I ought to be pleased.

The protests and demonstrations that followed the raid led to the huge celebration on June 28th, which Gerald told me about when I returned from England last week. There were more than fifteen hundred people at Grange Park, he said. The papers described it as "an afternoon of fun and frolic," a new beginning for gays and lesbians. But I remained pre-occupied with thoughts of Martin.

We finished all the wine Gerald had opened, though Ann, protecting their unborn child, drank little enough, and it was only when we were going to bed that Gerald told me about tonight's vernissage, suggesting I might like to go, if I got back from London in time. The artist, Christopher Lewis, was gay and quite open about it. They thought I would like him, so I said maybe ... well ... sure ... thanks ... I'd let them know. My mind was focussed only on the trip ahead of me. Was something terrible happening to Martin?

My dreams that night were of rope ladders that catch fire when buildings burn, knots that are never to be undone, and pieces of ribbon too short to tie even the smallest present for a child at Christmas.

XX

I've never thought much of astrology. No matter how the planets lined themselves up at my birth, it wasn't as a special favour to me. Tables don't rattle at seances, and I've heard no voices from across the river Styx. If any divinity has been shaping my end, I've not been aware of it. And yet, on the plane to England, I thought something was. I sensed a gathering of energies focussed on some future event, whose shape had already been determined but left unfixed in time. The cold waters of the Atlantic, far below where I was flying in the sun, had all the strength of lunar tides pulling me into darkness.

Morley was at Heathrow to meet me. I fired questions at him immediately. What was he doing there? Why had he met me? Did he have something serious to say? Was Martin all right?

He told me to calm down, before leading the way through what looked like the Commonwealth of Nations to get us to the Underground, where no Cerberus was at this other gate. We boarded the train, stowed my only suitcase, and began a dialogue that took us all the way into the city.

He said he was sorry to hear about my father, and should have written. I thanked him for his sympathy, even as I dismissed it, saying I wasn't upset. What I really wanted to talk about was Martin. How was he? Were things bad?

Yes, they were bad. They had had an argument, the night before, worse than any they had ever had, so Morley had left. He just couldn't take it any more. He walked out. It had been awful, but still, he knew he couldn't leave Martin altogether. He knew he would have to go back.

Did Martin realize he'd be coming back? No, but he'd told him he was only going to the hotel around the corner, so he wouldn't be far away. When I asked what the argument had been about, he said it was the usual. Martin had been drunk again. He simply shouldn't drink. He was an alcoholic. Always it was the same old story. He would come home from school, pop a few pills, take a few drinks, and be away. Nothing could stop him. Morley had tried, other friends had tried, even their charlady had tried. AA didn't work either. He just wanted attention. That was it.

He added, with more passion in his voice than I had ever heard, that if he was going to save Martin, he had to save himself first. He couldn't get pulled under. Martin was having a rotten time, but he had to help himself. He was thoroughly irresponsible. He couldn't behave like that at his age and get away with it.

Morley had ordered a cake from a patisserie nearby. It would be a surprise. Martin had accused him once of never doing things like that, never buying him little presents, flowers, books, chocolates, and so on. Today was Martin's birthday, and Morley would pick up a cake.

"Do you still love him?" I asked.

"Do you?" he asked me.

Neither of us answered the other. We fell into our private

reveries, trying to wrap the hard experiences of life around a soft four-letter word.

By now the London Underground was truly underground, threading its way below the thousands, even tens and hundreds of thousands, who simply walked and slept and ate and loved and died in the vast spaces all above. And I wondered when it came my turn to die if I would join those who, in greater light, hovered above and around those who journeyed below in dark tunnels. Could Ann Drinkwater, who stitched the Victorian sampler, possibly be right and my father wrong? "Let my soul from whence it goes / Eternal life inherit."

At Oxford Circus, Morley and I got out and began the familiar walk to the flat. I said I didn't mind the walk, even with my suitcase, which was light, although my heart was heavy. I would, after all, soon see Martin; and it had been along this same route that we had also guided the drunken Hugh to The Rising Sun.

We had come to the corner of Berners and Mortimer and had to stop for the light to change. I put my suitcase down for a rest, even as others were pressing forward, all waiting for the same light. Morley, who had been looking across the intersection, turned back to face me. I took the opportunity to ask about Hugh.

There on the sidewalk he told me Hugh had died the previous Tuesday in the Middlesex Hospital, not far from where we were standing, but it was a merciful end. His liver gave out, and no wonder. He had asked that there not be a funeral service. Maybe he thought that none of his friends would attend. He hadn't treated most of them very well, especially towards the end. He was scared by what was happening to him, Morley thought, but he and Martin had tried to be loyal. They had visited him right up to the last day. And you know, the wonderful thing, according to Morley, who was almost moved to tears when he spoke of it, was that the nurses allowed them to sneak Tango, Hugh's spaniel, up the back stairs of the hospital to visit him. Tango would just lie there on the bed and look quite happy. Morley had always hated dogs, but he thought Tango was different somehow.

There was by now more of a crowd around us in that London street, all waiting for the light, but either they didn't hear or they didn't care what we were saying and thinking. In another minute, we all surged forward as though life were normal and there would never be another traffic jam or another death.

Morley and I walked on in silence until we got to Charlotte Street, by which time I felt more in control of my heart. He gave me the key and told me to go on ahead and surprise Martin. He had no idea I was coming. We would have to allow him a drink this time, wouldn't we? After all, it was his birthday.

Morley headed towards the bakery just off Tottenham Court Road to pick up the cake, saying he'd be back in ten minutes. I unlocked the outer street-level door. The entrance no longer smelled of urine. I climbed the two flights of stairs, my suitcase bumping against the wall as I negotiated narrow turns. I wondered if Hugh had been buried or cremated. I hadn't thought to ask.

I got to the yellow painted door of the flat, put my case down once more — by now thinking it heavy — and thought

I would ring the bell before I entered, even though I had a key, so I could shout "Surprise!" when Martin opened the door.

Satisfied with my little plan, I rang the bell. There was no response. I rang it again. He may have been running a tap in the kitchen and not heard. Still no response. I unlocked the door, picked up my suitcase and went in. Everything looked perfectly normal — the long hallway with its mirror at the end, the crowded bookshelf, the coat rack, everything in place on the walls, the light on.

"Martin," I called. "Martin, it's me. I'm here. Surprise! Surprise! I'm here."

On one occasion, years ago, I had come into the flat in just that way, and he had been quietly hiding behind his bedroom door, ready to jump out.

"You can't fool me," I said and threw the door open.

He was on the bed, all dressed, lying on his back, eyes closed, holding his breath, being very still. I had seen this sort of thing before. He was good at it, but obviously I was going to have to play the game, too, so I went over to the window and drew back the curtains, letting a lot of light into the room. I went back to the bed.

"Okay, joke's over, party time," I said as jovially as I could but feeling also a little annoyed that I was having to participate in the charade more than I wanted to. I bent down and started to sing rather loudly into his ear: "Happy birthday to you."

Irritated because he still wasn't responding, I seized his right arm by the wrist to shake it. I let it drop when I found it was cold, and realized that he was not holding his breath.

He was dressed in grey trousers and a faded old blue silk shirt, one I had often said I liked. The bed was made up with white sheets, and his socks were blue.

For years, I had been haunted by that grey-blue figure on a rectangle of white. Just a print on a cottage wall, but the image had stayed with me. Now it was real.

"Don't do this, please," I whispered. "Why didn't you know? You really are my Arab Boy."

Death only makes fools of us when we ask questions which can't be answered. We might just as well try to heave mountains into oceans or make leaves spring green again from planks of wood or reroute the Amazon over the Andes as to keep the frail body of someone we love from going into the ground. And yet we try.

I sat on the edge of the bed and put my arms around and under his shoulders, trying to lift him a little, as though I could bring him back to life, like Lazarus. This was the body I had known so intimately, foreign to me now, earth's dust only. I felt the tears I had never felt for my father wrestling with his God, felt them for Hugh no longer young and pretty, felt them for Martin gone from every room in his house, felt them for myself, everything lost.

I noticed two envelopes, propped up against empty bottles, on the small bedside table, one addressed to me, the other to Morley. I reached to pick up mine. There was nothing to indicate it had been written in a hurry. The reverse was true. Each word seemed almost chiselled into an unforgettable place.

Dear Peter: Don't be upset. It had to be this way. I've been in all the rooms and I've had a good time.

*Everyone's gone now and it seems very dark, so I'm going
out onto the terrace to look up at the stars. Maybe I'll
learn what everything is all about. I still remember what
you told me that first night, that nothing is ever truly lost.
I'll always be your Arab Boy.*

I read it and reread it, despite the blurring in my eyes. So
much had been left unsaid. That's always the way, isn't it? I
reached out with my hand to touch Martin's face, now cold,
and to move my fingers slowly over lips I used to kiss. It was
happening again and again and again, Martin's ashes now to
be one with my father's and Rosemarie's and Hugh's and
one day mine, all mixed together in the unrelenting winds
and tides, a great pile of ashes and dust to be swept around
the world. But I had made a promise to Martin I had tried
to keep, and I was there.

It was soon after that that Morley arrived with the cake,
asking immediately what was going on, but no reply was
needed. He knew right away. I pushed the note meant for
him into his hands, and put my arms around him while he
read it, after which he handed it back to me, without
comment, more words to find a place in memory:

*My dearest Morley: I know my actions caused you pain.
I'm sorry. You deserved better, but I was born under a
different star. Forgive me and try to remember the good
years. They were many. There's a note for Peter also.
Please send it to him. I loved you both — in my fashion.
Remind him I was eighteen once. Everything seemed
possible then. I love you. Martin.*

Morley and I must have stayed that way, simply supporting each other, unable to move, for a very long time. I do not remember. Finally, he asked what I was going to do. I would go back to Canada, I told him. What would he do? He would stay there. What else was there to do? We looked down at Martin, who had reached at last his quiet containment, no fists flying, no cries of rage or pain, death itself the only form of shocking behaviour.

We noticed then, tucked under the alarm clock, a third note which Morley read before passing it over to me. Martin's instructions in it were that he wanted to be cremated, with half his ashes scattered in the old world and half in the new, because he had always felt divided between his life here and his life there. Morley promised to take half the ashes to Gloucestershire and scatter them in the garden of what had been their glorious country house. I pledged to find a suitable spot in Canada for the other half.

I repeated my earlier question: "Do you still love him?"

"Do you?" was the reply.

I had a lot of time on the flight back here to Toronto to think about where I should honour the pledge I had made. The first thing I did was to hire a car at the airport, and head for Stratford.

I drove a familiar route for several miles beyond the town to the quarry at St. Mary's, where I parked on the edge of the road and walked for half a mile into the woods, to that magical spot where Billy and I used to make love. It was as peaceful as I remembered it, with just the sound of mourning doves flying from tree to tree, singing their four haunting notes, and ghosts sighing in the evergreens.

It was there I untied a small piece of yellow ribbon which held together the gathered top of a plastic bag I was carrying in my pocket. As I walked about under the trees, I scattered all that was left of my Arab Boy in a truly fine and private place.

"May you find peace forever in this largest of all rooms," was the only prayer I spoke, and only the mourning doves answered.

XXI

One step forward, two steps back. With Shelley's baby unable to speak a language quickly forgotten, the celestial city has become a mirage, and all figures mere shadows. Shame, defeat, and loss are never easy things to talk about, even when thrown in with the good times, and now Martin had gone.

In light of all this, I wasn't in the best of moods for any vernissage. In fact, after telling Gerald about Martin, I said I wouldn't go tonight. He was sympathetic and didn't try to push, but he and Ann were still going and he hoped I would change my mind. They would meet me there, if I did. I knew it was to be in a small Yorkville gallery, and I knew the artist was gay, but *Works by Christopher Lewis*, I confess, meant nothing at all to me. I convinced myself that the place would be full of poseurs and the pretentious, a phoney élite who would look more at each other than the work on the walls. But the thought of seeing Gerald and Ann was enough to persuade me. They, at least, were genuine, and they were my friends.

The place had its fair share of those who pretended to know more than they did. I heard them chattering about postmodernism and all the latest trends, as we moved about the gallery, doing a quick round before we started to look more closely at the paintings. I admired the oils and pastels, figurative, representational, flower arrangements, portraits of friends, interior scenes, full of refracted light, tables with bowls of fruit, casement windows that opened onto a wider world, porcelain figurines, pianos and chandeliers, bottles of wine and empty glasses, evidence of friends who had been at a party, mantelpieces, fireplaces and grates, candlesticks and mirrors, everything suggesting a life of beauty and com-posure in an otherwise violent world. At that moment, even without knowing the artist, I felt I could trust him.

Gerald and Ann and I said little as we moved from one painting to another, able to appreciate them better now that most of the crowd had left the gallery, bidding all sorts of extravagant *bon soirs* to Marie Lachapelle, the *propriétaire*, draped in her layers of pink chiffon. We came at last to the one wall we hadn't looked at, with three male nudes.

We took a few paces back to admire especially the one in the middle, so simply framed with its thin edge of stained wood, nothing detracting from the work itself. Naturally, I thought of Billy and his drawing of me.

It seemed obvious to me that the artist had wanted to capture interior qualities beyond physical attributes. He had positioned the model on his back in a rumpled bed, exposed, vulnerable, sensitive, and erotic, but with no hint of the pornographic. The body was at a diagonal in the frame, with the head in the top left corner, partly resting on a thrown back left arm, the right arm off the edge of the canvas. The eyes seem fixed as much on the viewer as on some distant place. The face is in repose, thoughtful, not stern, lips full, mouth closed.

I heard Gerald say, "Peter, I want you to meet the artist."

And when I turned around, there I was, face to face with the artist, Christopher Lewis.

You.

No, please, don't say anything yet. Please. I want you to hear my first impressions, as though you were hearing me talk about someone else. Then you can speak, tell me if I've got things right, if I've remembered what's important, if I've picked up the essentials. It'll complete my story to let you hear it this way.

It was your eyes I noticed first, their striking blue-grey colour, the intense gaze as though you can see what no one else sees, and your mouth which looks as if you are always ready to smile. There's your curly brown hair and dark beard flecked with grey, and your voice which comes from a far-off place where music is made.

I said I was sorry I hadn't discovered your work before, but hoped now to change all that.

Your reply was that the paintings were going to be there for a while and I could always come back to have another look, if I wanted. Besides, the gallery wasn't going to close for another half hour, and you would be around for that time. Then you walked quietly away.

I liked what I heard so much that I said so to Gerald. He smiled and said, "I thought you would."

You came back within minutes to join us, noticing that we couldn't tear ourselves away from contemplating that one particular painting. You said the male nude was hard to do, especially these days. The female form was everywhere. That too was beautiful, but the male was more challenging for a contemporary artist. You didn't want to do macho figures, the stuff of porno mags. You wanted to do something that was real.

For you — and this is something I want always to remember — the challenge was to live in an outside world and an inside world at the same time. The exterior world of events can only be faced and dealt with if the interior world is kept secure and full of love. I'd like to make that my goal, too.

Much of what you said about Maud Lewis seemed to reflect your own approach to the world. She was an artist with your surname, but not a relative, which I wrongly assumed she must be. Ann, who is more up on these things, seemed to know she was a Nova Scotia artist, but not much more than that, so you told us about her.

She was born in Nova Scotia and became a Grandma Moses sort of figure, a true primitive, and she died only about ten years ago. A tiny, tiny little woman who lived with her not very nice husband in a one-room house just nine feet by ten and a half, with a loft above. A little place called Marshalltown in Yarmouth County. Polio as a child crippled her arms, deformed her hands and affected her neck so that she could hardly raise her head, but when she did, her whole face would light up because she saw a world of colour and joy. She taught herself to paint and never took any lessons. Her hands were so gnarled and twisted it was a miracle she could even hold a brush. But once she started, she hardly stopped, and she painted absolutely everything — sleighs in winter, oxen in a field of tulips and flowering trees, big black cats with yellow button eyes, butterflies and birds, sea gulls and fishing boats. But she didn't just paint little pictures which people would buy, she decorated her whole house, transformed everything, painted everything, windowsills and doors, breadboxes and wash basins and stoves, the works. For her, there was joy and beauty in everything, in all the basic colours and patterns and rituals of ordinary life, which is also true of your own work. She never met another artist. She worked on her own, making her own interior world secure. She never travelled beyond a sixty-mile radius of where she was born, but she knew all about life. She knew about the exterior world. She knew it was big, even though she was so small herself. She was just not small in her imagination. In her imagination, she was almost as big as God.

You asked if we wanted to go out for something to eat, because you were starving. Gerald and Ann said they couldn't stay out late on account of the baby — Ann had to get her rest — but I was just as hungry as you were, so I said yes, of course I would join you. Off they went in one direction while we came here. Once we had settled and given our order, I asked you who you were, the same question I asked Martin when he was only eighteen. Does this mean that Time curves back on itself, the way some physicists claim?

When you spoke of the world you inhabit, you spoke of its magic and wonder, of climbing mountains near Kelowna, skiing at Whistler, backpacking, bird-watching, stargazing, discovering Emily Carr, aware of the power and mystery and movement in all she painted, learning who you were, having a mother who encouraged you to look for love, and a father who supported you in all the efforts you made to find yourself. I liked what you said about your years in Paris, meeting people, not just French but German, Italian, Moroccan, Chinese, other artists, writers, intellectuals, poets, dancers, everyone who lived in a world bigger than yours and showed you what you didn't know existed. While all that was wonderful enough, what made you even happier was that you finally met your adult self and came to terms with that. Ibsen discovered that long ago, so that Nora knew she had to slam the door of her doll's house and strike out on her own. It was what we all had to do, in fact, and not let anyone stop us.

You were still learning, you said, still searching, still hoping to get it right one day. I said that I wanted to get it right myself. I wanted to remember what Shelley's baby forgot. You asked me then what I was talking about, and now I've told you. It's taken a long time, but I've kept nothing back.

Chris listened to everything until Peter got to the end, by which time night had turned into dawn. Outside, through the glass window near their table, they could see all the shops and the places that had been closed opening up, and the street that had been empty starting again to fill with life.

Chris thought for some time before he said very quietly: "Let's meet again."

"Are you sure?"

"Very."

"I still need some time."

"We both do."

"So often these days, I feel as if I'm trapped in one of those eighteenth century mazes. You know the kind. You get in and you can't find your way out. You try one way and it's blocked. Another way, and it's blocked too."

"I've been there as well. But I'm convinced there's a way out. There has to be. Only we can't see it. Not by ourselves, that is."

"What's the point then?"

"The point is this: anyone who stands tall enough can see it, can see the whole thing, can see where to go, can see the pattern. That's the person who gets out."

"I've never been that tall."

"Neither have I. Not by myself, that is. But if we're both going to be trapped in the same maze, why wouldn't I stand on your shoulders or you on mine?"

"Is that possible?"

"Of course it is. Maybe that's what being human means."

It was clear that opposite Peter sat someone of faith, capable of transforming the world, making it a place of hope, pushing aside Peter's own sad thoughts of death.

"Yes," he answered, "we would both have the now."

It was quite simple after all, just as Shelley's baby must have known. There were no words left. Just thoughts and dreams.

They sat for some minutes longer in silence, only breathing, before they got up to leave.

"See you tomorrow," Chris said.

"Hope so."

One step back. Two steps forward.

ACKNOWLEDGEMENTS

I would like to thank all those who helped and encouraged me in the writing of this book, including:

Jan Geddes, Scott Griffin, Marta Braun, Gwendolyn Black, Joe Plaskett, Marilyn Lerch, Janet Hammock, Lesley Read, Eldon Hay, and Steven Beattie.

And a special thank you to my editor, Marc Côté, for his keen eye and unwavering faith.

> *Think where man's glory most begins and ends,*
> *And say my glory was to have such friends.*
> — W. B. YEATS